Highland Bloodline

Florence Love Karsner

Copyright © 2017 Florence Love Karsner

All rights reserved.

ISBN-978-1-943369-11-9

Readers' Comments for HIGHLAND HEALER

Adventure abounds in the Scottish Highlands in Karsner's debut novel, in which a special woman with untapped elemental powers tries to stay one step ahead of a ruthless soldier bent on exacting revenge. Overall, this is a mostly charming tale of magic and mages. Karsner works quickly and efficiently to establish her principal players . . . the author manages to imbue the simple plot with a real sense of tension and suspense. The first in a promising series filled with likable characters and fun adventures.--*Kirkus Reviews*

I cannot wait to see what happens next- an enjoyable read. I would recommend it for a fun, twisting story with magical realism intertwined . . .Kay

Truly enjoyed this book. My ancestors are Scottish. The story itself was really good. All the characters were easy to follow. I could picture each one as they came into the story. Really enjoyed this book can't wait for the next one . . . Charles

She not only shows you the characters, she shows you their souls. . . Chris

I really enjoyed this book. I typically read the historical romance novels but found this one very refreshing. It had no "sex" scenes and it did not need them! It was well written how the author was able to introduce three separate group of characters and how their paths crossed. And I love Willie! Definitely going to get Book 2. . .Carol

It was packed with suspense and romance. It is one of my favorite books. A must to read. Put this on your wish list of books to read . . . Kathleen

Readers' Comments for HIGHLAND CIRCLE OF STONES

For the second installment of her series, Karsner creates an elegiac battlement on the first novel's foundation. The narrative's strongest theme is family...it uses its fantasy elements sparingly, though it also depicts them beautifully, as when the wizard, Uncle Wabi, uses 'time weaving, ' moving 'at a speed that had stars melting...and the colors of Aurora Borealis racing across the sky.'...a savage finale tests the clan and should rivet readers...A sprawling cast and deep family history invigorate this sequel." - *Kirkus Reviews*

The writing is fantastic. The characters are so well penned that I came to know them and when I put the book down, I wanted to know what they were going to do the next day. You find yourself immersed in the mists of the Highlands among the clan of brothers whose family values come through in spades. . . Amazon Customer

I absolutely love this series of books! There aren't many that are safe enough for me to let my kids read and still be interesting enough for me to read. This is a good love story without all the dirty scenes you find in so many romance books. Once again, it is set in the Scottish Highlands, as was its prequel, which I love, and is a very interesting installment in this series of books. I love the way I have gotten to know the McKinnon clan even better and feel like the character development in this series was well done! I can't wait for the next book to come out! Thank you Florence for this wonderful story! . . . Sherri

This book was very well written and kept me engrossed from the very beginning! I completed it in a few hours because I simply could not put it down! Very well done! I also loved that it proved almost a cultural lesson by providing meanings to words native to the setting. Truly loved it! . . . Shilohna

I loved this second book in the Highland Healer series. The characters are well written. The devotion of the main characters to each other and to each family is admirable. The attention to small details such as items in a room draws the reader into the story and makes you a part of it. The last chapter had me wanting more . . . Angel

SeaDog Press, LLC

313 Ebb Tide Court

Ponte Vedra Beach, Florida 32082

This book is a work of fiction. Any references to historical events, real people, or real places are used fictitiously. Other names, characters, places, and events are products of the author's imagination, and any resemblance to actual events or places or persons, living or dead, is entirely coincidental.

Cover Design: Dar Albert, Wicked Smart Designs
Ship Logo: © Dn Br | Shutterstock
Ouroboros Design: Elizabeth Pampalone / www.JaxComputerChic.com

Copyright © 2017 Florence Love Karsner

All rights reserved.

ISBN: 978-1-943369-11-9

The serpent is an ancient symbol of healing and is seen in early drawings wrapped around the caduceus of the Greek god, Hermes. Many ancient cultures regarded the serpent as sacred, and used it in healing rituals. A serpent devouring its tail is called an ouroboros. It is symbolic of immortality, the eternal unity of all things, and the cycle of birth and death. It unites opposites such as the conscious and unconscious mind. It has a meaning of infinity or wholeness, and is the Western world equivalent of Yin-Yang.

To Dorothy and Jackie

...the best of our bloodline

ACKNOWLEDGMENTS

As always, a huge thank you to my readers for taking time to read my work. Writing is much more enjoyable when I know it is appreciated. To those of you who have written reviews, please know that I appreciate your comments.

Elizabeth White, my editor, deserves special recognition. She very gently prods me until I produce a much better product than the one I started with. You can be sure to see her touch on all my work.

Finally, much credit goes to my husband, Garry, and my daughters, Caroline and Taylor for their never ending support. They read everything I write and give me unsolicited, but very helpful feedback! Couldn't do this without them.

1

The MacKinnon lodge was a most inviting place this evening. Oil lamps and candles burned softly, while a small fire kept the damp chill at bay. The hills and moor were coming to life again after a long winter, and even though it was after eight in the evening it was still light outside.

All the bairns were abed and the MacKinnon men were enjoying a wee dram after a trying day. To an outsider peeking in, the scene was one of perfect calm and peace. Were that outsider to enter, however, he would be steeped in the anxiety and tension that sizzled in the room.

The topic of conversation was the same as it had been for several nights now, rumors the British military were rounding up Jacobite supporters who had survived the Battle of Culloden and either putting them in prison, executing them on the spot, or sending them to the islands to be sold as slaves.

These rumors were not new, and many supporters had already been captured. It had been some time since the battle and the MacKinnons had avoided being captured. Their lodge was a difficult place to find, it being well hidden high up in the Highlands.

Alex came in the back door, having needed a word with Boder, the new hand they had hired for the lambing season.

"What did Boder want this time?" Jack asked.

"Another complaint about his living quarters. He's not too keen on sharing the cottage with Hamish and Kenny. Says they talk too much and keep him awake at night. Mostly he's miffed because I told him to put that cheroot out before he goes in the cottage at night as it wouldn't take much for that thatched roof to go up in flames. Don't think he much liked that. Thinks he should have a cottage to himself. He's a good hand, but I'm not of a mind to have the lads clean another cottage and make it ready just for his convenience. Let's see how he works out before we make any other arrangements for him."

From the kitchen, Caitlin was only half listening to the conversation. Her mind was occupied with the events of a few days ago. It wasn't every day she was called upon to use her extraordinary powers to save a loved one, and certainly it was not every day she caused the death of another human being. She was a healer after all, not a killer.

As she entered the room, her long skirt sweeping along the floor, Alex stood and turned his attention from Da and Jack to her, reaching for her hand as she came closer. He thought she was the picture of perfection. Her long, curly, flame-colored hair and sparkling aqua eyes seemed even more brilliant these days. Willie, her wolf companion and protector, trailed along beside her. He seemed to be aware of her condition and kept glued to her every moment. His role as her protector was one he never neglected.

"Lass, here, sit now, rest awhile. I know yer still worried about Charlie, but the ordeal's over and the little lad's safe. He's wounded to be sure, but he's young and he'll recover. Hear me on this now, *mo chridhe*."

Caitlin's large girth made sitting a bit of a chore these days. She and Alex were expecting their first bairn, and one look at the healer's body indicated the birth would be soon.

"I hope you're right. He's such a special lad, but he's had enough problems already. His deafness is quite a challenge for him, and since the incident with Drosera, he hasn't even made his usual sounds. Millie and Camille and I have worked diligently with him, and this is a major setback."

"Aye. But he's got this entire family to help him, lass, ye ken?"

Caitlin nodded and, finding the chair uncomfortable, stood again and walked to the window. As she looked out across the moor, Alex came up behind her and put an arm around her shoulders.

"*Mo chridhe*, ye don't need to worry so. Drosera was an evil woman if ever there was one, and if ye hadn't taken care of her she'd have killed our wee Charlie for sure. Don't forget, ye aren't totally responsible for her death. Yer bolt of lightning definitely started the process, but the shot from my pistol finished the job. So, I'm responsible also.

We both know it had to be done. If we hadn't taken action, she'd have found us again someday. Nae, ye needn't let her death weigh on yer mind. I know that's difficult for a healer, but let it go lass, let it go."

Alex thought he had gotten his message through to her, but Caitlin turned to face him, grabbed his shirt and jerked him closer.

"Alex, I killed a woman! A healer saves people, she doesn't kill them. I had no intention of destroying a life, I simply needed to save Charlie. I acted on an overwhelming instinct and in a matter of seconds I had taken Drosera's life. I don't want these powers. I'll never be able to control them!"

She burst into sobs and held her face in her hands. For a woman who remained calm in most trying situations, the emotional exhibition was out of character.

"Lass, ye saved the lad's life and that's all that matters. If ye hadn't stopped Drosera, Charlie would be dead now instead of that vile woman. Come now. Let's get ye settled here in the chair. We'll put yer feet up and I'll fetch ye a mug of Millie's hot cocoa."

He helped her into a larger chair and she sat quietly, sipping her cocoa and catching a few words of the discussion the men were having. Trying her best to turn her mind from her recent deplorable deed, she listened more closely to the men. She still found it amusing the true Highlanders spoke so differently than folks from other areas of the country. Their brogue was unique, certainly.

She had heard different accents in almost every village she came through on her way to the upper Highlands, where she now lived. She was originally from Skye, the largest island of the Inner Hebrides. And even though Skye was considered part of the Highlands, the accent was still different from the accent she heard up here. She loved the way these brothers said "ye" instead of you and "yer" instead of your. She'd grown used to it now, but still enjoyed hearing the men and their brogue. It was like a language from another era and she found it refreshing.

Da and Jack expressed their thoughts openly, but she knew

Alex would keep his thoughts to himself and only express them when he had worked out the details. But this latest issue, the Brits rounding up the Jacobites, this was a real problem and she could see the worry on Alex's face.

Her own thoughts, her worries, were about what would happen if the Brits managed to capture them, Alex and Jack. What would happen to the others? Da was still able-bodied but getting older now, as was Uncle Andrew. And Hector and Ian? Did the Brits know that all the brothers had been at Culloden? Would she and Millie have to fend for themselves and the bairns?

My life has changed so since coming to the Highlands. I was a carefree healer caring for the villagers in Skye and life was so easy. What was I thinking when I married this Highlander? It seems that we've gone from one calamity to another since we met. Of course, I was running from two men who were determined to kill me back then and Alex saved me from certain death. Oh, what a mess. I do love him so, but I wish life weren't so complicated.

These powers are very disturbing. I've used them twice now, and in neither case was I in control of them. Uncle Wabi says they were bestowed on me for a purpose, but I don't want them. I can just hear him now though . . . 'patience, dear girl, patience.' It seems to me if one is given powers, shouldn't they be able to control them?

Looking around the room, she saw all those she cared for gathered. If the Brits did manage to find them, Alex and Jack wouldn't be taken easily, but she also knew the Brits had plenty of soldiers and was aware there were informers, other Scots, who were aiding the soldiers in their quest. Brother had fought against brother in this battle, and in the end there was great heartache for all. There were too many unanswered questions. She had no doubt this problem was not going away, and time was not on their side.

~ ~ ~

For Alex, the leader of this band of brothers, his shoulders felt a heavy load of responsibility, as if they were carrying a heavy ewe, as they often had over the years. Da was still around, but he'd turned the reins over to Alex, the eldest son. Though they made decisions as a family, it was obvious the others looked to Alex to handle difficult situations, which certainly arose in such a large family. His intelligence was a great asset, but some situations were difficult to come to grips with.

Jack, the second oldest brother, and a very large Highlander, paced back and forth, his face flushed with excitement.

"But, Alex. We can't just sit here waiting on the Redcoats to come round us up. We've got to do something I tell ye!"

"I'm just as concerned as ye, Jack, but we have to think this through. We need a plan of action, not just a knee-jerk response that could get all of us killed. It's not just us menfolk now. We've got women and bairns to think about. Let's be rational about this and then take action." Alex had learned long ago to let Jack vent and then try to reason with him.

"Yeah, but if they show up tomorrow we might just be caught without a plan. What do we do if that happens?"

Then, as usual at the end of the day, a small voice called from the top of the stairs.

"Grandda, you promised!" That stopped the serious conversation, which was a good thing. No amount of talking had brought any answers so far anyway. They all laughed as Da stood.

Every evening he looked forward to story time with the wee ones. Reading to them brought back old memories for him and created new ones for them. The irony of the situation was that these were not even his own grandchildren. They were three orphans Hector had found hiding in Cameron Castle, an estate Millie inherited upon her grandmother's recent death. The orphans had been in the lodge for several months now and were an integral part of the MacKinnon family.

Just as Da rose to climb the stairs, there was a sharp rap on the front door. Alex was out of his chair in an instant. "Jack, pistols!" Fearing it might be the Brits, Alex hurried to the kitchen to retrieve the pistol he kept hidden in the pantry. Jack flew down the hall to retrieve his own firearm, moving quickly for such a large man.

Before the brothers could get back, however, Da had gone to the door.

"I'll get it. I'm up already." He opened the door and felt the blood drain from his face. *No. This can't be. He's here. And he's not a lad any longer, he's a man. No.*

His brain kept telling him it couldn't be, but his heart recognized the truth. There was the same shock of dark hair, and even darker eyes that looked into your soul, and long, gangly legs that had outgrown the rest of his body. And the final touch, the cleft in his chin that couldn't be denied.

Oh, Alice, mo chridhe. Ye should see him.

Da finally found his voice and connected it to his brain. "Good evening, lad. Can I help ye?" He held his breath almost dreading to hear the answer to his question.

The young lad quickly pulled off his tam and crumpled it, shuffling it back and forth from one hand to the other. "Yes ... sir. I'm looking for my father. I was told he lives here." The dark, intelligent eyes never left Da's face.

The old man nodded. "Yes. I believe he does. Come in then, lad."

The boy entered and Da leaned against the door for a moment, trying to regain his equilibrium and feeling his age as never before. Then he called out. "Alex, there's someone here who needs ye!"

Alex heard Da calling and quickly walked that way, his kilt swinging as his long, muscular legs covered the distance quickly. "What? Who is it?" He held his pistol tightly as he reached the door, coming face-to-face with the young lad standing there.
Certainly not the Brits. But who?

Alex, too, seemed to have the same problem Da experienced—lack of connection between his tongue and his brain. His mind reeled as he stared at the lad and he had no doubt he was seeing the very image of himself at that age—the thick, dark hair, rather scruffy at the neck, in need of a trim as Alex's always was, and long legs that were out of proportion with the rest of his body. The lad already stood close to six feet tall. But most telling of all were his eyes, so dark and deep Alex could feel them searing into his face. Likewise, his own dark eyes were taking in every inch of the young lad's features, as if to etch them into his mind. Then the cleft chin said it all.

Holy Jesus. What have I done?

What was he to say? How do you address a stranger who is so like you there's no denying it? But it was impossible. He had no children, except, obviously that was not true. But when, where, who? As Alex furiously ran a litany of questions through his mind, the lad looked away from him, then, turning back to face him, held his head at an angle that caused an avalanche of memories to come cascading through Alex's brain.

Yes, of course, Fiona. My English rose at university. Ye always cocked yer head in that manner when ye were about to question me about something I probably wasn't going to agree with. Why didn't ye let me know I had a son?

His held his pistol in his left hand, still pointed directly at the chest of the young lad, who stared at it as if he had never seen one. As his mind slowed down and reason returned, Alex finally spoke and let his pistol hang down by his side.

"Lad, I'm Alex MacKinnon. Please come in, join us." He held out his hand and offered it to the young lad. Much beyond that Alex wasn't sure how to proceed.

To his great relief, Caitlin had her emotions back under control and walked over to join him. The healer had only to take a quick look to understand the situation. The lad was the spiting image of Alex. And he was even more uncomfortable than Alex himself. That was apparent to her as she, too, offered her hand to the stranger.

"Hello, I'm Caitlin MacKinnon. And what is your name?"

"I'm Robbie. Actually, Robert Alexander MacKinnon."

"Please come in, Robbie. Come warm by the fire and I'll make you a cup of cocoa. That'll get your insides warmed up. It's still a mite cold out."

Alex was grateful someone had stepped in and taken the lead. It was apparent to him that both he and Robbie were having difficulty speaking—maybe a familial trait or genetic problem.

Da excused himself. Alex had no doubt that he, too, was relieved his daughter-in-law had sorted the situation quickly and was trying to assist in making things a bit more comfortable for everyone. In her usual fashion, the healer started issuing instructions.

"Alex, introduce Robbie to everyone and then you two come to the kitchen. We should have a few moments together and see if Robbie is hungry as well."

"Yes, of course, come in lad. Come in." Alex stepped back and the lad came through.

Robbie was surprised to find so many people in the lodge. His mother had told him only a few facts about his father. He knew Alex came from a large family with several brothers and that they lived in the Highlands. Other than that, he really didn't know much. He stood in the middle of the room wishing he could drop through a hole in the floor.

What was I thinking? That he'd welcome me with open arms? He didn't even know I existed before today.

Alex, usually very adept at handling social situations, found himself struggling to find the right words. Finally he managed to utter something that at least got the conversation going.

"Uh, Robbie, the beautiful woman making the cocoa is Caitlin, my wife. This other lovely lady is Millie, and she's married to my brother, Jack."

The lad continued to shift his tam back and forth in his hands as he nodded to the ladies and briefly made a quick handshake with Jack, who still held his pistol also. Young Ian stood up from his lying position on the floor. He, too, saw the unbelievable resemblance to Alex. The boy could be another MacKinnon brother from the looks of him.

"Hello, I'm Ian, Alex's youngest brother."

Robbie looked at Ian and felt a warmth he hadn't felt coming from the others. Perhaps it was that they were close in age. Whatever, it was a welcomed feeling.

Alex cleared his throat. "Um, everyone, this is Robert Alexander MacKinnon. Apparently he belongs in this family, so we'll get to know him. Now, Robbie, let's go to the kitchen and see if Caitlin has that cocoa ready."

Alex wasn't sure which was worse, standing with the lad, a son he didn't know he had, or seeing the expressions on the faces of his family. They were astounded.

The lad followed Alex and they took a seat at the old pine kitchen table, the one where all family matters got settled. Robbie liked the looks of the table, as there was something of permanence about it. There were many scars on the surface and someone's initials had been carved on one corner. Around the edges there were what looked like scratches made by an animal. But thanks to Millie's efforts, it was shining and smelled like lemons. In fact, the whole place smelled like a home should smell, not one that reeked like an infirmary with sick folk, like his own home had for the longest time now.

"So, Robbie, would you like a taste of Millie's apple cobbler? She's the main cook around here, and I assure you it's delicious."

"Uh, yes mum. I've not eaten all day, so that would be appreciated."

As for Caitlin, she had an ear that didn't miss the very proper pronunciation of his words. Apparently the lad had been reared with proper British English, and most probably proper manners as well. She observed that he waited for Alex to sit before he did, and he carefully lay his tam on the chair next to him.

She couldn't tell who was the most anxious, Alex or Robbie, and her heart was breaking for these two, a father and a son who had never met. She debated whether to retreat from the room and leave them alone to figure out how to communicate, or whether she should help them for a few minutes then take her leave. The healer in her desperately wished to bring some relief to the situation.

"Here, try this cocoa and have some cobbler. Your stomach will thank you, I'm sure. Alex, here's another cup of cider for you. I'll leave you two to yourselves now. You need to get acquainted, I believe." She left, holding her hands over her abdomen as she walked back toward the great room.

~ ~ ~

Da finished his story time with the bairns and stood at the window of the upstairs hallway, looking out over the moor. Thinking. Remembering. Alice, Mam, had a saying she used at times such as these: "Life is meant to be embraced, Daniel. If we run away from everything unpleasant or uncomfortable that is thrown at us, we'll cease to grow as people and never gain any new understanding. Rejoice in all experiences that ye encounter, even if ye don't completely understand them, and let them become part of yer soul."

Mo chridhe, this may be a great opportunity to embrace that which we don't quite understand.

He knew he must go down and lend Alex a hand, but thought he'd give him a few minutes alone with the lad then step in, as Alice would have done. Yes, she would have taken it all in stride. Eventually, he made his way slowly back down the stairs.

Jack, the largest of the MacKinnon brothers, and also the most hotheaded one who despised changes, accosted Da the minute he got to the bottom of the stairs.

"Da? Do ye think he's Alex's son? I mean, he looks just like him! What are we supposed to do? Alex has a son? Who would have ever thought that? And what are we to do with him? That's just more changes, Da, more changes."

"Oh, well, I feel sure we'll find room for him, don't ye? He's obviously a MacKinnon, so I don't believe we'll be throwing him out the door."

"No, but what will Caitlin think? She's about to have a bairn any day now and here, this evening, she learns Alex already has one."

"And she thinks it a very fine thing, too, Jack," a voice spoke behind him.

Caitlin joined them at the bottom of the stairs.

"The lad apparently is in need or he wouldn't be here. So, we all should make him welcome and try to see what we can do for him. He's fearful and anxious, certainly. I can see that on his face." The healer not only saw the pain in the boy's face, but she felt it at an even deeper level. Uncle Wabi had told her she would learn to shield herself from sensing others' pain, eventually, but as yet she still hadn't mastered that skill.

She was getting close to the end of her pregnancy and her emotions were riding a wave that crested high one day then crashed the next. The bairn wasn't due for several more weeks, and she knew these emotions were common in the last days, but she wished the child would get here, and soon.

"I think the best thing we can do this evening will be to find the lad a place to sleep and let him know we're glad he's with us."

Ian, the youngest of the brothers, stood again, which still took a bit of doing with his prosthetic foot. But he had no complaints, and didn't let his prosthesis stop him from doing most anything he wanted. Caitlin had been responsible for keeping him alive following a wound at the Battle of Culloden in which he lost his foot. The prosthesis was a gift from Da, Uncle Wabi and Uncle Andrew. The three had worked together to create it and now Ian was almost good as new.

"Let him come up to the attic with me. There's a small cot he can sleep on and I'll find some blankets for him. He'll like being up there. It's the best place in the lodge, trust me."

Ian would be returning to the Isle of Skye in a few days anyway, and his room would be vacant. The new lad could have full use of the room then. Being part of a large family had its good points, but Ian always liked that he could climb up to the highest part of the lodge and have his own space where he could light a candle, read to his heart's content, and watch out the window for the old stag that wandered the moor at night. He knew Robbie would like that too.

Millie and Jack made their way to the east wing where Millie's little daughter, Midge, was already asleep and they, too, retired for the evening. Jack and Millie had wed the same day Alex and Caitlin had. Millie, the former Lady Sinclair, had gone from being a lady in a castle in England, and wife to a despicable lord, to being wife to Jack, a Highlander whom she thought hung the moon. He had his strong points, and his weak ones as well. Most of all he disliked changes, but this past year had proved to him he didn't need to fear them. Sometimes they actually made things better.

"But, Millie. Another child, a lad, in the lodge? How many can we take in?"

"As Da said, we won't be throwing him out. I know how the lad feels, Jack. I, too, had no place to go and now I'm here with this family. It'll be alright."

With Caitlin and Millie having come into the family, the lives of everyone in the lodge had changed. Caitlin and Millie had become friends first, then Caitlin saved Ian's life after Culloden and the MacKinnons had come to her rescue in her time of need. Alex had been captivated by her from day one and had let nothing keep him from marrying her, not even family concerns about her.

The fact Caitlin possessed special powers had been a problem for Jack originally, but she had saved him, Alex, and Millie, as well as herself, on two occasions. That had gone a long way toward Jack accepting her and her abilities.

Caitlin slowly climbed the stairs, headed to the rooms she and Alex claimed in the west wing of the lodge. She particularly liked that wing as she had two large windows from which she could view the moor, and if she looked closely she could see the circle of stones at the top. She intuitively knew the circle was a special place and she longed to walk among the spirits that she was sure dwelled there.

This evening she found herself wondering what might happen next. Her handsome Highlander was her life, and his touch still sent chills along her spine. Watching him as he strode across the floor, his kilted body tall and muscular, was as appealing as ever, and the sound of his deep, resonating voice was soothing to her.

Her life was fulfilling and she never regretted leaving the Isle of Skye and Uncle Wabi, although she missed him greatly. He visited often and she could always "call" him if she really needed him. But this night she wished she could talk to another woman, perhaps

Mam. That woman had raised this house full of lads who were a credit to her and Da. And now, as Caitlin was about to deliver the next bairn in this clan, a new MacKinnon lad had shown up.

She undressed and began to brush her hair. Tying a ribbon around the mass of curls, she pulled on a high-necked nightgown and crawled into bed. She was tired beyond belief, but her mind wouldn't stop its churning.

Holy Rusephus! Alex has a son. But why did he not know about him? Why would any woman keep such a secret from a father? This will be a tale worth hearing. I sounded so sure of myself downstairs, but I don't know how to handle this situation any better than Alex. A son? Just one more calamity.

Alex would be up eventually, but she knew he would remain quiet about his feelings regarding Robbie until he'd sorted them out in his own mind. Only then would he discuss them with her.

She felt like an elephant as she tried to get comfortable in bed, and fell asleep wishing the bairn would be born this very minute—several more weeks was unthinkable.

~ ~ ~

"So then, Robbie. I think we might better try to get acquainted, ye ken?" Alex shifted uncomfortably in his chair, not sure how to get this conversation going.

"Yes ... sir. I suppose that would be the logical thing to do."

Alex noted the lad all but refused to make eye contact, and an element of anger and resentment inside the boy was palpable.

"Well now, it's fairly obvious the two of us are a lot alike, physically, that is. So we can agree ye must be my son. Is that how ye see it?"

The lad looked to the floor and, in a most sullen voice, replied. "I guess so. Mother told me I was to find you when she was no longer here with me. That's why I came here this evening. She died a fortnight ago and I've been trying to determine what would be the best course of action for me to take."

Alex could feel anger and resentment coming off the lad in waves. Unconsciously crossing his arms across his chest in a defensive manner, he took a deep breath and leaned back, fearing what the next words from the lad might be. The boy sounded like a much older person, and other than observing that the lad was nervous, what with him picking his tam up again and constantly fiddling with it, Alex would have assumed he was an adult.

Suddenly realizing his posture might be sending out a message that wasn't exactly welcoming, Alex released his arms and leaned forward to rest them on the table and gave the lad his undivided attention. Seeing his own dark eyes staring back at him gave him pause, but he began.

"Oh, lad, whatever caused her to die? She was such a lovely young woman when I knew her. It grieves me to hear she has passed away."

Still addressing the floor, Robbie began his tale. "She'd been ill for quite some time ... sir. When she wasn't teaching, she volunteered at the Old Tolbooth, the prison in Edinburgh, where she contracted typhus a while back. The doctors at the Royal Infirmary of Edinburgh treated her, but finally there was nothing else to be done so she asked to leave hospital and come home for her final days. Mattie, our housekeeper, arranged to bring her back home and nursed her through the last weeks. She died on April 14th, which is ironic, as that happens to be my birthday.

"Lad, that's a heartache for ye, to be sure."

"Yes ... sir, but actually, it's a meaningful day already so it seems appropriate somehow."

Alex sipped at his cider, trying to decide how to further the conversation along. But then, what did he want to know? Surely he would offer to help the lad, but how were they to get any kind of relationship going?

"To be frank with ye, lad, I don't know any other way of figuring things out except to ask ye questions, ye ken?"

"Alright. I guess that's OK. I'll answer them if I can. But you must know, I don't especially want to be here even though Mother said I should find you. I'm a British citizen, not a Scot."

"Aye. Aye. I see. Then, do ye understand I never knew I had a son?"

"Yes ... sir. And you should know I never knew my father was alive until a couple of months ago. Mother had a birth certificate that has my name as Robert Alexander Edwards ... and another one that says Robert Alexander MacKinnon. She told me my father had been a soldier in service of the Crown and that he was brave and died in a battle with a battalion of French soldiers. There was never a lot of discussion about him, other than she always insisted he was a most intelligent man, very handsome, and a fine soldier. She even showed me a few charcoal drawings she said were of him. Of course, I now realize she invented this man in order for me to believe I had been a wanted child, and that is exactly what she accomplished. I did always feel wanted and cared for. Only now, since she's passed away, I'm aware of new feelings, of being without roots, drifting, not sure what to do next."

"Aye. Of course, lad. Ye naturally would feel that. Then, ye can be sure this family, the MacKinnon family—yer family, I suppose—will welcome ye. And I should also tell ye we're probably quite different from folk down in the Lowlands or Edinburgh and London. Speaking of that, where did ye come from?"

"I've lived in London and Edinburgh. In my early life we lived in London for some years then, for some reason, Mother insisted we move to Edinburgh. She'd been a tutor at university there early on, then went back to London and was headmistress at Her Majesty's Preparatory Academy, a school for young ladies. She taught there for some time, but about five years ago she wanted to return to Edinburgh and the university. She had fond memories of her time there and missed the stimulation of the young students. So, we moved there and that's where I still live."

"So yer early years were pretty much spent in London then. I suppose that's why ye sound more English than Scot. But of course ye would. Fiona was English through and through."

"Yes ... sir."

Alex didn't miss the hesitancy of the lad to call him sir.

"But she always spoke highly of the Scots and their devotion to family and their strong work ethic. She was impressed with those characteristics. But not everyone I know feels that way about Scots."

"Then I thank her for that. She was a fine lady herself, and I never held it against her that she were English."

He smiled at the lad and the smile was returned briefly. But there was certainly a question written on the lad's face.

Ah, he seemed to take no offense and took that remark as it was intended. So, maybe we can get through this.

Robbie took a deep breath, then made his pronouncement. "I've always thought I was thoroughly British. But now, I guess I have to realize and admit I'm half Scot."

Alex thought for a moment before addressing this proclamation from the lad. The flat, non-emotional way in which he made the statement told Alex the lad would rather be a toad than a Scot.

Looks like I have a new problem to deal with. He was proud to be British, of course. Now he knows Scots blood flows in his veins as well, Highland blood at that.

"Well, then I suppose yer right. In my opinion a man, or lad, should be proud of his heritage, his country, and most of all his family. But I can understand ye might have some trouble agreeing with me on this. Ye've thought ye were British for some years now, and actually ye are half British, as it were. But there's goodness to be found in both peoples, I suppose, and areas where there will always be disagreements. Mam would have said 'that's life.'"

"Who's Mam?"

"Mam was my mother, yer grandmother. She's gone on now, but she always had sayings that seemed to fit most occasions."

And I know she could help me now if she were here.

"Robbie, we have a lot of catching up to do. It's late now so I think we'll call it a night and tomorrow we'll make more headway. Tonight ye need to rest and, again, ye are welcome here in our home. I'm not real sure how a father should act, but I'll do my best. I hope ye can find a way to understand that if I had known about ye, I'd have come looking for ye. This family cares for its own. Ye are my son. That makes ye important to all of us."

"Yes ... sir. Mother and I discussed you at length before she passed on. She held you in the highest regard and indicated I was to do the same … even if you are a Scot."

"I'm glad to hear that, lad. Then let's see where we're to bed ye down. Come, I'll see what Caitlin has in mind."

As they stood, Da entered and stood for a moment, staring at his son and grandson. Alex was certainly a handsome man, and wore his kilt with pride. The lad was clad in long, dark trousers and a dark matching coat. Obviously their clothing was different, but if they were any more alike Da would eat his tam. The lad was several inches shorter than Alex and certainly not as filled out, but then he still had a few growing years ahead of him.

Stroking his bearded face, Da ran his finger down through the cleft in his chin.

Huh. Well now, guess that's at least one trait the three of us have in common. Wonder what others we may have.

He walked over and put his hand out and the boy took it for a short moment.

"Lad, I'm yer grandfather, Daniel. Ye found yer way here, and now that ye have, we're glad to make yer acquaintance. We MacKinnons take care of each other, and ye'll be treated like one of us, as ye certainly are from what I see."

"Thank you ... sir." The boy hadn't known what to expect, but this was not an anticipated response.

They don't even know me, but are going out of their way to make me feel welcome. But they're Scots, known to be scoundrels and uneducated heathens. I know I can't trust them.

"If it suits ye, Ian would like ye to share his space. It's up in the farthest part of the lodge, the attic actually. He's about yer age, maybe a tad older, I think. So, take the stairs all the way to the top and he'll find ye a bed. We'll talk tomorrow. Night to ye now."

Robbie nodded quickly to Da. "Yes ... sir. That sounds fine to me."

The young lad looked about, not sure where he was to go. He made a quick trip back to the porch and returned carrying a soft, leather valise in which he had brought a few items of clothing, some of his mother's personal documents, and his ever-present writing pad. This pad was much more important to him than any of the other articles, however.

Da made his way to his room at the end of the hall, a book tucked under his arm as always, and Alex waited at the foot of the stairs for the lad.

"Up there, lad—Robbie. All the way to the top. Ian's got a place for ye to rest yer head. He'll be going to the Isle of Skye in a couple of days and then ye'll have the place to yerself. So if you can manage to share a room a couple of nights, it will be helpful."

"Of course ... sir."

Alex hardly knew how to react to such a formal, polished young man. On the one hand, the lad obviously disliked learning he was half Scot and had made that very clear. But on the other, he had the manners of a young gentleman. Alex tried to remember himself at that awkward age. He was quite sure he was not polished, but Mam would have insisted on good manners. And if he was rebellious, then Da would have given him some extra chores to work off his angry feelings. No doubt, though, this lad was as much a MacKinnon as any of them.

Robbie lifted his valise and began the climb up the stairs. And it was a climb, too. Once he got to the top, he saw the faintest light coming from beneath one of the doors. He knocked and waited a second. Just as he was about to knock again, the door opened and Ian nodded to him.

"Aye, this is the right room. Mine. And I think ye'll like it, too. Come in."

Robbie slowly walked through the doorway and felt as if he had entered a room that had been designed with him in mind. There was an old wooden desk in front of one of the tall, many-paned windows. A candle had been lighted and there were several maps and drawings lying on the desk. He came closer and took a quick glance at them. The maps were very old and Robbie thought they were from a much earlier period, perhaps from early Roman times, and there was a scent in the room that was most pleasant—an herb, something green and fresh. Maybe rosemary.

"Put yer bag in the corner. I've put some blankets on the cot and that should keep ye warm enough. Ye'll find it's actually warmer up here than any other place. Da says it's something about the heat rising. But still, it can get cold up here in the Highlands, even in the spring. Probably different from where ye came from. Where was that exactly?"

"I came from Edinburgh, where I lived with my mother. She died recently and I'm not sure what I'm to do now."

Ian found himself searching for the right words, but wasn't sure there were any. "Oh, then, don't worry too much. Alex is a very intelligent man. He'll figure out the best thing for ye to do. I know how it is to lose yer mam, though. Ours passed on a couple of years ago and we all felt like our world had turned upside down. Maybe that's how everybody feels when their mam dies. But I'm learning that because she died doesn't mean she's lost to ye. She's just in a different place now. Ah, listen to me, going on so. Come over here and take a look out there."

Robbie walked closer to the tall window, the two young lads standing side by side. Ian snuffed the candle out and it was pitch-black in the room. Suddenly, the moor was easily seen beneath the light of a glowing moon. The snow that had covered the ground for so long had melted now as the days were warmer, even though the evenings were still chilly. The highest peaks of the mountains were still covered and pockets of snow could be found in the crags, but the green, spring sprouts were beginning to show and the heather on the moor was blossoming quickly.

"Now look just at the edge of that stand of pine trees on the left side, look closely."

"I don't see anything. There's nothing there but trees. No, wait. Oh! Is that a stag?" Robbie stared at Ian, his face registering his excitement.

"Yeah. He's been here as long as I can remember. He shows himself sometimes on an evening such as this. I sometimes wonder if he can see me too."

Robbie continued to look at Ian. The two could have been brothers. But there was something about this young lad Robbie didn't quite understand. He acted as if Robbie was not a stranger but had always been here, in this lodge, as if he had always been a member of this family. There was also an element of mischief, or adventure that emanated from him. But then, there was an element of warmth, also. Robbie had lived in London and Edinburgh, but he had never come across a young person who was as interesting as Ian.

"Do you think he can see us now?"

"I'm learning that the animals know a lot, and we've a lot to learn from them if we only will. Just some of the things Uncle Wabi is teaching me."

"Uncle Wabi? Who's that?"

"He's actually Caitlin's uncle, but he feels like mine too so I call him Uncle Wabi. He's a very unusual man and I'm studying with him. I'll tell ye about him tomorrow. Right now I think we'd better get to bed. If I know Alex, he'll be expecting both of us to be down in the kitchen early, ready to listen to his instructions for the day." He smiled when he made this remark and Robbie smiled in return.

2

Alex removed his shirt and kilt and placed them on the chair under the window. He eased his body into bed, snuggled up to Caitlin's back and reached over and stroked her large abdomen. He was still in awe of how a woman's body could change so much. She was so small, yet now her middle was enormous.

I hope she's not having twins like ye did, Mam. I don't think I could take that, losing a bairn. May the Creator be with us.

Caitlin was dead to the world, as she always was by nightfall these days. But Alex's mind was on fire and running in a thousand directions. He couldn't seem to stay on track with one thought before another one rushed in. How was he to deal with this new information?

Information, my arse! It's a young lad, my son. I've gotta get my thoughts together now and figure out how I'm to deal with him. And whatever must Caitlin be thinking about me? That I just left a young lass with no thought for her condition? But then, I didn't know about her condition. And if I had? Would I have stayed in Edinburgh with her? Nae, that wouldn't have been my first choice. But, maybe I ... ah, Jesus!

Alex covered his head with the blanket in an effort to shut out any more thoughts that might come rushing in. His body and mind had had enough for one day. Tomorrow would be soon enough to tackle this latest problem.

He was awakened a few hours later by Caitlin moaning in her

sleep. He sat up quickly, looking down at her.

"Mo chridhe, are ye in pain? What is it, lass?"

She mumbled something he couldn't understand, but the next moment she sat up and called out loudly.

"Holy Rusephus! It can't be coming this quickly. First bairns are always late. Help me up, now!"

Alex jumped out of bed, quickly donned his kilt and helped Caitlin to stand. She grabbed her stomach and groaned as a searing pain crept from her back around to her abdomen.

"What? What do I need to do?" Alex had birthed lambs and calves in his time, but this was his first experience with a bairn, and this one his own.

"Just help me to Mam's sewing room. That's where I want to birth this bairn. It's a special place, Alex. Take me there."

"Aye, lass, aye."

"And send Jack for the midwife. Maria, I think her name is. I thought I could handle this by myself, but this bairn is coming early and quickly. I may need some help. Then come back up here and help me get down the stairs."

"Maria? I don't think I know her, lass."

"No. I met her in the village a few weeks ago. She's Lourdes' aunt who just arrived here from Spain. Lourdes says she's a very competent midwife. I believe she lives in the cottage next door to the kirk—a place McGuire arranged for her. But she's old enough to know her business. Hurry now."

Alex fled the room before Caitlin even finished her sentence. In a few seconds he was at the other end of the hall calling out loudly.

"Jack! Get down here brother, I need yer help!" His booming voice probably awakened the entire household, but Alex was not concerned with that.

It was a known fact Jack was not at his best when awakened abruptly, but Millie roused him and helped him get moving. As soon as Jack came running, Alex was giving orders.

"Go to the village and get Maria, the midwife. Caitlin's having the bairn early and it looks like she needs the midwife to help her. Don't think she had planned on needing any help, but the midwife might be useful. Go now. She lives in the cottage next to the kirk."

"I'm going, I'm going. But who's this Maria person? I thought the midwife was old Harriet. That's who Mam used."

"Caitlin says Harriet passed away and this woman, this Maria, knows her business. Just get yerself there and back, quickly now."

Jack had never seen Alex in such a state. He usually took everything in stride and stayed calm when others might be agitated. No sooner had Jack gone than Millie came running to Caitlin's room, pulling her dressing gown together, her long, dark hair streaming behind her as she hurried along.

"Caitlin, are you alright? Is the bairn coming?" Millie's voice was soothing and well modulated, always the lady's voice. She found Caitlin pacing from one end of the room to the other.

"It looks like this first bairn is determined to make an early appearance. My calculations said it should be several more weeks now, but this one's got a mind of its own, just like the rest of the MacKinnons I suppose."

She grabbed at her abdomen, trying to tell herself to slow down her breathing and stop fighting the pain. She knew the more she fought it, the more severe it would become. How many times had she said those words to women in labor? And she remembered the looks they often gave her, ones that said they'd like to slap her face if they could.

Well, healer, looks like you didn't have any idea what they were truly enduring, now did you?

Alex took the stairs two at a time and was back quickly. Caitlin was standing next to the bed holding on to the bedpost.

"Here, help me get down the stairs. Just hold me under the arms and I'll manage."

Alex nodded, then as though he had not even heard her instructions, picked her up and carried her down the stairs as if she weighed nothing at all, with Millie following closely behind them. Millie well remembered this stage of the birthing process and it wasn't a fond memory. Of course, she'd had Caitlin at her side and all went well for her and her bairn, Midge.

Alex set Caitlin down carefully. "Here, lass, come lie down now. Let's get ye off yer feet."

"No, I have to stand up, walk around. Get some hot water, clean cloths and bring my medicine bag from the pantry. It's up high on the top shelf where the bairns can't reach it."

Even in this time of distress, Caitlin managed to keep her

thoughts in order and was determined to keep her wits about her. Actually, though, she didn't feel much in control and wondered what was keeping Jack and the midwife. It may be that she'd deliver this bairn by herself, but she'd rather have help standing by.

Millie left them and busied herself in the kitchen preparing tea, as she was sure the whole family would be there shortly. Having Caitlin at her side during the birth of Midge was something she would never forget. She often thought she would not have survived her ordeal in the forest on that cold, snowy night without Caitlin's help. That was the beginning of their friendship. Now here she was only able to make a cup of tea for Caitlin. She didn't have a clue about what she could do to help a laboring woman, but was glad Jack was bringing Maria.

In the last few weeks Millie's days had been even more hectic than usual. Caitlin literally waddled about, so Millie did most of the running back and forth between the lodge and classroom.

Just yesterday, as she loaded up her arms with books and school supplies and headed across the yard, the new hand, Boder, appeared as he had several times the last few days.

"Here, I'll take those for you. A lovely lady such as you should have servants to do her bidding. What are you doing at this Highland lodge anyway? It's obvious to me you belong in a fine house, perhaps even a castle somewhere."

He put a hand at her back, ostensibly to help her walk, and just his touch made Millie cringe.

"Thank you, but I can manage."

Millie felt his fingers as they pushed back a lock of her hair that had blown across her face. Then his eyes moved up and down her body and he smiled as he bowed and walked away.

She vowed to herself to keep out of Boder's way and not mention the exchange to Jack. She knew he would not take kindly to Boder's comments about her belonging in a castle. She wondered if perhaps Boder was someone from her past. Did he know about Lord Sinclair's death? Did he know her father? She no longer thought of either of them.

She had just poured herself a cup of tea when she heard voices coming from the stairwell.

"Daniel, we've been through this more times than most. The lass will be alright I tell ye. She's delivered many bairns for others and knows what to expect. The best thing we can do is keep Alex's mind occupied."

Uncle Andrew's voice was soothing and he was aware Da cared greatly for his daughter-in-law, as did he. No matter how many times they'd sat through the long birthing process when the lads had been born, they both always dreaded that the child may die, as Alex's twin sister had so long ago.

Jack rushed in the back door practically pulling the midwife behind him. She was an older woman, a bit on the rotund side, and wore a long, full-skirted dress and a colorful scarf tied around her thick, salt and pepper hair. She spoke with a certain amount of authority and had a strong foreign accent. Jack wasn't sure where she came from, but had no trouble understanding her. In fact, she probably had more trouble understanding his Scottish brogue, which only got thicker when he was anxious.

Alex refused to leave Caitlin even as she insisted she didn't need his help, but he was relieved when Jack entered with Maria. He knew when he was out of his element, and this was one of those times. But still, he wanted to stay with Caitlin, not let her go through this ordeal alone.

"Come on, brother. Let's go down and have some tea. Millie's got it all ready for us." Jack wanted to get out of there himself.

"Nae, I'll stay here with her. I can't leave her, ye ken? She's mine and I'll not let her go through this without me. I'll be staying."

Jack nodded and looked over at Caitlin, who gave a quick nod to him indicating she agreed with the decision—Alex could stay. But the midwife wasn't as happy about that decision as they were. In her heavily accented voice she addressed Alex.

"I can take care of her, Señor MacKinnon. Birthing a niño is not something menfolk usually want any part of. You should go now. I'll call you when it's over."

She approached Caitlin's bedside and began to lay out the items she would need to assist in the birth. But she apparently knew nothing of the MacKinnon men. Changing their mind on something they'd decided was not an easy undertaking.

"As I said, I'll be staying," Alex replied as he pulled up a small stool next to Caitlin's bed and sat down. He took her hand and she gave him a small smile as another searing pain had her in its grip. She pulled Alex's hand and placed it on her abdomen, letting him feel every movement of the bairn as it struggled to make its appearance.

The midwife put her hands on Caitlin's abdomen also.

"It's not quite time, señora. Slow your breathing down now. Slow your breathing down. But it'll not be long now. I'll tell you when to push."

She did sound like Lourdes thought Alex, the same accent. Lourdes was quite a bit younger than her husband, McGuire, very attractive, and even smaller than Caitlin. Her talent was working with flowers and plants and she and Caitlin had become friends. Alex hadn't quite figured out how McGuire was able to convince her to come to the Highlands with him, but then, Da had convinced Mam to do the same so it did happen.

But the accent was the only thing the midwife had in common with Lourdes. There was something about the woman that disturbed Alex, but he couldn't put his finger on it. She was not especially to his liking, but he knew he needed her so he'd put his dislike aside for the moment.

Jack left the room and found his way to the kitchen, where Uncle Andrew and Da were sipping their tea. They looked up as he entered.

"Everything alright with Caitlin?" Da asked. He tried to keep his worries to himself, but Andrew could read his face very well after all these years.

"Yeah, but Alex refuses to leave her. The midwife's not too happy about that, but ye know how Alex is when he makes up his mind."

"Aye. Kinda like the rest of us, huh?" Da said.

They all laughed and began to once again discuss the latest rumors about requirements the Crown was going to impose on the Scots.

The Battle of Culloden had been disastrous for many Scots, particularly those who were members of the Jacobite Uprising, in which the MacKinnons had played a part. Lately there had been a few travelers from London and Edinburgh relaying information that the Crown was working harder than ever to find and punish Scots who had participated in the uprising.

The rumors were that their lands would be forfeited and the men either imprisoned, executed or exiled. Further, the Scots would be forbidden to speak Gaelic and the tartan could not be worn. Word was many had already been rounded up and sent to the Caribbean as slaves.

"What do ye think, Da? Will the Brits really come looking for us? And take our lands?" Jack asked. He wasn't one to believe everything he heard, but this subject had his attention.

"These rumors are just the latest of many, lad. The ones in charge always try to control those not in their power. It's not anything I'd give a lot of thought to. Besides, we're so far up in these Highlands the Brits would get lost just trying to find us.

Nae, time will pass and this Battle of Culloden will fade in their memories. I remember the uprising of '15. It was the same as now. Just a lot of bluster, but not much action. As for taking our lands, that might prove to be a bit more difficult than they think. The clans that live up here will stick together as always. A few generations ago we MacKinnons actually lived mostly down around the Isle of Skye, but following some disputes some of us came up here, which is where we've been for some time now. I don't think we'll be going anywhere."

That eased Jack's mind. If Da wasn't too concerned, then he wouldn't be either.

~ ~ ~

The brightness of the full moon surrounded Wabi's cottage and he stood looking out his kitchen window at the water lapping the rocks down on the edge of the beach. He was not surprised to see a large winged bird swoop down and alight on a perch that had been built just for him. Owl. He walked outside and called out.

"Ah, my dear friend. I was hoping you'd get here soon. I'm sure you, too, know where we're headed this beautiful evening. It seems I just got here and now I have to turn around and make another trip."

Yes, Master. The time has come, and even though I detest time weaving I know we must get to the Highlands quickly.

"Right you are, Owl. Caitlin's in labor and knowing that girl, she'll hurry through it like she does everything else. It's important I be there when the child is born. But I promise to keep the time weaving to the shortest route and not make any detours to extend our trip."

He laughed and gathered his old crooked staff, his long dark cloak and a small leather pouch that he flung over his shoulder.

"Then let's be off."

With a nod of his head and one quick wave of his staff, the two of them disappeared in a spinning whirlwind that took Owl's breath. No matter how many times he traveled in this fashion with Wabi, he still found time weaving unnerving. But he had to admit, it was an expedient way to get somewhere when time was of the essence. He even agreed that the sights he often saw—when he was brave enough to open his eyes—were extraordinary. The universes melded together in a rainbow of colors he had never before seen and a myriad of sounds assaulted his ears with such glorious music he could almost enjoy this trip. Almost.

The Highlands were only short minutes away. Sometimes, however, Wabi's and Owl's landings were not as eloquent as their departures. Gentle landings were not something Wabi had ever stopped long enough to perfect. He was usually in such a hurry to get to a specific place that he just got up and went, and often landed in a most jarring manner.

Tonight he was certainly in a rush. Only a few hours earlier he had sensed vibrations he knew were coming from his niece, Caitlin. He was a bit surprised as he thought the bairn wasn't due for another few weeks. However, he also knew bairns changed their mind often and didn't ask permission from anyone as to their arrival time.

He and Owl arrived at the steps of the lodge. Owl took roost in the rowan tree by the porch, and just as Wabi raised his staff to knock, the door opened and Ian greeted them.

"Uncle Wabi, I thought ye might show up. There's a lot of activity going on inside. Most of it's coming from Jack, Da and Uncle Andrew discussing the Crown's plans for us Scots. The rest of the noise is coming from Caitlin. She's calling out loud enough for ye to hear her in Skye. And every time she screams, Willie howls even louder."

Wabi grinned, then noticed another young lad standing behind Ian. Before he had a chance to ask about him Ian made the introduction.

"Uncle Wabi, this is Robbie, Robbie MacKinnon. Alex's son, ye ken?"

Wabi didn't miss the sullen look on the lad's face, nor the strong resemblance to Alex, but knew this was not the time to ask questions.

"Hello, Robbie. Good to meet you, lad." Then he turned back to Ian. "You say Caitlin's making herself heard? Then I got here just in time. She hasn't delivered yet, apparently."

"Nae, but ye can hear her screaming at Alex to sit down and stop pacing. She's actually yelling at him, Uncle Wabi. Ye should hear her."

"That means everything is as it should be. Just one of the phases of birthing a bairn, my lad."

"Maria, the midwife, is with her. But I heard Caitlin yelling at her, too. Glad I'm not in there."

Wabi smiled and walked to the kitchen to speak to Da and Andrew. The three oldsters had become friends and Wabi was glad Caitlin was a part of this family. It suited her for sure.

"Wabi, come, come in. Didn't know ye were due a visit, but we're always glad to see ye. Here, sit and have a cup of Millie's tea. It's even better than mine. We'll drink tea now, and save ourselves for a wee dram when the time comes." Da laughed.

The fact Wabi just showed up unannounced no longer phased the MacKinnons. He had earned his place in the family and his eccentricities were accepted by all of them.

A voice coming from Mam's room had them all turning their heads.

"I have to push, now! Stop telling me to not push! Get out of here!" Caitlin's voice was clearly heard above the other two. "I said get out of here, now!"

The next sound was that of a door being slammed, then total quietness for a moment. Shortly, Maria walked into the kitchen muttering to herself in her native language.

"¡Madre de Dios, ella es imposible!"

None of them spoke Spanish, but they all understood what she meant. Caitlin had a temper they had all witnessed, and a determination even greater. That she had sent the midwife out was not surprising to them at all. She usually managed to be in charge of most situations in which she was a participant. No one said a word, but offered Maria a cup of tea instead. Before the midwife finished her tea, they heard the next cry.

"Alex!"

Caitlin called out, then let out a scream that had everyone on the edge of their chairs, afraid of what exactly they did not know. Willie's long, mournful howl further set their nerves on fire. Finally, the wail of an infant filled the air, and this cry was almost as loud as Caitlin's and Willie's.

After waiting for a few minutes, Wabi excused himself and went to Caitlin's room and entered without stopping to knock. He was greeted by Willie, who licked his hand then ran back to the bed and put his front paws up on the edge of it, as if he'd had a hand in the proceedings. Wabi found Alex kneeling next to Caitlin's bed, trying to wrap a blanket around a wriggling, very pink bairn. The look on his face was so amusing Wabi wanted to laugh.

"Ah, Alex, so you survived then I see." Wabi smiled at him, then went over and placed a kiss on Caitlin's forehead.

"Uncle Wabi, you came. I'm so glad."

"Of course I came. I have work to do just as you did. Now, if I may, I'd like to hold your daughter."

"How did you know I had a daughter?"

Removing his cloak and standing his staff in the corner, he turned to his niece.

"That's a long story, Caitlin. But at first glance, I'd say she's healthy and certainly her lungs are working well. I was at the birth of your grandmother, Ci-Cero, you mother, Flinn, and of course yours. At each birth I performed a ritual I would like to perform with your daughter as well."

"What kind of ritual? I don't know anything about any ritual. Why would you do that?"

"It's part of the Creator's plan for me, as well as for you and all the others in your line of healers. It is simply a way of marking you that identifies you as belonging to this particular line. It's harmless, not painful, but important."

"What kind of mark? I don't have any mark."

"But of course you do, my girl. You may not have ever seen it, but it's there. I placed it on you myself."

"Where? Why haven't I seen it?"

"It's behind your left ear, just at your hairline. I suspect Alex has seen it."

"But, what does it look like?" She ran her fingertips behind her ear, but could feel nothing. Alex spoke up.

"Oh, you mean that small circle? I have seen it, assumed it

was a birthmark. I've never actually examined it closely."

"Yes, you're right. It is a circle. To be precise, it's an ouroboros, which is a serpent with its tail in its mouth, a symbol of healing for millennia. Many ancient cultures regarded the serpent as sacred and used it in healing rituals. It's symbolic of immortality, the eternal unity of all things, the cycle of birth and death. Simply put, it's a sign of wholeness and infinity."

Alex stared at his newborn daughter, who already looked so like his Caitlin. Her hair was abundant and as flaming as her mother's, and she was so tiny he feared he would break her. Carefully handing her to Caitlin, he nodded his agreement with the ritual.

Wabi reached inside his old leather pouch and brought out a small rowan twig and held it above his head, high in the air, as if presenting it to some unseen entity. He reached out his arms and Caitlin placed the crying, squirming, bairn in them.

Wabi held her gently to his chest, then closed his eyes, all the while softly chanting in a language known only to a few. He carefully touched the twig to the area behind the bairn's left ear. As the twig touched her skin, a small droplet of a deep blue fluid dripped from the rowan twig and a small circle appeared.

Caitlin held her breath, thinking perhaps the liquid would burn the child's skin. But the bairn quieted and stayed perfectly still, as though she intuitively knew this ritual was the bestowing of a gift. Wabi continued to chant as he sprinkled the droplet with silver dust that sparkled for a moment then was gone, leaving behind a perfect ouroboros behind her left ear.

"And now she, too, has been marked. She belongs to your line. The Creator will have his own plans for her destiny, for her life."

He placed a kiss on the child's forehead, just as he had on Caitlin's, then handed her back to her mother. The wailing had ceased and the child slept quietly. The line of healers continued.

Caitlin looked at the ouroboros. "Uncle Wabi, that looks like some kind of blue ink. What is it?"

"It's fluid from the woad plant. It's been used for centuries by many peoples, and most certainly originated with your people."

"Woad plant? But, Wabi, that's poisonous isn't it?"

Wabi smiled and waited, as he could see Caitlin rummaging through her very fine mind searching for some lost information. Then she spoke.

"Oh, yes, the plant my ancestors, the Picts, used on their bodies. I've just started reading my grandmother's journal, *The Wolf, The Wizard and the Woad* in which Grandmother Ci-Cero tells the story of her people, my people I suppose.

They were a very fierce people who often went into battle with their bodies tattooed with blue fluid from the woad plant. The Romans began calling them Woads after losing to them in battle. It's said that Hadrian's Wall was erected in order to keep the Woads to the north of it because they were such fierce warriors. Most probably folklore, but the name stuck. I had no idea I came from such early folk."

Wabi nodded. "Ci-Cero's mother, Katalani, your great-grandmother, was indeed a Woad, and perhaps the earliest of this line of healers. I met Katalani only briefly, at the birth of your grandmother, who later was given the name Ci-Cero by the native tribe she lived with in North America."

"Yes, she tells how she received the name in her journal. It's an engrossing story. I'm afraid I haven't read much of it yet. But then, you lived through it yourself, so I don't need to tell you about it."

Wabi nodded to his niece.

"You must make time to read the entire story. Your people, the Picts and Vikings, are proud people. You have blood from both and you are so like your grandmother, Ci-Cero, even more so than like your mother, Flinn.

"Memories of that time are forever etched in my brain and heart, my girl. And they live on through you and now this bairn you hold. She has a destiny that will find its own path as all the others have. The Creator has honored me by allowing me to be a part of his plan for this line of healers. It is my destiny."

Wabi excused himself then and left the two new parents, who were busy counting fingers and toes and grinning from ear to ear.

"What are we going to call her, lass? We've talked about several names, but I haven't heard ye mention any lately." Alex looked at the two, his Caitlin and now his daughter, amazed to see the likeness—as alike as he and Robbie.

"I would like to honor both our mothers by naming our daughter after them. How does Alicia Flinn MacKinnon sound to you?"

"Aye. Aye. Mam would be pleased to know her name is

carried on."

"I never knew my mother, but perhaps if we keep her name alive her spirit may find a place with us. I was thinking we would call our child Flinn. Is that alright with you?"

"Flinn, aye. Flinn it is."

~ ~ ~

Millie breathed a sigh of relief when the new bairn announced her arrival. It wasn't that long ago she had been through this same ordeal and she'd not forgotten what a difficult time it was. She would forever be grateful Caitlin had been there when she needed her help. Now, perhaps she'd return that favor by offering to tend the new child for a while so Caitlin and Alex could get some much needed rest.

Knocking lightly, she entered Caitlin's room. She almost laughed as she watched Alex struggling, trying to wrap the bairn in a blanket. This man, who was so very capable of doing most anything, had a look on his face that told her he was out of his comfort zone. One quick look at Caitlin and the two shared a smile they both understood.

"Well, now. What have we here? A playmate for Midge, I believe?"

She took the child from Alex, who looked relieved to let someone else hold his bundle. He stood and spoke a few words to Caitlin, kissed her, then went down to the kitchen to share his excitement with Da and the others.

Millie gathered the child to her breast and inhaled the warm, sweet aroma that every mother recognizes.

"Ah, Caitlin. She's such a beauty. Look at those sparkling eyes. And that hair. Don't think I've ever seen a lovelier child. Well, maybe Midge, of course."

That brought a smile to Caitlin's face and, for some reason, tears to her eyes. She wiped away her tears and looked again at her friend holding her child. Strange events had brought them together, and something told her they would share even more events in the future.

"Well, now. First things first. Why don't you give this child her first meal? This is the one time she'll know exactly what to do without any help. Then I'll take her so you can rest awhile."

"Thanks, Millie. But I think I'll just keep her here close to me.

Somehow I'm not ready to let her go just yet. I don't understand it, but she seems more a part of me now than she did when I carried her."

Millie smiled but kept her thoughts to herself.

Yes, and that feeling will never leave you. There will be days when the responsibility of having a child is overwhelming, but even then you'll hold her close and feel what all mothers feel—never-ending love.

~ ~ ~

Alex's grin grew even bigger when all the men folk, and even Maria, stood as he entered the kitchen. Each of them had a cup of cider and raised it to him.

"And a toast to the latest MacKinnon, I say. And to her da and mam." Da tossed his cider back and the others followed.

Alex found himself speechless, a most unusual state for him. "Aye, and to the wee lass. A beauty like her mam." He had in mind to say more, but his throat was near to closing up on him so he stopped with those words.

Maria gathered her belongings and medicine bag. "As Señora MacKinnon's not in need of my services, I'll be off then." She was accustomed to being in charge of births, but this MacKinnon woman definitely had a mind of her own. However, Maria had to admit the woman had handled her own situation very well.

"Aye. Ian and Robbie will get the cart and take ye home then, Maria. I don't know what to tell ye except that Caitlin can be determined when she sets her mind to it." Alex looked about the room and observed nods all 'round.

"What matters is that she and the little one are well. That's all I need to know. Now, come young señor, I'm ready to get to mi casa."

Ian was more than glad to have been assigned a task. All the screaming coming from Caitlin and the howling of Willie, plus the anxiety reeling off Alex, was taxing his emotions. He had often spoken to Mam of feeling others' pain, a trait he shared with Caitlin. Mam had told him it was something he would learn to control, but as of yet he hadn't developed that ability either.

This evening was as painful for him as it had been for Caitlin and Alex, and he had been glad when Alex asked Robbie to go with him. He was sensing the uneasiness of this lad, too, and knew he would welcome a chance to get out of the lodge for a brief time.

"Good night, Maria," Ian called as he and Robbie left the midwife a little while later.

"Buenos noches, señors," Maria called out as she closed the door to her cottage.

The two lads climbed back on the cart. They were not in a hurry to get back to the lodge, so the cart creaked along the path and the two talked as easily as if they had known each other for a lifetime.

"So then, I suppose ye being Alex's son would make ye my nephew." Ian smiled broadly at Robbie, who returned it in kind.

"Yeah, I guess that's right. I believe you're maybe a bit older than I am. Seems strange somehow. As of this evening, I have a father, a stepmother, a grandfather, three uncles, two aunts, a cousin, and a half-sister."

"Did yer mam never tell ye about Alex or his family?"

Robbie avoided looking Ian in the eye. He'd already decided he wasn't going to like anyone at the lodge, but was now finding that difficult. Ian was just so interesting.

"No. She was a great storyteller and I suppose she just made up a story she thought I would like. She told me my father was a soldier who died in battle. According to her, he saved many lives by his heroic acts and died on the battlefield. And that was what I believed until just a couple of months before she died. It was then she told me the real story and who my father really was, or is. The story of Alex and his Highland family."

"So ye never knew anything about Alex before then?"

"No. But when she told me about him, she spoke of him with such feeling I wondered why she didn't come to the Highlands with him. When I asked her, she simply said she knew she needed to be in the world of art, literature and academics. Most of her friends were from those backgrounds, and she was always happy with them. She never lacked for friends, but I can't recall any special man now that I think about it. It appeared her work, her teaching, and her friends were enough for her. Of course, most of them were English, although she had a couple of friends from India, too."

"Aye, then I'm glad ye know the truth. Uncle Wabi believes truth will always be that which frees us from our troubles."

"Uncle Wabi. The old gentleman I just met, right?"

"Aye. He's like a member of the family now, and as ye'll find out he's a wizard of sorts, if ye ken what I'm saying."

Ian wasn't sure Robbie would have any understanding of the true nature of Wabi, or him as far as that went. So he thought it better to keep some information to himself and let Robbie figure out a few things on his own.

"Well, the truth is I'm not just British, but am half Scots. And my mother lied to me my entire life about who my father was."

Ian's antennae picked up on the lad's extreme agitation and anger. But even at his young age, Ian knew this would be something Robbie would have to work out for himself.

"Alex is a man ye can be proud to have as yer da. Even if he is a Scot."

Robbie made no comment to that remark, but just stared ahead.

As they returned to the lodge, the menfolk were still in the kitchen discussing the situation regarding the Brits. The MacKinnons had barely escaped the Battle of Culloden with their lives. The Battle was over, but the repercussions of it were beginning to be felt throughout the land, even into the upper Highlands where they lived.

Ian and Robbie exchanged a look, and with no words being said, decided not to participate in the conversation but to go on up to the attic space and watch the wildlife they might get a peek of when it was quiet and the moon was bright. The uncle and the nephew appeared to be more like brothers than new acquaintances and both were aware of it.

~ ~ ~

Wabi had left the lodge shortly following the birth of Caitlin's bairn. He had an inkling, actually more of an uncomfortable feeling, his presence was needed in Skye, so he took leave in his usual fashion—time weaving.

That evening, Ian and Robbie stayed up late watching out the window, looking out over the moor. Finally, to their delight, the old stag once again showed himself.

"Has he really been here a long time? I mean, how do you know it's the same stag?"

"That's easy. Next time he shows himself, look at his rack. The left side is missing part of its upper portion. Da says he ran some poachers off years ago. He believes they shot at the stag and nicked his rack."

"Ok. I'll look next time I see him."

Ian turned over in bed, hoping sleep would come, but so far his mind was restless and was as unstoppable as the water rushing down the crags when the snow begins to melt in the springtime.

I wonder if the old stag knows I'm leaving for a while. Will he still be here when I return? When will that be? This is my home, but Wabi tells me there's so much I must learn that I may be gone for some time. Mam, can ye hear me?

He lay in his bed remembering his conversation with Alex earlier, and understood his brother was eager for him to go to Wabi's.

"Go, lad. If the Brits do find us up here, then ye'll be safe with Wabi. He'll not let anything happen to ye, ye ken?"

Several hours later, when it became obvious to him that he was never going to get to sleep, Ian got up and gathered his small satchel of clothes along with a few important items. The first item was a gift that had come from Caitlin. It was a very old map of Scotland and the Isles, including Skye where she came from. The second was a compass Da had given him some time ago, and he'd told him to never travel without it. He'd liked carrying it in his pocket as a small lad, but this trip would be the first Ian had ever made on his own, so maybe it would be helpful now.

The last item was the sparkling amber stone he had found at the old kirk. He now knew it was instrumentally a part of his power, and he had a vague memory of seeing Mam holding it, but the memory was so faint as to almost be a dream. He carefully packed the items in his bag and headed out the door.

Robbie heard Ian moving about so he, too, got up and with a nod from Ian, followed him down the stairs and outside to the stables. They were ever so quiet, creeping slowly down the stairs in an effort to not wake the household.

"Are you going to leave without saying goodbye to your family?"

"Aye. They'll understand. They all know how I hate goodbyes. This way is better."

"When will you come back? Will I see you again?"

"Of course. This is my home. I'll always return to the Highlands. My family is here, but my place now is with Uncle Wabi. Once I've learned what I can from him, I'll find my way back here. Until then, take care of our room and don't let Alex and Jack work ye to death. Hector will show up soon, and ye'll like him too. He's quiet, but will listen to ye. But if ye ever need anything, Alex will find a way to make it happen. He's a very fine brother and yer lucky to have him for yer da. He's fair and very intelligent.

Jack's got a quick temper and can be loud, but he'll keep ye safe and he'll come to yer side if ye need him. And Da? Well, Da is the backbone, the one who keeps the family together. He's always the one to go to when ye can't figure out yer problems. He'll tell ye he's just an uneducated old Highlander, but don't ye believe him. He's more knowledgeable than most anyone I know. Mam had a real hand in that, I'm sure. He's our rock."

"I wish you were going to be here. Then I'd have someone close to my own age to talk to."

"Trust me, Robbie. There will be more folks to talk to than ye can believe. There will be times ye'll hide out in our room just to hear yerself think."

He laughed then grabbed Henson, his feline friend—with his black-tipped ears and tail— and put him in the saddlebag. Merlin snorted and pranced as if his hoofs were walking on hot coals. Robbie pulled the horse's head down, whispered in his ear quickly, then threw a leg over him and was ready to begin his journey.

"Oh, and Robbie? Caitlin's a very special woman. If there's any real trouble, find her. She'll know what to do."

Robbie stood in the doorway of the stable and watched in silence as Ian nudged Merlin's side and left moving at a brisk pace. Part of Robbie wished he were off on an exciting adventure such as Ian. But another part of him was fearful. Should he run back to Edinburgh? Or did he want to find a place in this family, his family? It was a dilemma he would struggle with for a long while.

3

Ian had no idea the distance from the lodge to the Isle of Skye was so great. The other time he'd traveled to the Isle, he and Wabi had used time weaving as their mode of transportation. But on this trip he was bringing Merlin with him so he had to travel in the same manner that all others did, and that way was very slow. Actually, though, the slow pace was not unpleasant. He saw countryside he'd never seen before and the majesty of the Highlands was even more seared into his brain than ever. There couldn't be any other place on earth as glorious as his Highlands.

It was late and he'd been traveling all day, still not sure how much farther he had to go. His compass was a great aid, and he kept on a south-southwest bearing as Wabi had told him. But both he and Merlin needed rest and food, so he thought it would be a good idea to look for an inn for the evening. He wasn't worried about Henson as he just disappeared occasionally into the forest and always came back licking his chops. It was still amazing to Ian how large the cat was. And that black tail and black ears gave him a most intriguing appearance.

Moving on slowly, he could barely see the rooftop of a building in the distance. It was too far to see much detail, but he headed in that direction and his exceptionally keen nose told him he was close to the coast as the air had a salty, pungent smell he found especially to his liking.

"Ah, smell that? That's the same scent that fills the air at

Master Wabi's cottage. The Isle can't be too much farther now, Henson."

He'd been on the road for a few days and had seen no one, which surprised him a bit. Surely people lived in these areas, as he'd passed several villages yesterday, but only a couple today. The day had started out with a low-lying fog that still hovered above the ground, and Merlin stepped gingerly, making his way along the narrow path. Shrub was growing taller than one would expect, but it was a path at some time apparently.

"Huh. This path doesn't look as though it's been traveled in quite some time. I wonder if we've strayed off the main road somewhere."

Henson stuck his large head out of the saddlebag, lifting his nose as if to get his bearings. Ian wasn't exactly sure when he had started talking to his traveling pal, but it kept him from feeling quite so alone.

"What do ye think, Henson? We need to find an inn for the night if we can. That might be one up ahead there, but can't tell from this distance."

Henson jumped from the saddlebag and tore off in the direction of the distant building.

"Henson! Dang you, cat. I can't find ye in that thicket. Ye'll just have to find me, then."

As he neared the building, he stopped briefly, looking about. Apparently he was in luck, as just above the heavy door was a wooden pole adorned with a garland of greenery. All inns used this as a way to tell travelers they were indeed an inn, sort of a welcome sign.

He quietly walked up on the porch and looked about, doing exactly what Alex had taught him—seeing where he was, who's about, and most importantly, where's the nearest exit. Assuring himself he was alone and taking note of only one door going in and a window on either side, he opened the door. Calling out loudly, his voice echoed off the walls of the empty building.

"Hello? Anyone here?"

He waited a long moment, then having received no response, continued into the interior of the inn. The sun had set long ago, which meant the place was rather dark inside. As his eyes adjusted to the dim conditions, he saw several tables with chairs pulled up to them and candles set about in small niches along the walls and at each table.

Calling on one of the new skills Master Wabi had taught him, with a nod of his head he lighted the candle on the table nearest to him. Tinderboxes with flint and steel were always part of his traveling kit, but once Wabi had taught him how to light candles with a nod of his head (and a whole lot of mental preparation), he never lighted a fire any other way, unless someone was in the room with him. He kept this ability to himself as Wabi had taught him.

The light from the candle revealed a rather small room with several tables along the walls. The place was vacant, but had been used recently. There was a large chunk of oat bread on a table up front and a half-full bottle of wine stood next to it.

On another table beneath the window there was a plate of baked partridge or grouse, certainly a bird of some kind. Three of these tables had been set with four plates, four mugs and a couple of bottles of wine. One of the bottles had been opened and the mugs all had a small bit of liquid in them.

Hmm. Looks like dinner was interrupted for a number of folks. What's happened here?

Slowly making his way to the kitchen at the rear of the inn, Ian saw rooms off either side of the narrow hallway. Once again reviewing his options for a fast escapc, he noted there was a back door, and it was standing ajar. All the rooms on either side of the hallway were empty, but from thc looks of them, they had been occupied. He saw clothing folded over chair backs and lying on the beds.

Strange. Something is amiss here.

Taking a peek out the open window at the rear wall, he saw another dilapidated building just a few meters behind the inn and decided to check that out. He walked out the door and started toward the outbuilding. As he got closer, he saw it was a small stable with a couple of stalls. There was also a tack room at the rear, with several saddles, a couple of blankets for the animals, and leather reins hanging from nails.

But there are no horses. How did these folks get to the inn? It's too far from any village for them to have walked here. Perhaps if the fog weren't here I could check for tracks, but it's impossible to see through this misty cover.

He returned to the inn and, after one final tour of the place, the stable and the immediate surroundings, decided he would stay there for the night. It was far too late to continue and he knew he would be wise to stay inside rather than out in the elements. But first, he brought Merlin inside the stable and gave him some hay and water. The run-down stable was better than nothing. He still hadn't seen Henson, but he knew he'd show up—at least he usually did.

After seeing to Merlin, he tinkered about the kitchen and found more of the freshly made oat bread and some boiled potatoes. Anything was better than the dried lamb and days old bannocks he had in his saddlebag. They were nutritious enough, but these fresh vittles were much better. He thought briefly about trying the wine, but something told him he'd better pass on that idea. Fresh water was plentiful and he washed his meal down with that instead.

The first room on the right had two small cots side by side. Ian chose the first cot, intending to rest for the evening and begin moving on toward Wabi's place early the next morning. The instant he closed his eyes, he was sleeping soundly.

A few hours later, but which only seemed like a few moments to Ian, he was awakened. Unlike his brother, Jack, Ian was alert the first second his eyes opened.

What woke me?

Keeping perfectly still and putting all his senses on alert, he listened. Next he sniffed the air, much as Willie or Henson might, and opened his eyes as wide as possible. Nothing.

But something woke me. I still sense it. There's something here, or someone.

Lying there, still unable to hear or see anything, he recalled one of Wabi's first lessons:

"Ian, my lad, you must learn to trust your instincts. Most of the time they will serve you well and keep you safe. Don't question them, just respond to them."

As he quietly rose, his nose registered a scent that was unknown to him, a wild scent, of that he was certain. Then, before he took another step, his ears were ringing with a sound that had his hair lifting from his scalp.

He'd heard animal sounds in the Highlands, any number of cats, or wolves, but this sound reeked of a wildness he was unfamiliar with.

That unnerving sound was followed by a frightening, prolonged, deep-throated, gargling growl that filled the dark night.

Was that first sound a scream? Was it a woman? No. No. I don't know. And the second sound? That was a wild animal for sure.

The sound was so close and loud Ian thought the animal must be inside the inn with him. It was quiet for a brief second, then the chilling scream came again.

This time he knew it came from the stable. For a moment he couldn't decide what action to take. Should he run toward the sound? Should he run in the opposite direction?

The next sound–the high, terrified neighing of a horse–made his choice of action easy.

Merlin—something's after Merlin!

Ian dashed out the rear of the inn and fled toward the stable, knowing Merlin was in trouble. But the scene that greeted him was not one he had thought to find. There was indeed a wild animal in the stable, and it was clinging to the back of a man who had hold of Merlin's halter. The animal appeared to be some sort of mountain lion thought Ian, and from the looks of things this man was trying to steal Merlin.

"Help me, lad! Help me! Here. Ye can have yer horse back, just shoot that cat!"

Ian immediately sized up the situation and a few things fell into place. He knew a highwayman when he saw one. They were known to take anything they could and kill anyone who got in their way.

He pulled out the pistol Da had insisted he take with him and pointed it in the direction of the highwayman.

Holy sheep shite! Do I shoot the cat or the man?

As Ian got closer, the great cat leaped to the ground and flew out of the stable in a mad dash.

"So, ye'd take my horse would ye? And the people from the inn? Did ye kill them and take their horses too?"

"No, I didn't kill them. No, I wouldn't do that. Just put the pistol down now, lad."

Ian came a bit closer, wanting to look the man in the eye. He had never killed anyone before and didn't especially want to now, but Da had given him the pistol for a reason. And no doubt this man was evil. He'd stolen horses and it appeared he had killed those people who had been having their supper at the inn.

"If ye didn't kill them, then where are they?"

"Here. Take the horse. I'll just go on my way now."

Ian hesitated for a moment. Should he shoot the highwayman? Should he just tie him up? What? He was learning much from Wabi about using his newly found powers, but at the moment he didn't know how to handle this situation. Da had taught him many things, but he'd never been faced with a dilemma such as this. He looked about, silently wishing someone would come along to help him figure this out. But no, he was alone with the highwayman.

"Here, lad. I'm laying the reins down on the ground now. I'm not going to take your horse. See?"

The would-be thief carefully lay the reins on the ground and stayed on his knees. As Ian walked another step closer, the highwayman rose up quickly, catching Ian under the chin with his large fist.

"Ugh! Wha?"

Ian blacked out momentarily and crumpled to the ground. He never saw the highwayman as he fled the stable, disappeared into the woods and was gone from sight. When the room stopped spinning and Ian finally got his bearings, he was highly irritated with himself.

Jesus. Alex would hang me by my heels for making such a stupid mistake!

He got to his knees and stayed there a moment, as the room was still reeling a bit. He got to his feet as Henson ran up to him, rubbing along his lower legs and making a loud, soothing, reverberating sound Ian could actually feel through his leg. Most cats simply meowed, but Henson's sound was more like a growl you might hear from a dog, or maybe from Willie.

When Ian started walking toward the inn, Henson took off to the rear of the stable, calling out again with his feline growl. He quickly returned to Ian and began rubbing his leg once again.

"What? Is there something out there?"

Ian was aware he was more alert now than he had been earlier. Perhaps he'd just been tired and not paying enough attention. But Henson was obviously trying to tell him something so he looked about, being careful to hold his pistol tightly in his hand.

"Come on then. Let's see what it is."

Ian was learning to listen to Henson, as Wabi had taught him animals often know things before we humans do. It appeared the highwayman was long gone and that was just fine with Ian—but he had not exactly acted in a manner he was proud of.

Henson was leading him behind the stable into a wooded area. There was enough moonlight for him to see, but the mist was getting thicker by the minute and there was only a short time before it would totally cover the area. As he rounded a large stand of yew trees, he heard voices calling out.

"Help us! We're in here!"

Ian listened for a long moment, then followed Henson as he dashed under the bushes.

"Hold on, I'm coming!"

When he pulled back the shrubs that were preventing his forward movement, he could see a faint glow in the distance.

"Where are ye? Call out to me so I can find ye."

"Hello! We're here, in a cave of some sort."

No, no. Not another cave.

Ian couldn't help but recall his recent experience in the cave where Caitlin had been captured. He also remembered another cave in which he and Master Wabi had brought down a most evil foe named Nezerra, an old woman who had spent a lifetime scheming to kill Wabi for a curse he had put on her eons ago. And her scheme had almost been successful. But the two wizards, Wabi and Ian, had prevented the disaster and removed her from this earth.

"I'm coming, I'm coming."

Ian hurried into the cave, keeping his eyes trained on the light coming from within. Apparently the highwayman must have needed light to find his way about the cave and in his haste had left a torch burning in a niche in the wall.

Ian spied the group immediately and one of them called out to him. "Oh, thanks be. Ye found us," an old bearded man mumbled as he spied Ian. "We need yer help, lad."

"What happened? How did ye get in here?"

Ian began to untie the prisoners, which took some time as the highwayman had used leather ties with which to bind them and they had gotten tighter and tighter. There were half a dozen men and four women all trussed up like turkeys, their hands tied behind them and their ankles secured as well. A couple of them had rubbed their wrists raw trying to free themselves from their restraints. They didn't seem to be harmed other than that. All of them had been gagged, but the old bearded man had managed to struggle and get his gag away from his mouth and call for help.

"We really thought we were goners when that mountain lion showed up. He was huge! Did ye encounter him?"

"Only for a moment. He was clawing his way across the back of a highwayman I met in the stable. But as soon as I arrived, he took off."

"Lucky for ye. He could have attacked ye as well."

"How did ye get here, in this cave?"

"That highwayman ye spoke of. He came into the pub brandishing a pistol. He took our coins and our horses. Then he marched us into this cave and tied us up."

"I see. Well, he walloped me a good one and left in a hurry. Ran into the forest, I guess. I don't even know which way he went."

"Did ye see our horses anywhere?"

"Nae, I didn't. My bet is he has them stashed away somewhere and he'll return for them."

"Aye. But right now, if ye'll untie us we'll get back to the pub. There's food and room for everyone to rest. We'll look for the horses in the morning light. We need to be inside in case that mountain cat decides to come back. Ye've come at just the right time, lad."

Ian got everyone headed to the pub and he, too, wasn't keen on spending the night outside with a large mountain lion wandering about. Eventually everyone got settled in the pub and all was quiet.

When daybreak came, Ian and Henson were nowhere to be found.

4

Alex had been as patient as he could possibly be with young Robbie. He had bit his tongue on more than one occasion knowing the lad was struggling as much as he was to form some sort of relationship. Being a teenage lad was not the best time to learn that what you had been told about your father had all been a mother's fictitious tale. Still, Alex would not give up on his son. Just looking at him daily made his heart ache for the years that had been lost to him.

"Caitlin, it's like watching myself every time I see him. He even thinks like I do at times. It's verra unnerving. But for the life of me I can't find a way to reach him. He refuses to even look me in the eye when I'm talking to him. And he doesn't seem to even be trying when I try to teach him how to throw his dirk. It's almost as if he wants to disappoint me, and it's obvious he's verra unhappy about being a Scot. Well, that's just a fact he'll have to come to grips with."

He leaned his forehead against the window, staring out at the sheep grazing high up on the moor. Failure was not an experience that he was very familiar with.

"Perhaps you might be exaggerating a bit, Alex. Robbie's bound to be going through a very difficult period right now. He's not who he thought he was, his father was just a figment of his mother's imagination, and now he finds himself living with a family he has nothing in common with other than blood. But as Uncle Wabi will tell you, blood always wins out. Give him time. He's extremely bright and I'm quite sure he understands more than he lets on."

So now here they were once again, Alex working with Robbie, who still didn't seem to understand the importance of learning the basic skill of throwing a dirk.

"Ye gotta know how to throw a dirk, ye ken? The Highlands have many dangers and your dirk can save yer life, lad. Now, try once again."

Robbie slowly pulled the dirk from the rear wall of the stable. Alex had demonstrated once again how to execute throwing a dirk properly, lodging it deep within the planks. Robbie walked back to where Alex was standing.

The lad had been with the MacKinnons for some time now, but so far there had been no progress in his skill level, nor in their relationship. Alex thought teaching Robbie the skills Da had taught him would be a good place to start, but that plan wasn't working so well.

"It's no use. I'll never learn how to do this. Can't you see that?"

"Just give it one more try. It'll come."

But with his next attempt the dirk never even reached the stable wall, falling to the ground short of its target. Alex could see the young lad was defeated, and it was true the boy was no better with the dirk now than he had been several weeks ago when they first started his training.

"Don't worry so, Robbie. I'm verra sure it took me some time to learn the process, and we'll not quit on it. Ye'll get the hang of it. But let's call it a day."

Robbie was not at all sure that was true, but he nodded just the same.

Alex tucked the dirk back inside his belt and they headed to the lodge, walking side by side.

"Is Ian coming back any time soon? He said he would, but now I wonder." No matter how hard he tried, Robbie's speech sounded stilted, even to him.

"Oh, aye. He'll turn up. He's studying with Wabi and Da believes it's what he was meant to do. He's our brother, but he's got a few different talents the rest of us don't have."

"What kind of talents?"

"Oh, just special ways. When ye've been here a while longer

ye'll understand what I'm telling ye. Wabi is a most unique man, too, ye ken? But our mam always taught us to accept folk as they are and not to try and put our ways and beliefs onto them. It may be that they know more than we do. Wabi, Caitlin, and Ian have saved us from harm on more than one occasion, so I'll not question their ways meself."

"I saw him off that morning, after the bairn was born. He said he didn't like goodbyes so wanted to leave before all of you were up and about."

"Aye. I figured as much. Ian's got a soft place in his heart, which is a good thing most of the time. But he sometimes feels things that make it difficult for him to act. It was just as well he left quietly, and I'm glad ye saw him off. The two of ye probably have a lot in common, being so close in age."

"Maybe. He told me he's sixteen and I'm fourteen, so, yes, we are close in age. But he's a lot more accomplished than I am. You should have seen him astride that black horse of his. The animal snorted and pranced about until Ian whispered something in his ear. Then he put that big cat in the saddlebag and threw his leg over Merlin, without using the stirrup. He fairly flew out of the stable and never looked back."

"Aye, well, he does that sometimes." Alex was not ready just yet to try to explain Ian's and Wabi's eccentricities to Robbie. "So then, have ye never been on a horse, lad?"

"Oh, yes ... sir. But not one like that one. I'm not very good at riding either I have to tell you."

"Not to worry, lad. Ye just need to know that Ian's been on a horse since he was old enough to walk. It was one of those things Da made sure all of us learned to do. Ian was just particularly good at it, as is Da. We'll have ye riding like Ian in no time. Ye'll take to it lad. Yer a MacKinnon after all."

"Yes ... sir." What the lad didn't tell Alex was that he wasn't particularly fond of horses. He'd actually taken a spill from one when he was small and hadn't cared much for them ever since. But living up here, it was obvious he would have to learn a few things in order to survive.

Living in London and Edinburgh was a bit different. Of course there were horses there too, but most of the time he and his mother would take a carriage to their destinations and someone else was in charge of controlling the animals.

Standing quietly at the edge of the stable door, Da had witnessed the exchange between his newly acquired grandson and his son. The strain between the two was obvious to everyone. Apparently the others thought time would take care of the situation, but Da wasn't so sure about that. So, as was his habit, he discussed his worries with Alice.

Ah, mo chridhe. It's a delicate situation I'm dealing with today. This new grandson, Robbie, looks exactly like our Alex, but in every other way he couldn't be more different. Well, other than his intelligence, that is. He's such a bright young lad. Ye'd find a way to make him part of the family, but I'm not sure I can. 'Course I know ye'd tell me, "Daniel, just treat him like ye did the other lads." Aye, Alice. I know that's what ye'd tell me.

Even before they reached the back door, Alex and Robbie could hear voices coming from the kitchen, but were too far away to distinguish words.

"I can't stand that odious man! If he touches me again I'm going to scream." Millie clinched her hands together and tried to regain her ladylike composure.

"Maybe you should tell Jack. I'm pretty sure he'd put a stop to Boder even coming close to you." Caitlin didn't care for him either, but was surprised when Millie told her about his advances.

"Oh, aye. But that's just it. I hate to think what Jack would do to him. Probably beat him to a pulp—or worse. No. I'll just be careful to keep out of his way."

"Yes, I'm sure you're right. Jack would make mincemeat of him, I'm afraid. But that man reeks of something dirty and foul. Alex says it's that cheroot he keeps in his mouth. Most of the time it's not even lighted, but he still chews on it just the same."

"Well, let's not mention it to Jack just yet. Hopefully Boder will keep away. I'm quite sure he understands I don't like his attentions."

Millie left and began to prepare her lessons for the next day and Caitlin got back to her potions.

As Robbie opened the door, Alex again heard voices, and this time he could tell whom they belonged to, and Caitlin's was loudest of all.

"Dugald MacKinnon. Get yourself back upstairs and stay there until I come for you. There will be no stealing from others even if they are your brother or sister. Now go!"

"My name is not Dugald MacKinnon! It's Dugald MacGregor!"

"I said go. Now."

Alex and Robbie walked into the kitchen, where Caitlin was busy making herbal remedies and tinctures for her clinic. Their new bairn was resting in the small crib that had been here as long as Alex could remember. The most recent bairn to use it had been little Midge. She had gotten too big for it, and now it was occupied by the latest MacKinnon, the one they had decided to call Flinn. Willie was resting beneath the crib, and though he never made a sound his eyes took in everything that was happening around him. He was most definitely Caitlin's protector, and now he had decided he also had a new little mistress to watch out for.

"Problem, *mo chridhe?"* Alex asked.

"No, not really. Dugald took a couple of wooden soldiers Da had whittled for Charlie. Seems that Charlie went looking for them and found them in Dugald's secret hiding place. Some hiding place if a lad as young as Charlie can find it.

But, no matter, stealing can't be tolerated and I've told him he has to stay upstairs until I come for him. He hates being inside more than anything, so that's a real punishment for him." She smiled as she stirred her potion.

Alex walked up behind her, put his arms around her waist and sniffed her hair, which smelled of lavender, as always. He'd never tire of this woman and he thought she was even more beautiful now than when he first met her. It was his belief that motherhood agreed with her and she glowed from within.

"I wouldn't be too hard on him. He's just a young lad. Jack stole my keepsakes more times than I can remember and I never let Mam know. We usually just duked it out and settled it on our own."

"Well, Charlie's a good bit smaller than Dugald, so I'm not sure that would be a good solution."

"Don't let his size fool ye, lass. Hector was always smaller than Jack and me, but he could always take care of himself. And, of course, I was always the best lad of all."

"Yes, and I hope Mam's not listening right now."

She laughed and Alex was glad to see her back to her normal size and seemingly taking motherhood in stride. She was ready to resume her clinic hours and the lodge was full of activity, with Millie still teaching in the crofter's hut out back.

Camille, Uncle Andrew's lady friend, apparently was staying permanently and that was good. They didn't know much about her yet, but she was a godsend as far as Millie and Caitlin were concerned. In fact, even the orphans were growing to like her. The two younger ones, Bridgette and Charlie, could often be found visiting her in the crofter's hut where she lived with Uncle Andrew.

That relationship, Uncle Andrew and Camille, had brought happiness to both and the family was pleased for Uncle Andrew. He had lived in the lodge for many years after his Florence passed away, and now the lodge had another empty room since he'd moved to the large crofter's hut that Millie and Caitlin had turned into a very hospitable home for the couple.

With Uncle Andrew out of the lodge, and Old Jamie having passed on a few months ago, and Ian gone to Skye, it was quieter than it had been in some time. But today the quiet was disturbed by the new bairn when she began to fuss and cry. Caitlin's hands were busy adding herbs to her concoction and she looked at Robbie.

"Robbie, would you please pick Flinn up and walk her about a bit? She's been fussy all morning, but refuses to nurse. I'll be finished with this brew in just a few minutes."

"Me? You want me to pick the bairn up?"

"Well, yes, if you would, please."

Robbie stared at Caitlin, his eyes shifting toward Alex, perhaps hoping for some help from that corner, but Alex kept quiet.

"I've never held a bairn in my life. I don't think I know how to do that."

Alex finally did speak up. "Well, she is yer half sister, ye ken?" Alex reminded him.

"Yes ... sir. But she's so small."

"Aye. That she is. But I've already learned she doesn't break. Just pick her up and hold her close. She smells pretty good too. Well, most of the time, that is."

Robbie stepped closer to the crib, and just as he was about to lift the child, Willie raised him head, causing Robbie to step back.

"Caitlin, I don't think your wolf will let me do this." Fear was evident on his young face, and both Alex and Caitlin saw it.

"If Willie didn't like you, Robbie, you'd have known it by

now. He's just making sure you know he's under there. He's had his paws stepped on more than once and has yet to retaliate."

Cautiously, Robbie stepped forward and lifted the bairn, holding her out at arm's length.

"Now, just bring her close to your chest and let her rest her head there."

But Robbie didn't bring her close. He held her out in front of himself, letting her legs dangle in the air, and the child ceased her crying and quieted. For the longest moment she seemed to search Robbie's face the same way he was searching hers. He then pulled her close and she let out a long sigh, closed her eyes and drifted off to sleep.

"She's got the same eyes as you, Caitlin. And her hair is the same too. But I don't see anything about her that looks like Alex—uh, my father—my da."

"That may be, but I have a feeling she's a MacKinnon through and through. She already has a way of letting you know when she wants something and how soon she wants it. It's a trait I've learned runs in the family," Caitlin responded.

Robbie looked to Caitlin as he held the babe and finally asked, "She's sleeping I think. What do I do now?"

"Just walk around the room with her a bit. She'll learn to recognize you by your scent. Uncle Wabi has convinced me that infants are just like small animals. They know those around them mostly by scent and sound rather than by what they see."

Alex stood in the corner observing Robbie as he walked about the room, softly rubbing the bairn's back as he did so.

My children. These are my children. Mam would have said the Creator has found me worthy and blessed me.

He left the room before his emotions got the better of him. Fatherhood was indeed a new experience, and one in which he felt unsure, an almost foreign feeling for the very able Highlander.

Later that same evening, Robbie returned to his attic hideout. Writing in his journal that evening, as most evenings, he put his thoughts of the day down.

I don't think I quite realized what a quiet, solitary life I lived until now. The library was my favorite place to visit and at home I pretty much stayed in my room, writing and drawing. But there's so much to see up here. I want to explore, but I'm afraid I might get lost. Then what? Alex, my father, would think even less of me then, more than he does already.

~ ~ ~

Early the next morning Robbie was surprised to hear a soft knock on his door. Opening it, he found his grandda standing there.

"Alex and Jack are out early looking for some strays. Mrs. Sutherland complained they've made her garden a mess and are eatin' her new flowering buds. Spring has its own problems I guess."

"Yessir, I suppose so."

"Well then. Since those two are out of pocket, let's sneak some of Millie's scones and a mug of coffee. We'll head to the stable and see if we can't make a bit of headway with your dirk throwing."

"I don't know . . . sir. I think I'm one of those who can't even hit the broad side of a barn, or stable in this case."

"Not to worry, lad. I taught the other lads and they're all able to throw it quite well. I expect ye'll manage it too. Come on now."

Robbie was reluctant to attempt this particular skill again. He'd really rather stay in his room and write a story or record something in his journal. But Grandda fell into that same category as Ian. Something about him was to Robbie's liking, even if he didn't want it to be.

The two armed themselves with several scones and coffee and took their mugs, making their way to the back of the stable.

"Umm. Millie makes the best scones in Scotland. Ye agree?"

"They're a lot better than Mother's. She wasn't much of a cook, but Mattie, our housekeeper, she was. She kept us fed pretty well I guess."

Daniel nodded. "Alright then, lad. Let's see what's going on with yer dirk throwing. Here, take mine and see how it feels in your hands. This dirk's a tad smaller than Alex's and lighter in weight, which is the way I prefer it."

Grandda reached out and handed the dirk to Robbie, who took it in his hands and shifted it back and forth from one to the other.

"Yes, it is lighter than Alex's, and shorter too, I think."

"Aye, lad, it is. But if ye throw it properly, it'll do a lot of damage if ye need it to."

Robbie nodded, still hesitant to try his hand at this feat again. "I'm not sure this is something I'll ever be good at Grandda."

"I hear ye, but I'll be the judge of that. Now then, lad, let me watch ye a couple of times. See if I can spot anything that needs a little work."

Robbie ran his hand along the blade, then took the dirk by the handle. He walked off the paces from the back of the stable as Alex had taught him to do. He stood for a long moment, then finally flung the dirk with all his might. The knife traveled fairly straight, but barely touched the wall before dropping to the ground. Robbie turned away, unwilling to see the disappointment in Grandda's face at his feeble attempt.

"I told you. This is not something I can do! Why can't you and Alex just accept that?"

Grandda retrieved the dirk and brought it back to Robbie. "Most things that are worth doing take time and practice, ye ken? Now, try once more. Here. Take the dirk."

Da watched Robbie slowly count off the paces once more. He pulled his arm back and stepped forward once again, throwing the dirk even more awkwardly this time, losing his balance as he did so. With this attempt, the dirk didn't even reach the stable wall. It just dropped from the air midway and fell to the ground, seemingly as defeated as Robbie.

"Now can we just go back inside? I want to write more on my story." This was about as much humiliation as Robbie could take this early in the morning.

"Just a moment, lad. I'm asking ye to try just once more. If ye don't make any headway then we'll both go inside and find our breakfast. Here, take the dirk."

Releasing a long sigh, Robbie reached out with his right hand to take the dirk from his grandda.

Daniel pulled the dirk back away from Robbie's outstretched hand. "Wait a second, Robbie, take the dirk in yer left hand."

"But I'm right handed, Grandda."

"Just do as I ask ye. Now, when ye throw the dirk this time, step out on yer right foot, not the left as ye've been doing."

"What? Throw with my left hand and step out on my right foot?"

"Aye. That's right. And when ye release the dirk, keep yer arm extended. Don't let it drop until the dirk hits the wall and stays put."

"It hasn't hit and stayed put yet, Grandda."

"Aye. I can see that."

Robbie stepped off the paces again then took another deep breath. He stood tall, held the dirk in his left hand, pulled his arm back, stepped out on his right foot and let the dirk fly, keeping his arm extended.

TWACK! The dirk hit the wall with such force it was still vibrating seconds later.

"But ... but ... I'm right handed, Grandda! I always have been."

"Well, I'm not sure yer left hand will agree with ye lad." He grinned in spite of himself. The next two throws were just as successful as the first one, and Robbie had to work hard to keep himself from grinning too. He had no idea how he had done that, but certainly liked how it felt.

"Looks like ye might conquer this skill after all, eh?" Daniel put his arm around the lad's shoulders and felt the tension in his grandson's body release as they made their way back to the lodge.

~ ~ ~

All the men were gathered in the stable looking over the pony Da had bought the week before. He was a sturdy little fellow with brown and white spots on his rump. Da liked him the moment he spied him. The animal was good-natured and didn't flinch when he and Andrew gave him a once over from nose to tail. He was to be Dugald's, and Da was looking forward to teaching the lad to ride.

"Ye think Dugald's old enough, Da? He's only about eight or so," Jack said.

"Aye, but ye lads were even younger when I first put ye on a horse's back. Dugald's on the small side, but he'll learn quickly, mostly because he's wanting to, ye ken?"

Alex ran his hand along the pony's back and was rewarded with a nose nudge. Finally he voiced the thoughts that had been running through his mind for a while now.

"Da, what do ye think about me and Jack going down to the border for a couple of days, just to listen about for a while? McGuire stopped by yesterday. Said he heard rumors the Brits had rounded up several Jacobite supporters—clan leaders actually—down near the Black Isle. Word is they were sent to the Caribbean Islands where they'll be sold as slaves. I kinda find that hard to believe, but it might be good to put an ear to the ground and listen a bit."

Uncle Andrew nodded and put in his own two cents.

"Aye, that's the word in Edinburgh, too. I talked to a couple of mates at Barclay's Pub. They all tell the same story. I'm headed back there tomorrow to pick up a few of Camille's possessions that she values highly, mostly some important papers and a few keepsakes.

Not sure Edinburgh's a safe place to be. Can't tell the Jacobite supporters from those who opposed us, some of them our own countrymen. But Camille's decided to stay up here permanently, so I'll take a coach down and get those items for her. Doesn't seem like too much to ask, I'd say, so while I'm there I'll give a listen and see if there's any new information." He walked off toward his cottage.

"Da, we still don't know much about Camille. Has Andrew told you anything?" Jack asked.

"Only that she has a small home in Edinburgh she wants to keep. At the moment she's let it out to an elderly gentleman who's recently widowed and he takes care of it. Andrew has always kept a lot to himself, and that's his business. Camille brings happiness to him and Andrew says she's excited about teaching the bairns. And Dugald, Bridgette and Charlie have taken quite a liking to her."

Alex paced back and forth as he talked. "Three women, three orphans, and the youngest bairns, Midge and now my own, Flinn. If it were just us menfolk as it was not too long ago, I'd not be so concerned. But we've got a large family now and we need to have a plan for keeping all of them safe."

The pacing was an indication to Da that Alex was well into a plan already, but not quite ready to discuss it. His oldest son would always consider every angle before voicing his thoughts about any situation.

"Aye, lad. Ye've got a point. Maybe ye and Jack should go down. See what ye can learn. Meanwhile, I'll be here with the ladies and bairns. And the new hand, Boder, he'll be here, too. Andrew will be back in a few days and then we'll put our heads together. Aye."

"Da, Boder's not here anymore. He left yesterday."

"Oh? What brought that on? I thought ye said he was a good hand."

"Aye, that I did. But he had a way of asking too many questions and I was tired of his suggestions for how I should run the farm more ... efficiently, I believe was the word he used. He thought I should sack Kenny and Hamish, didn't think they carried their weight. Those lads are part of our family and in my opinion they do just fine."

Da nodded. "I only saw him a couple of times. He kept himself out with the sheep mostly. Then good riddance. Glad ye sent him on his way."

"Millie never liked him much, but she never said why," Jack reported.

"Caitlin says he smells funny. You know how keen her nose is. Probably that cheroot he's always chewing on."

"Huh. Women. They have some funny ideas. I'll never understand them," Jack said, shaking his head in bewilderment.

"Well then, that's that. But Robbie's here now, too. And I've noted he handles the younger bairns pretty well. Caitlin and Millie are quite self-sufficient, and Mrs. Sutherland will lend a hand if we need one. But let's wait another day or so. Hector should be here later today, or tomorrow at the latest. He needs to be in on our plans as well."

"Yeah, but if he's not here tomorrow I say we go ahead. We may not have time to wait for him," Jack replied. Waiting was never a good idea in his opinion.

Da agreed. "He's to bring Dorothea with him this trip. Millie asked her to come help with Midge. She was Millie's nursemaid when she was a bairn, ye ken? At the moment she's taking care of the young ones at the Sanctuary, and Hector says she's very good at her job. With Old Jamie gone now and Andrew out of the lodge, we have plenty of room for her and her young lad."

5

Millie carefully retrieved the small porcelain vase little Midge had taken from the table in the great room and placed it on the top shelf of the pantry.

"No, that's not for bairns to touch, Midge. Here, play with your doll." The vase was one Mam had brought when she and Da came to the Highlands. No sooner had Millie removed the vase than Midge was climbing on a chair reaching for a biscuit on a tray on the table.

"No, Midge. No biscuits until after supper."

The bairn started to cry and, as usual, someone came running to her aide. It was suppertime and Jack had already come in and was cleaned up, ready for a good meal and a quiet evening. He reached down and picked her up.

"Here ye go, lass. Let's go see where the other bairns are off to." He still carried Midge everywhere even though the child was walking these days and Millie was forever moving items up high out of her reach.

He met Caitlin coming down the hall and one look at her, what with her curly hair coming down in ringlets about her face when it was usually pinned up neatly, told him all was not well. She was carrying a very unhappy Flinn who was crying nonstop.

"What's wrong? She never cries." Even Jack knew this was unusual for the newest bairn.

"I'm not sure. But she's running a fever and she refuses to

nurse." Before she had even finished her sentence, the back door opened and in came Robbie herding the orphans along. Bridgette was crying loudly, making for a situation he had no idea how to handle.

"Caitlin, my throat hurts. Can you make it better?" Bridgette pulled on Caitlin's apron to get her attention, then promptly vomited in the middle of the kitchen floor.

"Jack, go get Alex. I need some help here. I think he's still upstairs getting a bath."

Jack headed up the stairs and met Da coming down.

"Here, I'll take the bairn." Da stepped closer and gently took the bairn from Caitlin. He was thrilled with his first grandchild, Flinn. She looked so like Caitlin and his Alice—that hair and those aqua eyes that appeared to take in everything about her.

Standing at the top of the stairs, all Alex could see and hear was a crying Midge, a crying Flinn, and a crying Bridgette.

"What's going on? Jack, how did ye manage to upset three lasses at once?"

Jack smiled. "I don't think ye can blame me for this racket. But Caitlin's face tells me she's concerned, which has me worried. I'm hoping we don't see lightning on the horizon, ye ken?"

Alex and Da laughed. "She's not brought the lightning in some time now, brother. She usually manages to handle things in other ways. But why are they all crying?"

Walking back into the room after cleaning up Bridgette's mess, Caitlin looked at her Highlander.

"Good question. I'm not ready to say for sure, but I've a good idea of what may be going on. All three have a red throat—that much I can see; none of them will eat; Bridgette's just vomited; and all three are irritable as a hornet. I'd say it's something contagious, but not sure just what yet."

"OK. Yer not sure exactly what, but what does yer gut tell ye?" Jack never did like beating around the bush.

"Come over here Bridgette. Let's take a peek at you. Lie here on the sofa and let me get a closer look."

"I'm cold, Caitlin. Can I have a blanket?"

"How can ye be cold, lass? It's warm as an oven in here." Jack shook his head. He kept walking the floor with Midge, but she still cried. Da, likewise, was unable to quiet Flinn.

"I don't know much about bairns, Caitlin, but I can tell

something is wrong here," Alex chimed in.

"Alex, ask Millie to find a blanket for Bridgette. Let me check her out a little further. I don't like the looks of this."

"For God's sake, Caitlin, will ye tell us what ye think?" Jack's temper always jumped forward when he was the slightest bit worried or angry and by this time, Caitlin knew that about him. Alex and Da stopped in their tracks, both anxious to hear her reply.

"I hope I'm wrong, but take a look here on Bridgette's neck and face. See those raised bumps? I found those on Flinn's back this morning, and Midge has some too. All these symptoms—lack of appetite, vomiting, being cold when it's not cold weather, sore throat, and now this rash with raised bumps—I've seen them before."

"Aye. And what does all that mean?" Jack asked.

Caitlin looked at each of the men, as if trying to decide whether she should voice her findings. Finally, she answered Jack's question. "These are all symptoms of Scarlet Fever."

The silence that followed Caitlin's pronouncement was deafening. All three men looked at her as if she had spoken in a foreign language. Scarlet Fever meant one thing—death. This disease was perhaps the most dreaded of all simply because there didn't seem to be a treatment to stop it from spreading from one family member to another. They all knew of families who had lost one or more loved ones to the disease.

"Lass, are ye sure?"

"No, Alex, I'm not sure. But it certainly looks like it."

"Do ye know how to treat it?" Jack felt the anxiety building inside and knew the others felt it also.

"No, I don't have a potion that will cure this disease. I can help with the fever and may have something to slow down the vomiting, but this disease will have its own timetable."

"Are ye saying there's nothing to be done, then?" Da asked. He'd not forgotten some years back when one of the local families had lost two children to the disease. Mam had taken food over and left it at the door as even Highlanders knew how quickly the disease could travel from one family to another.

Alex began pacing. "Nae, ye can't be saying there's nothing ye can do. Surely something can be done. Doing nothing is not my idea of dealing with any situation." Alex simply wouldn't take that as an answer.

Caitlin looked at him, actually feeling the anxiety building within him. She had never known a more determined person, except maybe herself.

"There is one thing we can do. We can keep these three away from the others, put them in one room and I can try to reduce the fever and vomiting. I've been exposed to Scarlet Fever, actually had a light case as a child according to Uncle Wabi, so I should be fine. But all of you need to stay away and keep the other bairns away as well."

Alex nodded his agreement and Jack likewise.

"Jack, tell Millie to have Kenny and Hamish go to all the families and let them know the school is closed for the time being. Tell the parents to keep their children at home until this passes. Hopefully it'll stay confined in these walls and I'll tend to these three.

"Let's take them up in Old Jamie's room. We'll put Midge and Bridgette in the big bed and bring the crib in for Flinn. Go now, we need to act quickly."

Caitlin's ability to act in a dire situation and treat sick patients was definitely one of her greatest assets. But this particular situation was a bit different as one of these patients was a very young bairn, and it was hers.

~ ~ ~

The lodge was rather quiet at supper. Caitlin stayed upstairs with her three young patients, and Dugald and Charlie were sleeping over at Camille and Andrew's cottage. Camille thought it would be better to keep those two over there away from the three ill ones. Caitlin agreed and she knew they were in good hands with the couple. Mothering seemed to come naturally to Camille even though she didn't have any children herself.

Millie rose from the table, then cleared her throat. "I'm going to go up and help Caitlin. Midge is my child and she needs me."

Jack stood and came over to put an arm around her waist. He so liked that Millie was tall and thought she was six feet of beauty both inside and out.

"Millie, Millie, ye gotta listen to what Caitlin says. She said none of us are to go into the room. She's trying to keep the fever from spreading. She'll take care of Midge. Ye know that."

"Yes, I do know that. But I can't stand feeling so helpless. Midge is crying, I can hear her!" The tears she'd been holding back came streaming down her cheeks now, which was not a good thing, as Jack could handle just about anything except crying women.

"Come now, lass. Let's pass out some of your clootie dumplings I see in the kitchen. Our Midge is being cared for by the best healer I've ever known. She'll be alright."

Da began to clear the table and dish out the dumplings. Alex poured everyone a cup of cider and offered his own thoughts.

"He's right ye know, Millie. Caitlin's a verra fine healer. She saved Ian when we thought he was gone for sure. She'll do the same for our children. We just need to let her be in charge and we should do what she tells us."

Suddenly it dawned on Millie she wasn't the only person who had a sick child.

"Oh, Alex. I'm sorry. Your bairn is in there too. I'm not myself just now. Please forgive my outburst. I know Caitlin is skilled and I will certainly follow her plans." She took a deep breath and the "lady" was back in control once again.

Alex smiled at her. "No apology needed, Millie. We're all troubled these days, and now, with this Scarlet Fever, it's just one more worry on our heads."

Millie dished out more dessert. "Here, let's take ourselves back to the kitchen table. That seems to be where we do the best thinking."

Sitting back down at the table, Da chimed in. "Aye, lass, Alex is right. We've got some worries to deal with. But we always do, and we will this time, too. Now, let's the four of us sit here a minute and see what we can figure out amongst ourselves. Caitlin's in charge of the sick ones, Camille and Andrew are taking care of the other two, and we have to give some thought to that nasty British problem."

"Da, ye don't really think they'd try to find us up here, do ye?" Jack asked.

"Nae, lad. Ye gotta know how to get up here, and even if they did find their way we could post some men to alert us before they get here."

Da sipped his cider, knowing this situation was one they hadn't had to deal with before. He knew Jack and Alex were looking to him to have an answer to the problem, but at the moment he felt drained and tired. He'd had a very busy day as it was, and presently he was looking forward to his bed. He'd feel better after a night's rest.

"Aye, Da, that's not a bad idea. But if they should get this far up, then we've got another problem. What do we do with them? There would likely be more of them than there are us, so what then? Nae, we've gotta think more on this." Alex wanted a more detailed plan.

"Well, yer right, lad. But, first things first. Right now we're not making use of all our assets. And as ye know, ye should use everything ye have to come up with a good plan."

"Aye. What are we missing, Da?" Alex asked.

"Ye lads have always made me proud with yer abilities to think logically and listen to each other, realizing that several brains are better than one."

"What are ye talking about, Da?" Jack looked at Alex and shrugged.

"We're all here, except for Hector, and he'll show up at some point."

"Aye. No doubt he's heard the rumors, too. But we can't count on him at the moment."

Silence reined for several very long minutes. Then, as if having been struck by one of Caitlin's lightning bolts, Alex stood up.

"Jesus. Of course. Robbie. He probably knows more than any of us about the Brits. He'll have heard much in Edinburgh this past year. Da, yer way ahead of me."

"Don't know about that, but I've spent some time with the lad lately. I can tell ye he's got a verra fine head on his shoulders. I know he seems a bit proper and unsure of himself, but he's got a quick mind and I believe we'll learn he's wise beyond his years. Just a thought, mind ye."

Alex went to the top of the stairs and called out. "Robbie, can ye come down here for a minute?"

The lad spent a lot of time in his attic lair. Ian had been right. The space was special. He was never disturbed up there and could write and draw into the night if he wished. Alone, as always. Alone, but not lonely now.

"Alex? Uh, Da? What's wrong?" Robbie stood in the doorway and Alex once again saw himself as a young lad.

"We're having a family meeting in the kitchen and we'd like ye to join us, if ye will. We've got several important decisions to make. Could ye do that?"

"Oh, yes ... sir. Of course. Just let me put my candle out." He walked over to the desk, pinched the flame with his fingers, closed his journal, then joined Alex and they returned to the kitchen, where Jack's temper and impatience were front and center by this time.

"The Brits are threatening our way of life and our families. I can't imagine my life without Millie and Midge and I'll be damned if I'll let those Redcoat bastards take me away from them! And who knows what they might do to our women and bairns?" The need to protect his family was overwhelming.

"I say we go on. Every day we wait is another day the Brits are closer to finding us. Hector wouldn't expect us to wait around for him. He'd want us to try to get as much information as we can, as fast as we can. If he shows, Da can bring him up to date."

Alex was ready to take action too. His family meant more to him than life itself. And like Jack, he'd die trying to protect them.

"Aye, I agree with ye. We should have acted long before now, but I had hoped this whole Culloden mess and Prince Charlie would be forgotten, just as Da said the rising of '15 was. But looks like we've got to find out all we can and make our plans accordingly. We'll tackle this problem like we always do. We'll gather the facts, then act in a manner that will keep all of us safe."

"Well, Mam would tell us, 'if ye don't see an answer to yer problems, lads, then create one.'" Jack was ready.

Robbie answered every question they threw at him relating to Edinburgh and the British soldiers. He'd always thought of them as his countrymen, but now he wasn't so sure.

"My home, my mother's home, is located up on the High Street, actually right next door to Major Ashford. He's a very important British officer and there are always a lot of comings and goings at his residence. But I have to tell you, he always treated my mother and me with respect."

"Then ye know yer way around Edinburgh well enough, lad?"

"I know every street and alley, and I'm friends with every merchant on the High Street. I've explored the castle and all the buildings surrounding it. I've even been in the Old Tollbooth prison, even though Mother forbade me to go there. She thought I was too young to be exposed to such as those inside. But I did sneak in a few times, and that was enough."

Alex was surprised to hear that bit of information.

"Then looks like ye might have a streak of Highlander in ye

already, lad." Jack laughed. He was still taken aback at times when he watched Robbie. It was just like looking at Alex at that age.

"Then we're in agreement. If Hector's not here by morning we'll go on to the border."

Da nodded and excused himself. His bed was calling him after a long day.

~ ~ ~

"Are ye sure ye can handle this without help, *mo chridhe?* We'll only be gone about a week or so, but if ye wish me to stay then I will. But Da says he's in agreement that we should get ourselves down to the border and listen in at a couple of pubs, see what's going on."

"I'll be fine. This fever will wear itself out in a few days and the bairns will be running about as usual. Go now, see what you can learn. It just seems to me that Culloden took enough men already, so why can't the Brits leave the rest of the Jacobite supporters alone? The Brits won the battle, and we all just want to live our lives as best we can."

"Aye, we all want that. But there are enough rumors floating about that we need to check them out. We believed in the cause and did our part, so that's history now. I rather doubt the Brits can remember the names of Prince Charlie's supporters, so I'm not too worried they'll remember the MacKinnon brothers. And as Da says, we live so far up in the Highlands they'll have a hard time finding us. But still, it's better we know what the thinking is in Edinburgh and London."

"Then you two go and get yourselves back as quickly as you can. Millie, Camille and I can care of the bairns, and Da and Robbie will be about if we have any trouble."

~ ~ ~

Caitlin kept busy 'round the clock, bathing fevered foreheads and all but forcing her medications down the throats of the three bairns. Her skills were limited when it came to a disease such as Scarlet Fever.

A knock at the door got her attention, but before she could call out the door opened to reveal Millie standing there.

"Millie, you can't come in here. Go back down stairs now. I don't need you to become my next patient."

"But I can hear Midge. She's crying. I must hold her."

Caitlin gently closed the door, but spoke loudly in order for

Millie to hear her on the other side where Willie was standing watch. He had never harmed a family member, but his presence at the door gave them pause just the same.

"I know it's hard, Millie. And yes, she is crying, but that's a good sound. As long as they're crying and fighting back, I can help them. When they get quiet and stop fighting, then it's more difficult for me. Please go help Da in the kitchen and put some supper for me at the top of the stairs. I'll eat when I can and I'll try to get something down the children, but that may be difficult. And don't forget to bring up some brewed tea, with some honey if we have any. They'll drink that I hope, if nothing else."

"Alright then. I'll get busy. But I'm so very worried. She's never been sick before. I feel like I should be doing something, anything."

"Then make the tea and send Robbie up. Da says the lad told him he had Scarlet Fever when he was a child, but I need to make sure before he comes in here. I'll ask him. Now just be calm, Millie. And don't forget to check on Dugald and Charlie. Camille handles them well enough, but Dugald can be a handful for someone who's never had children. Trust me, I know about that."

Shortly afterward Robbie flew up the stairs taking two at a time, just as Ian always had. He stopped abruptly when he encountered Willie at the door. The wolf stood and Robbie felt fear rising from his toes to the top of his head, and the impulse to flee was almost overwhelming.

Willie came closer and, for the first time, rubbed his nose against Robbie's leg, a sure sign of acceptance and an indication he understood the lad was to be trusted. Robbie swallowed and released the breath he had been unaware he was holding. Then, in a very brave move for him, he knelt on one knee and scratched the wolf behind his ears as he had seen Alex do many times.

Robbie knew if his mother could have viewed this scene she would have expired from fright. She never would even let him have a dog in their home, as she was afraid of just about anything with four legs. He rapped quickly on the door and waited.

"Caitlin, it's Robbie. The lady, uh Millie, says you need me."

"Robbie, yes. Da says you had Scarlet Fever as a young lad. Is that right?"

"Yes. Mother kept records of everything I did, especially

illnesses. I've had chicken pox, mumps and, yes, Scarlet Fever. She wrote in her diary I almost died and she went to the kirk every morning to pray for me. She wasn't a religious person, so it seems she must have been very worried. Oh, and one more illness, I guess you could call it that. I had lice at one time, too. Mother was horrified, but I survived the scrubbing with lye soap she insisted on. I still remember that treatment very well. My skin was raw for several weeks, but I guess it did the trick."

"Lice, huh. Well then. If you're sure you've had Scarlet Fever, I could use some help in here. At the moment I need some medications that you'll find in the upper part of the cupboard in the kitchen. Bring me the basket filled with herbs and some clean cloths so I can give these bairns a bath to ease their fever. Several of my herbs will help with this. There's not a whole lot I can do, but these measures may help them somewhat."

"Right. I'll get what you need. Be right back." Robbie rushed down the stairs relieved to have something to keep his active mind busy. He'd spent the morning with his grandda and was still thinking about that. The old man was a lot like Alex, but somehow very different also. Robbie was trying to figure out that difference.

6

Next morning, Alex and Jack were up early, both chomping at the bit to get a move on. Hector still hadn't arrived, so they were leaving without him.

When the sun peeked over the mountains they made their way to the stable. Da came out shortly, followed by Caitlin, Robbie and Millie. Willie stood next to Caitlin as if to let Alex know he'd keep her safe. The men had already said their goodbyes to their women and bairns. No more needed to be said.

"Da, we'll be back in a few days, as quickly as we can. Andrew should be here tomorrow or maybe the next day. And Hector will get here eventually, too."

"Aye. Ye lads go and find out what's going on. Then get back here and we'll figure out our strategy. I've got a very capable grandson, three fearsome women and a wolf on my side. We'll be alright."

Alex and Jack rode out, Alex astride Zeus and Jack on Millie's Arabian, Dillon, the horse she stole from her late husband, Lord Warwick, when she fled his castle so long ago. The steed was a very large animal and able to carry Jack's weight easily. Normally Jack would have ridden Goliath, his own large bay, but he needed to put a new shoe on that one's left front foot, something he'd planned to do this week. Millie's Arabian was an exceptionally fine animal and Jack smiled to himself when he pictured Millie, the lady, stealing him from her abusive husband.

After being on the road for slightly more than a day, the brothers stopped at a pub for a bite to eat and to listen to the gossip, which was always plentiful in any pub.

Approaching the pub just before sunset, they tied their horses at the edge of some trees. As they entered the establishment, they had to quickly step aside at the entrance as they were almost overrun by several British soldiers dragging a man out the front door.

"Ye British bastards! Ye have no right to come to our country and steal our lands and properties. I'll go to me grave spitting on ye!"

The middle aged man, a Highlander from his outward appearance, cursed and kicked at his captors but to no avail—four Redcoats were more than he could handle by himself. There were a number of other Highlanders in the pub, but they knew in addition to the four who were hauling the man out there were seven more sitting at a table close to the front window, and all were armed.

"Alex, ye think we better make ourselves scarce? Could be that bunch knows we were supporters of the prince."

"Aye, ye've got a point, brother. I don't know how they know who the supporters were, unless some of our own are giving us up. But no matter. I agree we should keep ourselves out of sight. Let's move on."

They made their way back to the horses, mounted up and headed back into the forest, still making tracks toward the border.

The two Highlanders were very adept at keeping deep within the woods and avoiding someone on the trail. Da had taught them survival skills at a very early age. But now, they weren't sure who the enemy was. Was it the British soldiers who seemed to show up everywhere these days? Or was it some of their own countrymen who were perhaps giving information to the Brits in order to save their own hides?

They came to a small copse of hardwoods and dismounted. "We'll rest a couple of hours then move on down to the border. If the rumors of our clansmen being sent to the islands are true, then we have some very hard thinking to do. If it were just us men folk, we could disappear from the place for a while, leave the sheep to Kenny and Hamish to take care of. The Brits can look at those two lads and know they're too young to have been supporters. But now we have Caitlin, Millie, Robbie, all the bairns, and Camille, too. What can we do to protect them?"

They rested on the ground and pulled their plaids close around their bodies. Alex closed his eyes and tried to order his thoughts, but it was impossible. One moment he was thinking about placing sentries at the edge of their property to alert them to anyone coming, and the next his thoughts were of holding Caitlin close, burying his face in that glorious hair and breathing in the lavender scent that was a part of her.

"We'll figure this out, Jack. We will. Let's try to rest now."

"Aye." Jack trusted Alex's abilities and hoped he would come up with a plan that would work for them. But this was a difficult situation. Would their home be taken away? Would he and Alex be sent to the islands, or be imprisoned? And what about Hector and Ian? Hector was still running the Sanctuary, which was fairly close to the border. Had they already found him?

Jack and Alex weren't so worried about Ian. He'd only been a boy and they doubted the Brits would be after him. Plus, they felt young Ian had skills and personal talents that would serve him well if he were in a bad situation. Woe be unto any Brits who rubbed that lad the wrong way.

A short time after they had settled down, Alex quickly raised up on his elbow.

"Did ye hear that?"

"What? I didn't hear anything."

"A twig snapped behind ye there, pretty close."

"I still don't hear anything."

Jack turned his ear toward the area where Alex was looking and moved his head from one direction to the other. Standing slowly, he still heard nothing. But just a couple of seconds later he felt something cold and sharp stick him in the side of his neck.

"On your knees, Scotsman. Put your hands over your head."

The bayonet on the end of the soldier's rifle dug further into Jack's neck, causing a trickle of blood to run down slowly. Jack raised his hands well above his head, his face as scarlet as the Redcoat's jacket. Getting caught by the likes of these two young sprouts didn't sit well with the Highlander.

Alex reached for his pistol, but as he did so a sharp blade struck him across the back of his hand causing his pistol to fly through the air and land a meter or so in front of him.

"I'd think twice about reaching for that pistol, Scottie," a second soldier remarked as he walked closer and retrieved the gun.

Blood poured from the cut on Alex's hand and the soldier stomped on the wound just to render an even more painful experience for the Highlander.

"Get up. Here, take this rag and wipe your blood off my blade. Wouldn't want your Highland swill to corrode my very fine weapon."

Alex took the rag the soldier offered and wiped the blade clean, then dabbed at his hand.

"Wrap your hand with it. Don't want you bleeding all over me either."

Alex bandaged his hand the best he could. He knew Caitlin would have told him it needed a number of stitches, but this would have to do at the moment. He flexed his fingers and was relieved to realize the cut was not as deep as he had first thought. It would definitely be sore for a while, but he'd have use of the hand, assuming he didn't develop an infection that is.

"Look at this, Trevor. It's two very fine horses these Scots have here. They'll come in handy for us. Here, climb up on that Arabian, big man. Where'd you two heathens get a steed like that one anyway? Stole it no doubt."

Once the two brothers were on their horses, the soldiers tied their hands together behind their backs, then led their horses.

"Don't imagine you'll much care for riding with your hands tied behind you, but you'll manage. Serves you right for stealing someone's horse, you uncouth, backwoods thieves."

The soldier was right. Riding with your hands tied behind you is a most uncomfortable position, one most men find difficult. But Da made sure each lad could ride well, and had instructed all of them personally. Riding with their hands behind their backs had been just one of the many positions he'd insisted on them learning.

"We'll go as far as the border tonight, then on to Edinburgh tomorrow. There's a very fine gaol there with a room reserved for you. Yep, the Old Tolbooth will welcome the likes of you two, and the major will thank us for this."

The two soldiers would be rewarded for finding the Highlanders. Their informant had told them there were three brothers and a young lad. They couldn't care less about capturing a lad, but the third brother would be found sooner or later. Their contact had told them he came and went from the lodge, but didn't know exactly where he was at the moment.

"We'll find the other one, too. You can count on that. You Highlanders need to be taught a lesson about siding against the Crown—not a smart move on your part. But then, you're not known for being especially intelligent, are you?"

Laughter followed and the two soldiers spurred their horses on just to see how the Scots rode without any help from their hands. When the soldiers looked back at the two, however, the Scotsmen sat tall in the saddle as if they were out for an enjoyable afternoon ride.

7

Wabi poured himself a mug of tea, a Darjeeling variety Aned Favŕe had brought over to him. As the steam rose above the mug, the old wizard added a dollop of honey and sniffed the tea, enjoying the tangy aroma that filled his nostrils. Finally he stood and stared out the window looking down toward the water below his cottage. The loch was white capping and as Wabi watched, an eagle swooped down, extended his great talons, and reached down into the turbulent waves and secured his next meal.

"Owl, my friend, I dislike leaving my cottage knowing Ian is on his way. But this is one situation that requires my immediate attention, as you well know. Ian is a very bright young lad and I have no doubt he'll manage on his own until such time as I'm able to be with him."

Owl sat on his perch listening to his Master. The two had been through adventures that made Owl's head spin, literally, and he was still with his Master. Being a companion of Wabi did not mean he was forced to stay. He was free to leave at any time, but he knew his place was with this old one. The Creator would never force any of the species to stay with another if they did not wish to do so. Free will was one of the Creator's laws.

You've experienced this phenomenon before Master. If the Creator so desires, you will return again and complete your destiny as he has planned. And I will be here, as always, waiting for you.

"Knowing you'll still be here when and if I return is comforting, Owl. I just wish this situation had come at a better time. There's so much turmoil in the country with the British government's demands on the Scots and I'm concerned for all of my countrymen, especially for Caitlin and her loved ones."

Alex and the MacKinnon family will take care of her, Master.

"Of course. But once I enter my hibernation state, I can no longer communicate with her, nor feel her vibrations; nor can I call Ian or hear him if he should call me. But I have no choice. Every day I feel less and less able to perform my duties the Creator has set out for me. My power is all but gone and I must go now, the time has come again.

"Only you will know where I'll be. I trust you'll keep this knowledge to yourself, and if the Creator so desires he'll allow me to go within and find that deep well of energy that will return my powers. If not, then I will continue to sleep forever.

"In just a short while, the Beltane fires will be lighted across the land. This is a time of celebration of the return of life and vitality to the earth, a rebirth so to speak. All creatures, including man, may find rejuvenation and a new connection to the Creator during this period.

"I shall enter my hibernation and dwell in the home of the Druids on the Isle of Orkney, a place of the ancients who share my blood. There is power in this place, and if it is my destiny I will harness that power and return to my assigned place on this earth.

"However, if I do not awaken before the great fires die out, then you have my permission to inform Caitlin and Ian that the time has come for me to move on to the next life the Creator has designed for me.

"I've traveled this plane and been the caretaker for this line of healers for generations now. My intuition tells me the latest healer in this line, just a child now, has been given power that may be greater than all those who came before her. If this is correct, then doubtless there will be extremely trying times ahead for all those who care for her and I pray I will be allowed to help guide her. She may be a challenge even for this old wizard. But as always, the Creator's wishes shall be done, not ours."

8

The spring morning air still had a nip to it, but thanks to the gardeners and Reggie's green thumb, Cameron Castle was teeming with colorful flowers and plants and the vegetable gardens had to be picked every day. The sight was pleasing to Hector as he made his early morning walkabout around the estate. He entered the kitchen through the back door and casually strolled into the kitchen hoping to snitch a scone from Ethel's pastry basket.

"Morning, Ethel. Have ye seen Reggie? I've looked all over but she seems to have disappeared," he said as he lifted the tea towel and pinched a buttered scone.

"Oh, aye, Mr. MacKinnon. She was here earlier, but I'm not real sure where ye might find her now. There was a wee problem, but she's quite a capable young woman so I expect she'll manage to deal with it."

"What kind of problem? Is it something I need to know about?"

"One of our kitchen helpers, Aileen, a young woman from our village, has difficulty some days, as most of the women do. And there's naught to be done I'm afraid. She lost her husband at Culloden ye see, and she's grieving still. I imagine Miss Reggie's trying her best to console her. The girl says she has family around the Lairg Fern area and would like to get back to them, but she has no means to get there and she's pretty poorly most days anyhow. Mind ye, she's good in the kitchen though, sir. She's almost as good a cook as meself." She laughed and turned back to rolling out her piecrusts.

Hector walked away, nibbling on his scone. With just a little thought, he knew where Reggie would have taken someone to console them—the rose garden. He often found Reggie there herself and wondered if she, too, weren't grieving over her own husband, who had died following a hunting accident some time ago.

As he reached the winding path that led through the rose garden he heard voices, and occasionally a sob emerged as well. Thinking perhaps this was not the time to interrupt, he turned and went back toward the stable.

He needed to talk to Clint about hiring one more helper. Apparently Winston was getting on in years, as was Clint, and needed a hand with the sheep. Presently, the flock produced enough wool to keep the estate working, and a younger helper would make things easier for the old ones.

But that problem was one he could fix. But there was another one he couldn't. This latest problem, the British breathing down everyone's throat, was something else. Hector felt sure the soldiers would show up at Cameron Castle eventually. Would they close the Sanctuary? Did they know he was a Jacobite supporter?

That evening, Hector and Reggie had their supper together in the small library next to the great room. It was quiet and they usually spent this time reviewing the day's events at the Sanctuary, and Ethel took special pains to make sure they were not interrupted during these dinners. Of course, she always included some of the fine wine from the Cameron Castle cellar—she knew the mistress would have approved of that.

It was obvious to Ethel these two were on the way to becoming more than just coworkers. Hector's face actually lit up when Reggie came into the room, and Ethel was delighted to see some happiness as there was so much grief and depression in all the women at the castle.

The Sanctuary was proving to be a safe haven for the women and children in this area. Most of the women had lost husbands at Culloden and had no place to go. Millie's grandmother had left her the estate and Millie had asked Hector to turn it into a refuge for the widows and their children. So far the project was working well, and finding Reggie to manage it for him was the key to its success as far as Hector was concerned. He took care of managing the financial end and she kept the staff organized and worked well with the women.

The most difficult situations usually involved the children. The mothers were hardly able to take care of themselves, much less their bairns. To Hector's dismay, there were many small bairns who required someone to feed them, hold them, and care for them fulltime if their own mothers were unable to do so. That was where Dorothea proved to be his savior. Taking care of children was exactly what Dorothea was meant to do, and she loved every minute of it.

Reggie, too, blossomed at the Sanctuary and greatly enjoyed being with Hector every day. He was nothing like her husband, and it surprised her that she found him so appealing.

In her opinion he was very handsome, with his dark hair and eyes, and broad shoulders that always pulled at his coat. At first glance he appeared imposing to her, something about his very large size, and his brogue took her a while to decipher. The Highlanders definitely had their own way of speaking. But once she'd gotten to know him better, she realized he was very intelligent and had the patience of Job.

He spoke about his family in the Highlands often and Reggie dreaded the day he would leave her and return to them. They'd had a number of conversations regarding how long he would stay at the Sanctuary, but he still hadn't given her any real idea of just what he had in mind.

"Hector, I have a personal understanding of how it feels to lose your loved one, your husband. But as terrible as that was, some of these women have so much more to deal with. Most of them lost their homes when their husbands didn't return from Culloden. They have no way of making a living, and some of them have children they can hardly care for. Some of them have even lost bairns to various illnesses. Life is most difficult for these women, Hector. What you have created here is a wonderful respite for them. Where they go from here is not clear yet, but today they are being cared for."

"Aye, today they're being cared for. Living in the Highlands had its own difficulties, but being cared for was something I never had to worry about. Mam and Da instilled in all of us a desire to care for each other, and we've spent a lifetime doing that. But now there's such uncertainty with the Brits I fear we may be in for some trying times."

"I agree. I know you told me you'd eventually be going back to the Highlands, but I hope it's not any time soon."

"Aye, that's my plan. But don't worry lass, I'll not leave ye by yerself just yet. We've still got more work to do here."

He poured another glass of the deep red claret for each of them. "Come, let's take a moonlight stroll through your rose garden."

As she stood, he placed her *arisaid* (a plaid wrap) about her shoulders and escorted her out the door.

By the time they returned, Hector had heard Aileen's story, and several others, which made him even more aware of the grief these women were experiencing. Some of the stories had him wishing he hadn't heard them.

9

Following his adventure with the highwayman, Ian was taking his sweet time roaming about the countryside, in no great hurry, and enjoying being on his own for the first time in his life. A week or so passed before he turned his mind to moving on to Wabi's cottage. He knew that once there his time would be taken with hours of instruction. He did love learning from Master Wabi, but this new freedom was certainly a treat for a young lad.

He stopped for a moment and returned his compass to his inside pocket. He knew exactly where he was now even without consulting the device. But Da was right, the compass had kept him on track all the way. On his last visit to Wabi's he'd scouted out the area around the cottage, so he recognized the stone circle next to the stream running along the east side of Wabi's property. These stones had been placed here eons ago and Wabi instructed him to go past them quietly, with reverence, which he certainly did now.

As he approached Wabi's cottage, his first observation was how quiet it was. Last time, he'd been amazed to see how many birds and various animals seemed to inhabit the grounds close to the cottage. But today he heard no birds, saw no squirrels nor foxes. The quiet was eerie and he slowed Merlin's trot to a walk.

As the horse ambled along, Henson reared his head from the saddlebag, as if to see for himself.

"Something's not right, Henson. No sounds, no animals. No smoke coming from his chimney. Wabi always keeps a small kettle heating on his stove for his tea."

The cat leaped to the ground and tore off toward the water. Ian had learned to trust him, and knew he would return before too long. Dismounting, he unsaddled Merlin and let him loose in the small pasture behind the stable. They both could use a rest after this journey.

He walked down to the water's edge where Henson had fled. Still no sign of Wabi, but as he stood watching the never-ending ripples on the dark waters, he spied a large bird on the wing and had no doubt who it was—Owl.

The bird traveled with Wabi and Ian was well aware they communicated constantly. As yet, Wabi had not taught him that particular skill. As he watched quietly, the great bird circled the cottage and made a spectacular, downward spiraling dive that had Ian grinning from ear to ear.

Jeez! How does he do that?

Ian marveled at how the bird could make such a maneuver without losing control. He had seen him do this before when he visited last time. Still smiling to himself, he started back up to the cottage, intent on going inside and seeing if there were any clues as to Wabi's whereabouts. Perhaps he had left him a note. He hesitated to "call" Wabi, as he had been instructed to only use that manner of communication when absolutely necessary, so he'd wait a bit before he resorted to that measure.

As he walked up the cobblestone walkway from the water, the great owl zipped by and alighted on the post at the rear of Wabi's cottage. The post had been placed there for him long ago. As Ian neared the post he stopped momentarily, finding himself feeling a bit dizzy.

Whoa. What's this about?

He thought he might sit on the steps a second. It had been a long trip, so he must be more tired than he realized. Once again, though, even sitting he felt dizzy, and then heard a buzzing sound, like a swarm of bees hovering about their hive.

He put his hands over his ears and thought to stand up again and try to make his way inside. When he did, however, the buzzing got louder and the dizziness came again full force, causing him to lose his balance and fall to his knees.

Holy sheep shite! What's happening to me?

From a faraway distance he heard another sound. Was it a voice? No. It couldn't be. There was no one else close by. Then, once again, the same sound. It must be a voice. Yes. It was a voice. What was it saying?

Yes, yes...

Then the buzzing drowned out the sound of the voice. Finally, the buzzing died down and the voice came through, more clearly this time.

Yes, Ian, I am speaking to you. Now open your mind and listen. You can hear me if you will.

Ian shook his head and looked about. Still no one around. "Mam? Are ye calling me? Are ye trying to tell me something?"

Oh, for heaven's sake! It's not your mam, it's me. Now look up here, look at me.

Ian looked up and saw Owl staring down at him.

"Owl? Are ye talking to me?"

Yes, I am. This is not difficult if you'll just pay attention. It took me forever to get through to Caitlin—please tell me you aren't going to be so dense. I expect more from you, young wizard.

Ian threw his head back and began laughing so hard he almost keeled over.

"This is unbelievable! I'm talking to an owl! And yer right, it's not difficult."

Then let's get down to business shall we? Master Wabi has gone into hibernation. At the moment you will not be able to communicate with him, nor he with you.

"What do you mean hibernation?"

There are times when my Master must retire to a place of quiet and peace. He must go deep within and seek renewal of his powers. It is an arduous undertaking and there are no guarantees he will return from this resting place, a place of the ancients. That is a decision the Creator alone will make. Master Wabi is a pawn in his hands and will obey the Creator's wishes.

"But where is he? I need to speak with him. There's a lot of unrest in the Highlands. I'm worried about my brothers, and myself, too. The Brits are capturing the Jacobite supporters and putting them in prison—sending them to the islands. They'll become slaves, Owl. I need Wabi's help!"

My master's instructions were that I tell no one his location. However, he has left a task for you, young Ian. It is his wish that you seek him, and through doing so you will make use of all the skills he has taught you. If you should discover his whereabouts, however, he will still not be available to you. You are to learn from this experience and take advantage of all knowledge that may be presented to you. It may be that there will be experiences coming your way that will deepen your understanding of this world and of peoples unknown to you before this time. Leave your prejudices aside and be open to the truth, even if it isn't what you thought it to be. Lastly, you are to remain steadfast in your own beliefs—they are well founded.

"So I can look for him, but even if I find him I can't talk to him?"

That is correct. But if he has set this task for you, then he will have had a good reason. My advice would be to not question but follow as he instructed. Master Wabi never makes any requests without a good reason. Trust me.

"I don't even know where to start, Owl. I have a compass, but that won't tell me where to begin."

I would suggest you spend a few quiet moments recalling the many lessons from Master Wabi, then proceed from there.

With that, Owl spread his great wings and lifted off his post. Within a few seconds he was but a black dot on the horizon, leaving Ian standing alone staring into the distance.

10

Throwing open the windows in old Jamie's room, Caitlin stuck her head out, taking in a deep breath as she did so. She'd been cooped up in this room for days now and a breath of fresh air was welcome.

Her nose registered scents that hadn't been there just a few weeks ago. The strongest scent came from the heather that covered the moor from one end to the other. She took in the freshness of the young pine saplings growing in the forests, and she could detect just the faintest aroma of primrose and mountain avens—spring, her favorite time of the year.

She turned her attention back to her patients and Robbie, whose help had been tremendous during this time.

"Thanks be, the fever has broken on two of our patients. The worst is over for Bridgette and Midge. But Flinn is still burning up. Robbie, run out to the stable and look in the old cupboard in the last stall. That's where I keep extra herbs until I need them. Find the bottle labeled yarrow. I'll make a paste of that and apply it to Flinn's body. Hopefully this will bring her fever down. Go now. Hurry."

The lad fled down the stairs and out the back door. For reasons unknown to Robbie, Willie took off with him, which was surprising. This was the first time the wolf had ever tagged along with him for anything. But he wasn't afraid of Caitlin's wolf anymore. The animal was just as much a member of the family as he was, maybe more so.

At least he's pure bred, not a half-breed like me.

Opening the gate to the last stall, Robbie located the cupboard and combed through the numerous bottles of herbs and liquid mixtures. Each one was properly labeled and tightly corked so nothing dripped. He found the small bottle of yarrow and put it in his pocket, then closed the stable gate behind him.

In one of his early lessons from Alex, he was taught to always close the gate to all stables or pastures or fences. This was a very large sheep farm and keeping sheep in their proper places took effort from all hands.

Turning back toward the lodge, he was startled when Willie let out an ear-shattering howl and went sailing past him. Robbie followed quickly and found himself in the first stall looking down at a body on the ground and an agitated Willie pulling at the hand of the old man lying there.

"Oh, no, no!" Robbie got to his knees.

"Grandda, can you hear me?" He held the old one's head in his lap.

"What's wrong?"

Grandda's eyes remained closed and there was no response to Robbie's words. The lad had no idea what to do. If he called for Caitlin, she'd have to leave the bairns and come through the house, which he knew she didn't want to do. That left only one solution. He'd have to carry Grandda to the lodge. There was no one else around so he took a deep breath and tried to lift his grandfather. Like all the MacKinnon men, even in his old age Grandda was quite a large man.

But so am I. I can do this.

After trying to lift him like he would have carried a child, Robbie finally resorted to laying Grandda over his shoulder as if he were a sack of feed. At this juncture he just wanted to get him inside where Caitlin could check him out. As Robbie struggled to lift Grandda, Willie took off to the lodge, howling as he went.

Caitlin's head snapped up when she heard the howling. Willie only howled when something was wrong. What could be going on? She needed to know, but really didn't want to chance spreading the fever by leaving the room. She'd had no choice but to send Robbie out, but she'd prefer not to leave herself unless it was absolutely necessary.

She listened at the door and knew the moment Willie arrived. She spoke softly to him and then she heard Robbie.

"Caitlin, something's wrong with Grandda! He's unconscious, I think. I don't know what to do. Help me!"

"Be calm, Robbie. Listen to me carefully. Take Daniel and put him in Mam's sewing room. You know which one that is. Take Willie with you and stay with him until I come. I'll be there shortly."

Robbie kicked the door to Mam's sewing room open and Willie rushed in first. Placing his grandda on the bed, he looked about for a blanket. Somehow it seemed the right thing to do. Willie lay down on the floor close to the bed and would remain there until Caitlin gave him leave. Some lessons he had learned a long time ago.

Robbie found a blanket and tucked it around Grandda, then stood, feeling totally useless.

Caitlin hurried through the door and was at Daniel's bedside immediately. She touched her hand to his forehead and completed the head-to-toe assessment she always gave her patients. If the heat she felt coming from him wasn't enough to help her make a diagnosis, the telltale rash on his neck was.

"He's got it too, Scarlet Fever."

"But don't just bairns get that?" Robbie questioned.

"No, I'm afraid not. Adults get it too and for them it can sometimes be even more disastrous. He's quite an old gentleman now and I've learned that the young ones and the old ones have one thing in common—they sometimes have more difficulty fighting off diseases than others. We'll have to be vigilant with him and try to keep the fever down. I'll need you to help me even more now, Robbie.

"Yes, of course. Just tell me what to do."

~ ~ ~

Robbie's only experience helping a sick person was with his mother, Fiona, just recently, and ultimately she had died in spite of all efforts to save her.

Fiona was an exceptionally intelligent woman with a great amount of fortitude. She was her father's only child and he had spent his life making sure she became an educated woman who would leave her mark on the world.

He had been sorely disappointed when she was born, as he

had needed a son to carry on his family's linage. They were, after all, one of the oldest families in the realm. In fact, he and the king were distant relatives and close friends.

Lord Robert Wellington brought tutors from several countries to teach Fiona languages, mathematics, science, and art, and had exposed her to some of the greatest minds of the time. She proved to be a quick study in most subjects, and to his surprise had become a beautiful young woman. He shouldn't have been surprised, however, as her mother, Lady Wellington, had been most attractive herself. She had been stricken during one of the many flu epidemics that had spread across Europe and had died when Fiona was just a child.

When Fiona informed Lord Wellington she wished to go to university, he hardly knew what to say.

"Women don't go to university, Fiona."

"But this one will. I know you have great influence and can help get me admitted."

"That would take quite some doing, my dear."

"Yes, I expect it would. But, then you do have a good friend who can make most anything happen. I would suggest you enlist his help."

Lord Wellington looked at his daughter. Yes, she was indeed his daughter…and apparently thought like he did. So, never one to refuse a challenge, he took the matter up with the king.

The most difficult aspect of the request was that Fiona wanted to attend Edinburgh University, not Oxford as he had assumed she would.

Her research had revealed that Edinburgh University was regarded as the best institution of higher learning at the time, with Oxford a very distant second place. Lord Wellington had to step on a number of toes to accomplish the task, but once again, having a royal relative—a most royal relative as it were—paved the way for Fiona to apply at university.

It was not until 1892 that women were actually admitted to the university—and so Fiona was never included in their official enrollment documents. However, having received pressure from the king himself, she was allowed to sit in on classes. It hadn't taken long for her intelligence and abilities to be noticed by her professors, and they made use of these skills for their own purposes. They allowed her to act as a tutor, and that was how Alex came to be acquainted with her. He was taken with her beauty initially, but shortly realized she was more than just beautiful, she was well versed in many subjects. He was enamored with her. She was truly his first love.

He was a bit younger than she, but that didn't seem to be a problem for either of them. Their relationship was tumultuous and hot, and they often argued about the differences between the Brits and the Scots. But the physical side of the relationship was more than satisfying to both of them.

Robbie smiled when he thought about how insistent his mother could be. When she had shown up at the Old Tollbooth, the prison in Edinburgh, and demanded she be allowed to visit with the women prisoners, of course the officials refused her, reminding her the women prisoners were kept in a special area of the prison and were not allowed visitors.

The English and Scottish folk were always at odds, but she had spent a lifetime confronting that situation. So when Fiona informed the officials she was the daughter of Lord Wellington, cousin of the king, she eventually gained access.

Though Lord Wellington was British, he was well known throughout Scotland. It was common knowledge he and the king were close friends, and he mingled with both the English and the Scottish aristocracy. It was also known that if he were opposed in any endeavor, those in opposition often disappeared without anyone knowing what had become of them.

Fiona found the conditions in the prison so appalling and hideous she could hardly believe it. She was not a nurse, but she was very adept at listening to the women's woes and often brought them a shard of soap, or a small bit of chocolate or cake if she could sneak it in. Most of all she just gave them an ear, and often read to those who could not read, which was most of them. Even if they could have, there were no books or reading materials of any sort.

It was during one of her visits to the prison that she contracted typhus, a most debilitating and painful disease, one that claims most of its victims.

In her last days, Robbie often sat next to her bed and read to her just as she had to the women in prison. And it was strange, he thought. She didn't want him to read anything new. She wanted him to read from her favorite passages in her novels, or perhaps read a few lines of Shakespeare to her, and she often drifted off to sleep before he could finish his reading. No doubt the medications to ease her pain also made her sleep. In the end she just didn't wake up again.

Now here he was once again called upon to help a sick person, a special old Scot who was his grandda. He had not even known him a few months ago, but today Robbie was very aware that he fervently wanted him to live.

~ ~ ~

Placing her hand once again on each child's forehead and listening to Bridgette's chatter, Caitlin breathed a sign of relief.

"And now my sweet lasses, you may go downstairs. I don't think you'll spread anything to anyone. Go, now. We all need a change of scenery."

Opening the door, she called out. "Millie? Can you come up and relieve me of this bairn who's calling for her mam?" Little Midge was beginning to make a few sounds, and MumMum came out most often. Millie came scurrying up the stairs and held her daughter for the first time in a number of days.

"Oh, Caitlin. I don't know how you did it, but you managed to bring them through this disastrous fever. I was so afraid we'd lose them all."

Robbie reached into the crib and picked Flinn up, holding her close. He'd become quite comfortable with her during these days of helping Caitlin, and he still marveled at having a sister so late in life.

"It was touch and go for a few days, I admit, but perhaps we had a little help from other sources, eh?" She smiled to herself as she took Bridgette's hand and led her downstairs. The child had been ever so quiet during her illness, but before they got to the bottom of the stairs she was calling for Charlie and Dugald.

But, no sooner had the group gathered in the kitchen than Kenny burst through the back door, gasping for breath.

"Caitlin, Millie, I've just come from the Black Isle. Alex sent me down there to see what they're getting for their wool these days. And it's a good price, ye ken?

But what I need to tell ye is there were British soldiers everywhere. There was talk they had captured two Highlanders last week. I'm worried it was Alex and Jack. They talked about one of them having red hair and said he was 'big as a giant.' I couldn't ask any questions, so I come back as quick as I could."

Caitlin motioned him to sit. "Easy, Kenny. Let's not jump to any conclusions. There are many Highlanders with red hair, and most of them are big men, too. But let me talk with Uncle Andrew and we'll figure out what to do. You go on now, go get some rest. That's a long ride from the Black Isle."

Kenny nodded and turned to leave. At the last moment he turned back to Caitlin. "What can we do? Mr. Daniel and Mr. Andrew are too old to go about the country looking for them."

"I agree. But we'll talk with Uncle Andrew. He may have some ideas. He's been through a lot of trials in his time. We'll think of something. Go rest now." The young lad nodded and headed to his cottage.

"Robbie, come with me. We'll talk with Uncle Andrew, see what his thoughts are. Millie can you manage a few minutes? And don't go into Mam's sewing room. The children are all past being contagious, but Da's still running quite a fever."

"Of course. Bridgette can help me make some biscuits. You two go on," Millie responded, taking Flinn from Robbie's arms.

The walk over to Andrew and Camille's cottage was a short one, but before they even got halfway Camille flung the door open and called out to them.

"Oh, Caitlin. I'm so glad you came. Andrew's burning up. It came on so quickly, just this morning. I sent Dugald and Charlie outside and told them to stay in the stable until I came for them. I don't know what to do." Caitlin hurried through the door and went to Andrew's bedside.

"Ah, lass. Looks like I'm not any more immune than Daniel. But we're old ruffians who can withstand most anything. Go on with ye, now. I'll be alright."

"I'm quite sure you will be, Uncle Andrew. Just the same, I'd like you to come to the lodge. We'll put a cot in Da's room and I can tend both of you that way."

"Ah, lass, do ye think that's necessary?"

"Aye. Let's keep this fever contained in one place if we can. Robbie can help you if you can walk a bit."

Andrew nodded to Robbie. "I can walk well enough, but a hand from ye would be appreciated, lad."

"Yessir." Robbie stood next to Andrew and let the old one put his arm around his neck.

"That'll work. Come on then. Let's get to the lodge."

By the time they reached the lodge, Andrew's strength had been totally drained and Robbie had to help him onto the cot. Daniel was awake, but still fevered.

"Andrew? What are ye doing in here? Ye need to go on now, Caitlin says this stuff moves like wildfire."

"Well, I thought I would just keep ye company for a while, Daniel. We've shared a lot of other things, might as well share this fever too."

There was no response from Daniel. He had already drifted off again.

Sometime later, in the wee hours, Andrew called out softly. "Daniel? Ye'll not forget our pact now will ye? It could be important."

Daniel smiled in the darkness. "Nae, Andrew, I won't forget. But I don't think either of us needs to worry about that yet. Caitlin says we're on the mend. She's a fine healer, ye ken?"

"Aye. Then I'll see ye in the morning, eh?"

~ ~ ~

The next morning found Caitlin still working with Uncle Andrew. As soon as Robbie had gotten him onto the cot, Caitlin had given him her undivided attention. As for Daniel, he seemed to have weathered the worst of the fever, but was still in need of care.
Andrew was another story. Like Daniel, his advanced age was not in his favor. She continued forcing medications down him, but more often than not they came back up.

"Here, Andrew. Let's try another cool bath, anything to get the fever down a bit."

Unexpectedly, Andrew grabbed her by the front of her blouse and tried to sit up. "Florence? Florence? Where have ye been? I've been looking for ye, lass."

Caitlin eased his hands away and helped him lie back down.

Robbie watched in amazement. "Who's he talking to? Who's Florence?"

"Florence was his wife. She died many years ago."

"Oh. So he's confused, I guess."

"Hallucinations are common with a fever as high as his. We've got to get it down somehow. Let's try the yarrow paste again."

The two of them worked diligently through the day and night, constantly bathing Uncle Andrew and applying paste. But as the sun crept slowly over the mountain and announced the arrival of a new day, Andrew's death rattle announced his departure.

~ ~ ~

At first light Caitlin went to check on Da once again before she left for the day's event. She met Robbie in the hallway coming from Da's room. Apparently he had visited him also.

She entered quietly. "I believe the worst is over, Daniel. You had me worried there for a while, but you'll recover now, with a lot of rest and some of Millie's delicious food."

"Lass, yer a Godsend to the MacKinnon family. I'm not real sure how Alex managed to convince ye to come with him, but we're awful glad he did. We need ye, lass. And we want ye, too."

"This is where I belong. This is my home and you are my family now.

Daniel gave her a small smile. "And Robbie. The lad waited on me hand and foot. He's a MacKinnon whether he wants to be or not, I say."

"I couldn't have managed without him, Da. Spending so much time with him lately, I realize he's more like Alex than I knew. Rather quiet, but always thinking."

Daniel looked at his daughter-in-law. "I know ye all have a task today, one I wish ye didn't have. Burying a loved one is difficult, particularly when it's one who was as fine as Andrew."

"Yes, he was loved by all of us," Caitlin responded. She nodded and swallowed, finding it difficult to hold back the tears that were threatening to spill over.

"Lass, would ye look inside that tin over there, the one where Alice kept her extra buttons and such—that small tin on the window sill?"

Caitlin walked over and picked up the small rectangular tin and handed it to Daniel. He removed the top and searched around inside it for a moment, his fingers finally finding what he was searching for.

"Ah, here it is. Would ye please take this gold crown and put it in Andrew's coat pocket for me?" he asked, handing the coin over to her.

"Of course, Da. But a gold crown? That's very valuable. I don't think Andrew's going to have any use for it."

"Well, ye see, lass, we made a pact some years ago. We agreed whichever one of us went first, the other was to put a gold crown in his pocket before burial."

"But why? That seems like a waste of money to me I must say."

"Waste? Oh, no, lass. Ye don't understand. It's just in case he needs it, ye ken? A bribe for St. Peter!"

Even in his grief he grinned at the memory of making the pact with Andrew.

Caitlin smiled and gave him a hug before she left him, then made her way up to the gravesite. The circle of stones still called to her and she could often be seen standing at the top of the moor, her fiery hair blowing in the wind and her long skirts whipping about her ankles. The spirits she encountered there always brought her peace when all else failed.

Today she offered her prayers then quickly joined the others at the recently dug gravesite. Hamish and Kenny had prepared the plot, and Andrew would be buried next to his Florence as he had requested. Millie had made a floral arrangement using the white primroses and pine boughs that were plentiful.

One more arrangement was brought to the site as well. This one was simply a single sprig of heather tied with a yellow ribbon. The ribbon belonged to Camille and she tied it around the heather, Andrew's favorite flower.

They bowed their heads as the vicar offered prayers for Andrew's soul. His family would treasure his memory and his name would always bring a smile to their faces.

There had been no choice but to bury him, as no one knew if and when Alex and Jack would return. At the end of the ceremony, family tradition was to spend the day bringing to mind fond memories of the deceased. But somehow, with Alex and Jack gone and Da in his bed, that didn't seem to be proper.

Caitlin, Millie and Camille walked slowly back toward the lodge, each keeping their thoughts to themselves. As they got closer, Camille decided to go to her cottage alone. Her memories of Andrew were ones she would keep to herself, and some of them would last her a lifetime.

Had Ian been there, perhaps he would have felt the presence of another grieving one. As it was, only Robbie was aware. He watched as the old stag stood at the edge of the forest for several moments before slowly disappearing into his wooded haven.

11

The Sanctuary at Cameron Castle was always a busy place. Children were constantly being herded from one room to another, the women called to each other across the grounds, and some days you might even hear a little laughter.

But for many of the residents, having a roof over their heads, being safe, and having food didn't take care of all their needs. The horror of Culloden seemed to have invaded the very souls of some of the women, and those were the ones Reggie worried about.

"Hector, I think we need to try to get Aileen to her family in Lairg. She has an older sister there who would take her in. Do you agree with that idea?"

Sometimes Hector had difficulty responding to Reggie. Today she was wearing a cornflower blue dress with a high collar. The blue color accentuated her violet eyes, and her honey-colored hair was held back with a matching ribbon. She glided quietly along, her long skirts barely skimming the floor. These distractions got his attention more than her words.

"Uh ... aye. Ethel tells me she's a great worker in the kitchen, but some days she's lost in her thoughts and stares off in space. Ethel's worried about her, too."

"Do you think we can arrange that? To get her to Lairg Fern?"

Hector stared down at his boots for a long moment, then

looked back up at Reggie.

"I'll be going to the Highlands in a couple of days. I need to see Da and my brothers. They're bound to be as worried as I am about the Brits. I'll take Aileen with me and help her find her sister. Lairg's one of the villages on the trail, so it's not out of my way."

"I knew you'd find a way, you always do."

She smiled at him and walked away satisfied this one woman would have a chance at life again now.

Next morning, Hector wanted to get underway as early as possible. The trek to the Highland lodge was always a long one, and he had a detour to make along the way this time. Aileen had been very pleased he had offered to take her as far as Lairg Fern.

"Mr. MacKinnon, I do thank you. I know I'm difficult for Ethel to deal with some days, but I do try. It's just that I'm so alone now."

"Lairg is not much out of my way, Aileen. I've never been there, but I believe it's just south and west of our own properties. It'll take us a while, but if ye get tired we'll just let ye rest in the back of the cart. There's a blanket and that'll keep ye warm enough. I've used this cart many times for just such trips as this one. We'll find yer sister, then I'll get on to my own family. It's an easy enough task, lass."

Originally he had planned to go by horseback, as that was quicker. But when Reggie had made her request he decided to take the cart instead.

Aileen was a small, thin woman with an abundance of long dark hair. She wore it braided and it hung down her back. She kept to herself and didn't talk much, according to Ethel. Reggie had been able to get a few details out of her, but you didn't need to know the details to understand she was in pain and getting her to her sister's was a good idea. So before the sun even considered raising its golden head, Hector and Aileen were on the trail headed upland.

"Reggie tells me your family is in the upper Highlands, too, Mr. MacKinnon." She was trying to make conversation, but found it difficult. She'd retreated inside herself some time ago and making small talk with others was a real trial for her.

"Aye. I've got three brothers, my da and Uncle Andrew. And there's Caitlin and Millie, who are married to my brothers. Oh, and Millie has a little daughter named Midge. Millie was married once before, ye ken? It's a long story, but she's part of our family now."

"All these people live in one cottage?"

"Well, Da always added a room each time a bairn came along. Then he added another room when Old Jamie moved in, and then another when Uncle Andrew joined us. Da just likes to build cottages, I think. So what started out as a small crofter's hut became a rather large lodge. And believe it or not, there are still some empty rooms." He smiled at the woman.

The two of them had traveled for most of the day when Hector decided to stop at an inn for a bite to eat. The inn was located on the south side of Cromarty Firth, which was where they would veer off and head toward Lairg. He'd taken the food Ethel had insisted on packing for him, but he thought Aileen would find dinner in the inn a pleasant experience, probably one she hadn't had in a long time.

"Whoa, now, whoa, Bess. Hold here."

Hector pulled hard on the reins and stepped down from the cart. Coming to the other side, he offered his hand to Aileen and helped her down.

"What's this place, Mr. MacKinnon?"

"This is an inn I sometimes frequent on my way. Ethel's cooking is great, but there's also a pub in here that will take care of my thirst, ye ken?"

He smiled at the woman and led her through the door. To anyone watching, they would appear to be a young couple stopping for dinner along their journey, which is exactly what they were.

Aileen looked about. She'd actually been a cook in an inn such as this, years ago now it seemed. She didn't like to remember those days, however, as they were from another lifetime, a time when her life was full of happiness and promise.

"Why don't ye enjoy a small glass of their wine, Aileen? It might help ye relax a bit."

"Yessir." And she drank not one, but two glasses of the rich red wine the innkeeper placed on their table. Hector had become used to the fine wine at Cameron Castle, but this wasn't too bad. If nothing else, it seemed to loosen Aileen's tongue a little and she began to tell him her story. Hector knew parts of it, as Reggie had told him as much as she knew. But he now understood there was much more to the story, and the telling of it renewed Aileen's sorrow and brought pain to his own heart as well.

Mam, if ye can hear me, I need yer wisdom.

Aileen waited patiently as Hector went to the counter and paid for their meal and wine. She was more relaxed than she could remember being in such a long time. Somehow, telling Hector her troubles was strangely a relief even though it brought back painful memories. It took Hector a bit longer at the counter than she thought it might, but she stayed put until he came back to their table.

"The innkeeper says we can't cross Cromarty Firth just now. They've had so much rain the bridge is under water. He indicated there's another path we can take to get to Lairg Fern. It will take us a little longer, but we'll get there."

"I see. If you think that's best, sir."

They had only gone a short way when Hector saw Aileen's head lean to the side. She immediately sat up straight, but in another few minutes her chin dropped to her chest and she was nodding off again.

Bringing the cart to a halt, he gently roused her.

"Here, lass, let's let ye rest a bit in the cart. The blanket will keep ye warm and we'll be to our destination before ye know it."

"Yessir. I'm just tired and sleepy, from the wine I guess."

And she actually smiled at Hector, the first smile he had ever seen on her face.

Hector himself was tired, but this trip was one he knew he had to make. The British were virtually crawling all over the country and it was only a matter of time before he and his brothers would be called on to take some kind of action. But that was the problem. What kind of action?

Hector had made this trip so many times he could do it in his sleep. In fact, he thought he may have slept the last few miles. But just the scent of the Highlands was enough for him to feel a warmth flowing through his body.

It had taken him longer than usual to get here, but it was still light, as this time of year the days were much longer. The Highlands were alive with every flower and plant pushing its way through the soil, seeking the warmth of the sun. As always, he pulled to the back of the lodge, where he knew all the activity would be taking place.

Looking out across the moor, he saw Hamish and Kenny working with the sheep, then he heard laughter coming from the stable.

Suddenly, he caught brief snatches of voices—voices of children.

"Grandda says he's still tired, but when he's better he'll teach me to ride."

Dugald was showing Bridgette and Charlie the new pony Da had brought to the lodge. They looked at the pony briefly, then ran around the corner intent on chasing Tess, the old Border collie, as she slowly sauntered by. She was so old now that running was not an option for her.

Millie and Caitlin heard the cart pull up and peeked out the window. "Oh, Millie, it's Hector. Thank goodness. And he's brought Dorothea. What a help she'll be."

Millie rushed out the door, anxious to greet her old nursemaid and friend. But she stopped just short of going down the steps.

"Caitlin, that's not Dorothea. I don't know that lady, do you?"

Just seconds later, the three laughing bairns came flying around the corner of the stable, headed to the back door. They came to an abrupt halt, stared for several minutes, then began to run toward the woman standing by the cart. Dugald was the first one to find his voice.

"Mum! That's our mum, that's our mum!" he yelled as he flew towards the cart. Bridgette stumbled and fell to the ground as she began to run faster trying to keep up with Dugald. She was on her feet again in a moment and once again darted forward.

"Mummy! Mummy!" she screamed, and she, too, was across the yard grabbing at her mother's skirts.

Aileen had sunk to her knees, and had not yet found her own voice. It was hiding somewhere between the sobs and tears. She knew she would find it eventually, but just now her arms did the talking and that was enough for Dugald and Bridgette.

Then, as if he didn't trust his eyes, wee Charlie stood very still, then slowly began to make his way toward his mother. The closer he got, the faster his small legs began to run.

"Mu, Mu, Mu."

This was his first attempt at making any words since his frightening event with Drosera.

Aileen finally uttered her first words also.

"Oh, Charlie, come here! It's Mummy! Come here!"

She gathered all three precious bairns in her thin arms and held them tightly, vowing to never let them go again.

Millie and Caitlin stood by observing the scene in awe, and found themselves crying too. They watched in disbelief and wonderment as this small family came together after being separated by events none of them could understand. Caitlin sent up a small prayer of thanks for her own bairn, Flinn.

"Uncle Wabi would tell you the Creator had a hand in this." She wiped her eyes and handed Millie the kerchief.

"Ah, Caitlin, Millie, 'tis good to see ye both." Hector greeted them with a MacKinnon hug, which left the two of them staggering.

"Hector, how in the world did you find their mother? I thought she was dead," Millie said. She and Caitlin had both been mother to these three for some time now, but certainly were glad their own mother had been found.

"It's a long, sad, story ladies. There are so many sad stories at the Sanctuary. All of the women have one, and each one will pull at yer heartstrings. But once I heard Aileen's story it didn't take much to realize the bairns I had found in Cameron Castle belonged to her.

I now know the children had left their cottage thinking their mother was dead. But apparently she was ill and had become unconscious for several days and when she finally did awaken, she couldn't find them. She came to the Sanctuary several months ago and has been having a most difficult time trying to get a grip on her life, a life without her husband and bairns. It seemed an impossible task for her and she withdrew more and more everyday.

"Then she's one of the lucky ones, I say. Culloden has taken so much from so many," Caitlin said.

And it may have taken Alex and Jack even as we speak.

"So tell me what's happening up here. Where's Alex, Jack?"

Millie turned away, preferring to let Caitlin tell Hector their own sad story.

"Alex and Jack left for the border about ten days ago. They were hoping to learn whatever information they can about the Brits in order to come up with a plan to keep us all safe, if that's possible."

"Ten days? That's a long time. Were they planning to be gone that long?"

"No, they had thought to be back within a week at most."

"Then, I'll go look for them. Today."

"There's more to tell, Hector. Alex sent Kenny down to the Black Isle to check on wool prices. He came back saying two Highlanders had been captured there the day before he arrived. The innkeeper at the local pub described one of them as having red hair and being big as a giant."

"Jesus! That's gotta be Jack. And the other had to be Alex."

"Yes, that's what we think, too. But, Da doesn't want us to do anything hasty."

"Where's Da? He's usually got one of the bairns on his hip or reading to one of 'em. And where's Ian?"

"We've had several weeks of Scarlet Fever here in the lodge. The bairns, Midge, Flinn and Bridgette, were first. Then Da and Andrew."

"Well, I see the wee ones are up and about. How are the old ones?"

"Go see for yourself. Da's upstairs in Mam's room. He's waiting for you."

Hector bounded up the stairs and was at Mam's room in seconds. He knocked and, not waiting for an answer, opened the door.

"Da? Are ye alright then?" Hector had never seen his father ailing. He'd watched him recover from a wound from a wild boar, but even that hadn't kept him in bed. At the moment he looked pale and gaunt.

"Ah, lad. It's about time. We hoped ye'd come."

Hector knelt next to Da's bed. "Caitlin says the fever got ye but that ye'll recover if ye take it easy a while."

"Aye. It's nothing worth talking about."

"Maybe, but she knows her business, Da. Ye need to listen to her, and I do have something worth talking about." He pulled up a stool, sat down and proceeded to tell Da the story of Aileen and her bairns.

"That's the best news I've heard in a long time. It's right that ye brought her here. A mother needs to be with her bairns. Now, I'm tired of taking it easy, and when I'm ready I'm going downstairs whether the ladies like it or no. Caitlin's taken good care of me, but it's time for me to get meself on me feet."

"Caitlin says Uncle Andrew had the fever too. Guess he's

over in his cottage with Camille."

Da hesitated a moment, looking out the window over the moor. Then he turned back to Hector.

"Lad, nae. Andrew's gone on to his next lodge, ye ken? He didn't make it."

Hector stood and looked at Da, seeing unbearable grief in the old man's eyes. He and Andrew had been mates since they were but young lads. They'd spent a lifetime together and when you saw one, the other was close by.

"But, Da. He can't be gone. He ... I ..."

"I know, lad. It's like me right arm is gone. The only worse pain was when Alice left me. But ye know, son, she'd say, 'he's only a thought away, Daniel, only a thought away.'"

Hector slowly walked down to the kitchen. It never occurred to him that his own family might be having their own problems while he was down at the Sanctuary helping others. Looking around, he saw Flinn asleep in her crib and Midge playing at Millie's feet as she and Caitlin prepared food for this large group.

Aileen and the orphans had come inside and Hector made all the necessary introductions. The woman looked so forlorn, twisting her hands and pushing at her hair as if to tidy it. They all said the proper words, but her discomfort was apparent to everyone. She looked at Hector, perhaps seeking his approval. He smiled at her, and in a halting voice she began to speak.

"I don't know what to say to you all. I thought my bairns were gone forever. But you have taken them in and cared for them as if they were your own. Whatever can I do to thank you? I have nothing, no money, not even a home for them now. But I do hope you'll understand I can't leave them again. Perhaps my sister will have room for us, if I can just make my way there."

Hector, in true MacKinnon fashion, came to her rescue immediately.

"Ye don't need to worry about a place for them, Aileen. They, and ye, can stay here as long as ye want. As far as we're concerned, they, and ye, yer all part of the MacKinnon family.

"Now, Millie, I'm well aware of yer skills in the kitchen. Ye'll be pleased to know, however, that Aileen has worked in several inns as a cook and for the last weeks Ethel has taught her how to make dishes I've never even heard of."

Millie spoke up quickly. "Another cook? Oh, Aileen you have no idea how much I would like that. I enjoy cooking, but with my duties in the school these days it's quite a chore to keep food on the table and prepare lessons as well."

Aileen nodded, and without any further invitation began stirring a pot of potatoes on the stove with all three bairns still holding on to her skirts.

"So, where's Ian?" Hector asked.

Caitlin sighed and shook her head.

"He left here headed to Skye to resume his training. But that was some time ago now and I haven't been able to communicate with Uncle Wabi, so I really don't know what's going on with those two."

"Communicate? With Wabi?"

"Oh, it's just something Wabi taught me to do when I'm in a dire situation. But no matter how hard I try, he's not listening, or chooses not to. I just don't know."

Hector knew about Wabi's unusual powers, but he didn't quite understand how he and Caitlin could communicate.

"So Ian is gone, but if Alex and Jack have been captured I should get down to Edinburgh and try to find out where they are."

A voice from the doorway got their attention.

"Nae, lad. Ye go back to the Sanctuary and take care of those women there. They're just as needy as Alex and Jack and that's yer place right now."

Da saw the thin woman standing at the stove with the three orphans clinging to her skirts. He nodded in her direction. She smiled briefly then turned back to stirring the potatoes. Da came closer and bowed slightly.

"I'm Daniel MacKinnon, mam. I understand yer the mother of my grandchildren. I'm pleased to make yer acquaintance."

Dugald and Bridgette ran over to their grandda and hugged him about the knees, as they'd not seen him since the fever had taken over the lodge.

Aileen couldn't stop the tears as they started down her face and her soul filled with joy knowing her family was secure.

~ ~ ~

Following the burial, Robbie had retired to his attic lair and found himself writing furiously in his journal. This outlet allowed him a way to express his thoughts and fears. He'd been so relieved to see Grandda pull through the fever, and now he was back to wondering about Alex and Jack. What had happened to them? Were they even still alive?

He closed his journal and decided to see what the ruckus was downstairs. His attic room kept him isolated from some noises, but there was definitely something going on down there.

As he came into the kitchen he saw Caitlin and Millie, and to his surprise, Grandda. There was another small woman and a large man standing next to her. For a half second he thought it was Alex, but then quickly realized it wasn't.

Grandda called out to him.

"Here, lad. Come meet yer Uncle Hector. He's the last one I promise ye."

Grandda smiled as he introduced the lad—and his pride in this new grandson showed. Robbie had become very special to him. "Hector, this is Robbie. Robbie Alexander MacKinnon, Alex's son, ye ken?"

Alex's son? Alex doesn't have a son.

That was obviously not true, as the lad standing there could only belong to Alex. Hector stared at the young man as if he couldn't take his eyes away. Even the arrogant lift of his dimpled chin rang of Alex. Finally, he stuck out his hand to the lad.

"Uh, glad to meet ye, Robbie."

Hector looked to Da, then Caitlin and back to the lad.

"I see there have been some changes since I was last here. Perhaps I'd better come more often."

Da nodded. "Yep. It might not be a bad idea. As ye can tell, there's never a dull moment at this lodge. Robbie, this is Aileen. She's the mother to these three children that have ye about the knees."

Robbie nodded to Aileen and pried Charlie from his legs. Charlie didn't talk but found it easy to be with Robbie and both of them liked that.

Everyone was gathered around the dining table for the evening meal when there was a light knock at the back door and Camille entered.

"Camille, come in, come in," Da called out. They were all glad to see her, as she had closeted herself in her cottage since Andrew's burial. She preferred to grieve alone, and they accepted her wish to do so.

"We've had a wonderful surprise today. Please come in and meet Aileen, the mother of our three bairns." Millie ushered her through the door and she held out her hand to Aileen.

"My, what a wonderful development. It's my pleasure to meet you, Aileen. Your children have brought much happiness to me and all of us, and with you back with them, I'm sure they will bring the same to you."

The dinner conversation tiptoed around the one subject on everyone's mind—what about Alex and Jack?

Finally, Da stood and announced he was going back up to rest. Robbie immediately came to his side and offered his help. Hector took this all in but made no comment.

Just before Da went up, Hector walked over and spoke quietly to him.

"Da, I'll need to get back to the Sanctuary quickly as Reggie has her hands full. We've got a house full of women and children and it takes both of us to keep everything running smoothly. But I'll be back shortly."

Da nodded and allowed Robbie to give him a hand.

Returning to the kitchen, Hector dug into the inside pocket of his coat.

"Millie, I almost forgot. I've a letter from Dorothea. She said she explained everything in the letter, but I know what she wants to tell ye is that we truly need her at the Sanctuary. She's as important as Reggie, and right now I just don't know what I'd do without her. She's so good with the wee ones. They listen to her and she seems to have found her calling. I know she doesn't want to disappoint you, but at the moment she finds herself being needed."

"Then that's where she should stay. Tell her I understand and I'll come down soon."

Next morning, quite early as always, Hector was busy rigging up Bess for his trip back to the Sanctuary. He was surprised to see Camille strolling across the path from her cottage to the lodge. She was dressed in a very fine, dark blue coat with a matching hat—traveling clothes. Even Hector recognized that.

"Good morning, Camille. What brings you out so early?"

"I know the stage goes to Edinburgh every Friday morning. I was wondering if I might get a lift to the station if it's not out of your way. Andrew brought happiness to me and I'll always remember those days. But, I must go on with my life now, and it's right that I go back to Edinburgh. I have a small home there and many friends to comfort me."

"I see. Have you discussed the matter with the family?"

"Yes, Caitlin and Millie and I talked at length last evening and decided it would be better for me to just go on and not create another emotional scene for the bairns. They've had enough of those lately. We're in agreement this is the proper thing for me to do." Hector nodded his agreement. "Then, let's be on our way."

12

Ian sat watching the waves as they stretched to reach the edge of the shore, their fingers pulling at the ropes that held the old wooden boat Wabi kept tied at his dock. The lapping of the water produced a rhythmic sound Ian found soothing. He'd been sitting on the dock for some time now and Owl was long gone.

Well then. What am I going to do now? I gotta find Wabi. I need his help.

He stood, walked to the edge of the water and stared at his reflection. The last year had brought even more growth and he was almost as tall as Alex and Jack now. Still on the thin side, but even he could see the MacKinnon features were becoming more apparent. In a short time he would be broad shouldered and well over six feet. Smiling to himself, he recalled how he never thought he would be as big as his brothers. It looked like he had been wrong about that.

The ripples in the water caused his reflection to be distorted and he continued to stare, again pondering what he should do now.

Alex would know what to do. He always knows what to do. But he's not here. So what am I to do?

He watched in amazement as a flock of seagulls soared overhead, with one leading the pack. Within seconds they were gone from sight and Ian wondered at such grace and skill. It had seemed so effortless. In his own life, nothing seemed effortless. Well, except for the skills Wabi had taught him—namely, lighting a fire with a nod of his head and being able to travel through time weaving.

Maybe I should have stayed at home with Da and my family. But Da had thought this was the right thing for me, and even Alex was in agreement. But now, maybe I'll just go home. But I need to find Wabi. He'll have some ideas. Perhaps I should ..."

His thoughts were running around in circles and he was still no closer to knowing what to do. He sat down, as if standing was just too difficult. Even his body language revealed his feeling of defeat. Just then, a large wave rushed in farther than the others and had him scurrying to get up and away before he was wet on his seat.

Alright then. What would Alex do? Ye know what Alex would do. He'd tell ye to gather yer facts, plan yer strategy and then get off yer arse and move. Alright then, I will. So what do I know? Owl said Wabi's power is beginning to wane, he needs to go deep within, and that he's in a safe place. No, no, he said a resting place, a place of the ancients. That's what he said, a place of the ancients. Aye! Some of Mam's old books in our library talk about a place of the ancients. But where was that place?

He thought for a few moments, then was off running toward the stable, his prosthesis never slowing him down. Rummaging around in his saddlebag, he finally came upon what he was looking for, the old map of Scotland and the Isles Caitlin had given him. She knew he loved history and this map had been in some of her Grandmother's belongings. It just looked like something Ian would want to have, and she had no use for it.

Ian carefully unfurled the rolled map and lay it on a bale of hay. The map was made of vellum, the soft skin of a very young calf. Though it was stained in many areas, it had held up well. Its edges were fragile, however, and he hesitated to touch them. Caitlin had told him she thought it was a map of some of the islands where her early ancestors, the Picts and Vikings, had lived before they made their journey to North America.

Ian scoured the map inch by inch. There were notations on every spit of land. Most of them were in a language he didn't understand, but some were in Gaelic and he could read that. He recalled conversations with Mam, who knew Scottish history better than anyone. She'd talked about a tribe, people called the Druids, some kind of holy men. Mam had said they were often called the ancients. But where had they lived?

The map covered mainland Scotland and the northern isles, the Orkneys. Studiously combing the document from bottom to top, Ian noticed some of the islands to the north had small blue triangles drawn next to them. On closer inspection, he observed the triangles varied in size. Some were small, others a bit larger. He had no idea what these might indicate, but knew they could be important.

Some of the names on the map were ones he had heard before, such as Maeshowe, Skara Brae, the Stones of Stenness. But were these Druids, these ancients, the same ancients Owl had make reference to?

With no better place to start, he did what Alex would have done. He gathered his facts, planned his strategy, and now would take action. And the first part of his plan would have him time weaving, already his favorite way to travel.

13

Wabi reached the crest of the hill and pulled his cloak closer as a chilly wind blew in from the sea. If he listened carefully, he could hear distant chanting.

He leaned on his crooked staff and stopped for a moment, absorbing the sights, scents and sounds of his surroundings. The chanting came from the small order of Druids that made their home here, here being a small island on the edge of the Orkneys. Wabi had been here numerous times and no doubt would come again. This was his chosen place, the place where he would be allowed to "go within" and be free from all outside interferences. It was a place of reverence and peace.

Wabi's timing of his hibernation period was done with great deliberation. The Beltane fires marking the Summer Solstice would occur tomorrow.

The Summer Solstice, also known as Midsummer's Day, brings to an end the period of time where the hours of daylight are lengthening and the nights are growing shorter. It is a time of casting off the darkness and celebrating the light. This period is dedicated to the life-giving and regenerative powers of the solar orb, the sun. It's a time of renewal and rebirth and the Druids on the island would perform their own rituals during this time. There would be many festivals across the land and many fires would be lighted.

As he approached the great stone structure, the henge, he

knelt and recited his prayer. This was the beginning of the ritual he would perform in order to cleanse himself before entering his time of hibernation.

The grass mound on which he stood was actually a cairn built in early times. It hid a large chambered cavern with a complex of passages throughout, and had been built of carefully crafted slabs of sandstone. Many of the walls had been etched with drawings of cattle, sheep, and oaks, trees that are sacred to the Druids. In several of the passages there were bones from previous inhabitants, some human and some animal.

Wabi walked slowly, enjoying the immediate feeling of peace he felt upon entering the cairn. The tight passage led to a large council meeting room and he stopped at the doorway. As he did so, a multitude of young Druids knelt and bowed their heads. They did not know Master Wabi but had heard tales of him, and even these new initiates felt the power that emanated from him. Just his presence in the room had the air sizzling with palpable vibrations.

"Ah, Master Wabi. I felt you coming. We are ready for you," a voice called out. Those words came from Danaan, chieftain of this order of Druids and a longtime friend of Wabi. He understood Master Wabi was of an ilk even higher than the Druids, and rendered him his due respect. He had provided sanctuary for Wabi many eons ago and was humbled to do so again.

"Come. Your chamber has been prepared for you."

"If the Creator desires, may our paths cross again and perhaps I will be of assistance to you, my friend," Wabi replied as he bowed slightly to Danaan.

Danaan returned the bow and led the way through a zigzag path of even more chambers. He, too, lighted candles along the way with a nod of his head. Even Druids could perform a little magick, apparently. When they reached the appointed place, Wabi turned to Danaan.

"You may encounter a young man, a lad called Ian, if he is successful in discovering my whereabouts. He is my apprentice and I have tasked him with finding me. It's a good test of his skills and provides me time for renewal. Please allow him to observe your order and perhaps learn of your ways. He is quite gifted, and I believe him to be worthy of instruction."

"Yes, Master Wabi. We will care for him as well."

"Oh, Danaan? Be aware he may be a trifle, um, challenging. Highland blood flows in his veins. Need I say more?"

Danaan smiled. "We will come for you when the Beltane fires have died. May you rest in peace and be renewed from within." He turned and made his way back to the surface, leaving Wabi alone—as he desired.

14

When Hector arrived back at Cameron Castle it was very late and he was surprised to see a candle flickering in the window of the library.

Ethel must have forgotten to put it out.

The old cook, Ethel, ran the kitchen like a military leader might and he didn't think the place would keep going without her. But leaving a candle burning was a dangerous thing to do.

He unhooked Bess from the cart and put her in a stall. This had been a very long day for both of them, and the old nag immediately began to nibble on the hay Clint had placed in her trough. He was old, too, but taking care of the animals was a duty he never minded.

Entering through the kitchen, Hector stopped long enough to see what Ethel had in her pastry basket. An apple tart quickly found its way into his hands.

He also found a half-bottle of claret on the counter and took it and headed to the library. He'd extinguish the candle, have a quick glass of claret and take himself to his rooms, which were located on the first floor. The women and children all lived upstairs.

The candle gave off a soft, warm glow and he entered the library quietly, ready to let this day end. He stopped abruptly when he realized he was not alone.

"Oh," Reggie sighed. "You're back. Thank heavens. I was

worried the British soldiers may have found you and I'd never see you again." She sat rigidly in the chair, relief evident on her face.

Hector took her hands and pulled her up, bringing her closer to him. "Reggie, what are ye doing still up, lass? It's late. Ye need yer rest."

"I couldn't sleep not knowing if you were safe. Now that you are, I'll go back to my bed."

"Since yer already up, sit with me a few minutes and I'll tell ye about my visit. It was a bit more exciting than I had expected it to be."

Hector explained the saga of Aileen and the orphans, and Reggie beamed when Hector told her the outcome of the story.

"Oh, Hector. Can you believe it? She never even mentioned any children when I talked with her."

"Maybe it was just too painful. I believe it was the two glasses of wine that allowed her to tell me her story."

Then, leaving out a few details, such as Alex and Jack being captured, he began to explain to Reggie that he needed to be away again for a few days. He knew she'd just worry if he told her his true plans.

"Da asked me to go to Edinburgh and check on some legal issues with Murdock, our solicitor. Da's managed to acquire quite a bit of property in the last few years, and he wants to make sure the British government can't get their hands on it. I told him I'd see to it."

"I see. Dorothea and I will manage for a short while, but only a short while. Then you get yourself back here, with me, where you belong."

She stood and started to walk away. Hector pulled her back and lifted her, holding her close.

"Oh, I'll be back. Ye can count on that, lass." He left her with a kiss to seal this bargain.

The next morning found him well underway to Edinburgh. Cameron Castle had several horses that could have kept up the pace he was calling for. He couldn't get to Edinburgh fast enough.

He knew Alex and Jack would be planning to escape from wherever they'd been taken, but another hand might be a good thing.

15

Camille and Andrew's cottage was now home to Aileen and her three bairns. She could hardly believe she had found them again and she still pinched herself every day to make sure she wasn't dreaming.

Dugald and Bridgette talked so much Aileen could hardly follow their conversations. Charlie still hadn't made any attempts at talking, but he was beginning to come out of his shell. Caitlin and Millie had been amazed when they saw how easily Aileen communicated with him. Somehow she had developed a kind of sign language and they both understood it. All in all, the small family in Uncle Andrew's cottage couldn't be any happier.

But life in the lodge couldn't be any more desperate. The only folk living in the lodge now were Caitlin, Millie, Robbie and Da, and the two small bairns. And the scene in the lodge this evening was anything but quiet, as one might have expected.

Caitlin walked quickly from one end of the room to the other, her long skirts swishing with her jerky movements.

"I know you don't like the idea, but I'm going, so don't try to stop me!"

Caitlin's temper was quickly getting out of control, and right now she couldn't care less about keeping it in bounds.

Millie towered over Caitlin when she stood, and she, too, had a way of expressing her feelings that sometimes almost made her forget she had been a "lady" in her early life. She looked down at

Caitlin with her hands on her hips, throwing her long dark hair back over her shoulder.

"You can't just leave and go to Edinburgh. It's too dangerous, Caitlin. Da would be very upset and so will I!"

"I've tried to call Uncle Wabi. He's not hearing me for some reason. For all we know, Alex and Jack may already have been shipped off to the islands. I must try to find them. I have no choice!"

"Neither Alex nor Jack would agree to this plan. And what about Flinn? Have you forgotten about her? She still needs someone to nurse her."

"I haven't worked out all the details just yet. I was hoping you might help me with that problem. You're very good with details, and if you will try to help me instead of getting in my way things will go better." Tears were threatening to spill over any moment.

Caitlin was a full head shorter than Millie. But there she stood, arms akimbo, looking up at her friend trying to get a handle on her anger. Her aqua eyes flashed as she looked about the room, as if searching for something or someone that might help her with the situation.

For a second, Millie worried about Caitlin getting so excited. She had witnessed her power before and knew it to be lethal. Finally, Millie sighed then walked over and put her arms around the small woman's shoulders.

"You've brought the bairns through an ordeal, and Da, too. And I'm as worried as you are. It just seems terribly dangerous for a woman to take off by herself looking for two captured Highlanders.

But alright, let's figure this out, then. If you're determined to go to Edinburgh, then get yourself ready. The coach goes every Friday, so you could get one tomorrow morning. I'll find a wet nurse in the village somewhere and Flinn won't starve. I'll make sure of that. But Caitlin, this is such a dangerous thing to do. Jack and Alex will tie us to a tree and flog us for sure!"

She laughed and the two women held each other for a long moment, each feeling the tension within the other.

"No, I won't take the coach. I'll ride Soldier and be there much faster that way. Now, wait here a moment. I've got another idea that may have some merit."

Running up the stairs all the way to the attic, she knocked on Robbie's door. It opened and Robbie stood there with a question on his face.

"Caitlin? What is it? Is it Grandda?"

"No, just me. I need your help again."

"What? Someone else has the fever?"

"Nae. I'm going to Edinburgh and I need you to go with me. You lived in that city and I bet you know every twist and turn in it. I'm going to search for Alex and Jack. If they get sent to the islands we'll never see them again, and I can't let that happen."

Robbie had never known a woman with this much determination. He'd seen his Mother stand her ground with a few disorderly men in a pub once, but Caitlin had a will of iron. He'd witnessed it while she worked with the bairns and Da and Andrew.

"I, uh, of course. And you're right. I do know Edinburgh. I know shopkeepers, librarians, blacksmiths, book publishers, some doctors, and even some British soldiers. Yes, I know a lot of people."

"That's good. We may need to call on them for help."

"But, Caitlin ... most of them are British. Still, they might help me if I ask. I've known them all my life. They were Mother's friends."

"Then get yourself ready. We leave early tomorrow."

"Right. I came here by coach and I memorized the coach schedule, just in case I wanted to go back home. It leaves for Edinburgh every Friday morning."

"We're going by horseback. That's a lot faster and I'm good at following a map and using a compass. Uncle Wabi taught me those skills many years ago."

"But, I can't ride. Not really. I was on a horse once, but I fell off and broke my collarbone. That's my riding experience."

"Don't worry. Trust me, by the time we get to Edinburgh you'll be as good a rider as Ian. And, Robbie? Da isn't to know about this. He's over the fever, but he's too old and too weak to go with us."

"He'll be mad as a hornet, Caitlin. You know that don't you?"

"He'll just have to get over it. Alex and Jack are in trouble and you and I are the only ones who may be able to help them. We leave at first light. I'll meet you in the stable."

~ ~ ~

After Caitlin's visit, Robbie sat on his bed for a few moments, then went to his desk and opened his journal. From a small pocket in the back of the book he pulled out a letter his mother had given him before she passed away. He'd not read it yet, and even now didn't really want to. But perhaps the time had come to find out what was so important to her she felt a need to put it in writing.

As he carefully opened the envelope, Fiona's unmistakable scent rushed to meet him, causing him to inhale deeply, as if in doing so he could bring her closer. Lilacs. Always lilacs.

Her handwriting was ever so perfect. Robbie would know it anywhere. It was like her—perfectly styled and artistic in nature. Everything about her had been like that. She would never leave the house without being perfectly turned out. Every hair would be in place, her frocks would have been ironed by Mattie, and her gloves and bonnets would match her clothing. Yes, she might have been a bit too meticulous about most everything, but Robbie had always known she loved him. In fact, he was the most important person in her life and he never doubted that.

As he unfolded the letter, the lilac scent again flooded his nostrils, and for a brief moment his heart felt like it would burst. She'd wanted him to find his father, she had told him that. He smiled now when he recalled her instructions to "be sure to wear a tam when you travel to the Highlands."

But this very minute he would have given anything to have her put her arms around him as she had when he was small and had a problem. Finally, he began to read her letter. He wasn't sure when the tears began to fall, but once they started they continued even after he finished and tucked her letter back in his journal. It would stay there always.

He blew his candle out and looked out over the moor for a while hoping to get a glimpse of the stag, but the old one didn't appear this evening. Robbie was alone and more afraid than he could ever remember being. His mother was dead and his da may be also. He and a headstrong young woman were the only ones to try and free him from a prison in Edinburgh. Surely this must be a nightmare.

~ ~ ~

Next morning Robbie was at the stable before Caitlin. He hoped he wouldn't embarrass himself by falling off his horse before they even left the lodge. This escapade, tearing off with Caitlin to save Alex and Jack, had to be the most daring thing he had ever done. He still thought of himself as a shy, quiet, studious British young man who lived with his mother in Edinburgh, but apparently that wasn't true anymore. Today he was most definitely behaving like a fearsome Highland Scot who loved nothing better than an adventure such as this.

A Scot? Have I become one after all? No, because if I were I wouldn't feel so scared. Alex and Jack never seem afraid of anything.

Inside the lodge, Caitlin and Millie said their farewells.

"Hamish and Kenny will stay close should you need anything. Aileen will help you with Flinn, and Da may be weak, but he's pretty self-sufficient." Caitlin continued her instructions as if she were perfectly sure that everything she was planning would succeed.

She held Flinn close for one last moment, inhaling the warm, unique scent that only an infant has. Then, without another word, she handed her to Millie then bent down and took Willie by the jowls, looking deep into his eyes.

"Willie, stay here with Millie. Look out for everyone. I'll see you soon." Then she hugged him fiercely and flew out the kitchen door. When she arrived at the stable she watched in amusement as Robbie stared at her, looking from her head to her toes. He was dumbfounded.

She had dug through her trunk and found Ian's outfit that she wore when she was running from Commander Campbell and Lord Warwick—dark brown knickers, long brown tunic and dark stockings, and her own leather boots. She had braided her long hair and donned Ian's dark brown tam just as before, and had put a plaid in her saddlebag for warmth, just in case.

"Caitlin? You look like a boy! Are you going to wear that? Women in Edinburgh don't dress like that."

"Don't worry so, Robbie. I rather doubt anyone is going to invite us for tea. I've learned this outfit works a lot better for riding than my long skirts and petticoats."

"Oh, I see. Right." He stared another moment, then asked a question. "How do I know which horse to ride? And I'm not sure I can saddle one anyway."

"Hamish saddled the horses earlier this morning. He put a new shoe on Goliath, so you'll ride him. I'll ride my horse, Soldier. Now stop worrying. These horses know this country better than either of us. Come on over here and talk to Goliath a moment. Let him get your scent and your voice. He's experienced enough for both of you."

Robbie walked to the next stall where Caitlin indicated he would find his mount.

"Goodness—he's huge!"

"Aye, he is. He's Jack's horse. He needed a horse that could carry his weight and Goliath has no problem with that."

"I don't know ..."

"Actually, Robbie, he's a lot like Jack—big and imposing, but all heart. No need to be afraid of him."

Robbie eventually worked up the courage to mount Goliath. The horse snorted and shook his head back and forth, but stood very still for the lad to climb on. Caitlin put a few more items in their saddlebags, mounted Soldier, and they were off.

16

Stopping only long enough for everyone to get off their horses for brief periods, the soldiers had kept moving and consequently they and their captives were exhausted. Bringing in two Jacobite supporters would ensure they got a couple of days rest before they were out again in search of others.

When they arrived at the corral behind the west wing of the prison, they dismounted and roughly pulled Alex and Jack from their mounts. Jack landed rather harshly on his backside and, of course, responded in his usual way. Standing up quickly, he roared at the soldier who had dragged him from his mount.

"Ye British scum! If my hands weren't tied I'd break yer scrawny Redcoat neck!"

"I'll just bet you would, big man."

The soldier slammed the butt of his rifle against Jack's cheek causing him to stagger, then black out for a moment before falling to the ground.

Alex saw red, but knew more angry words would only escalate the situation. But this was about all he could handle.

"Were those yer orders? To batter and torture yer captives? Any decent soldier would understand that all soldiers, regardless of which side yer on, can respect another one. Brit or Scot, makes no difference. We're all men fighting for our country and way of life. So ye've captured us now; ye don't need to add insult to injury."

"Shut your mouth, heathen," the soldier stuck his bayonet in

Alex's back just deep enough to cause a trickle of blood to run down.

Once they turned the horses loose in the corral, the soldiers and their captives entered the building by a side door. The taller soldier grabbed a lighted torch from its bracket on the wall and pushed the two captives along.

After descending several flights of narrow steps they entered a long, dark corridor. The stench alone told the brothers they had arrived at their destination—a prison in Edinburgh. Even in the Highlands they had heard of the Old Tolbooth. Its reputation for being the most vile place to be incarcerated was apropos; it was indeed unbelievably horrid.

The British had commandeered the Old Tolbooth in Edinburgh as a place to house their prisoners before they took them on to Tilbury Fort in London. Once in London, the men would either be sent to the islands to be sold as slaves, or they would be killed outright. Alex and Jack were under no illusions their fate would be anything different. If they were to survive, they had to escape from the prison in Edinburgh before they were sent to London.

"Move your clumsy feet, you big oaf. You too. Don't make me have to drag you to your new home. You might find this place just a bit different from that great lodge I've heard you have in the Highlands, though. The major says it'll make a great place for our regiment as we round up the rest of your kind. Ha!"

Alex and Jack looked at each other, both struggling to hold their tongues, and Alex knew that was a real chore for Jack. Both he and Jack towered over these two young British soldiers and that seemed to irritate the young men. Just now, however, Jack understood the unspoken message Alex was sending him.

Just keep quiet, brother. We're not done in just yet.

But just when Alex thought his brother was listening, Jack stopped, swung around and used his forehead as a hammer, striking the soldier in the mouth. Teeth went flying and blood spurted everywhere.

"You'll pay for that Highlander," the young soldier screamed as he raised his rifle and struck Jack in the same place as before, against the side of his face. That move flayed Jack's cheek open and sent him reeling backward.

Alex winched as he watched. He had no plan, but one thought gave him hope. During the first moments when the young soldiers had captured the brothers there was a lot of commotion, and after having slashed Alex's hand and having jabbed Jack in the ribs with the bayonet, the captors had taken their pistols, but had failed to check for other weapons.

Alex felt sure that just as he, Jack was carrying a dirk under his shirt, and probably one in his boot as well. This was just habit with them, one Da had instilled early on.

Presently, Jack's head hurt like the very devil and he felt blood running down the side of his face. His right eye began to swell and he knew it would be totally closed shortly. It took a lot to bring him down, but that second strike had been quite a hard lick with the butt of the gun.

The farther they went into the bowels of the prison, the more intolerable the stench became. The dimly lit, dank corridor had small cells along each side. Each cell had one or more prisoners, and none of them made a sound as the two new ones marched by. Water dripped from the ceiling along the way, making the floor very slippery. Several rats scurried across the path in front of them, causing the soldiers to curse and kick out at them.

"Damn disease-carrying vermin! I hate coming down here. No telling what we might pick up just delivering you two traitors. Move on now. I want to get out of this rotten pit."

The next scene, however, had Alex stopping in his tracks. In the small cell on his left were two young lads, not even in their teens yet. The two were clad in ragged, filthy tunics and their feet were bare. The young lads were so thin their rags would hardly stay on their shoulders as they stood watching, their hollow eyes riveted on the newcomers.

"Two little thieves, these young ones. Putting them in here for a spell might just cure that problem."

But they were yet to view an even more disturbing sight. When they heard quiet sobs coming from the other end of the corridor, Jack and Alex slowed their pace. They didn't want to witness what they knew their eyes would reveal. In the far corner of her cell a young woman sat huddled on a mucky bed of straw. Her fine clothing spoke of someone with means, and the fact they weren't rags yet told them she hadn't been here very long.

"And that's what happens to women who won't do as the major wishes. She's a real looker, but has a streak of independence in her. The major put her in here to teach her a lesson. My bet is it won't take her long to adapt her ways to his demands. Stupid woman."

They walked on, and when they reached the last cell at the very end of the corridor the soldiers shoved Alex and Jack through the doorway. Just as they stumbled through, a long, dark snake slithered beneath the bars and headed down the hallway. Jack jumped two feet backward.

"Jesus! Did ye see that? That was a snake I tell ye!" Jack wasn't nearly as concerned about the gun at his back as he was about a snake in his cell. He had an illogical fear of them and that was just a fact.

"He's gone now, brother. Don't worry about the snake."

The soldiers snickered. "Get yourselves in there, you two. You'll get gruel and water twice a day if you keep quiet and don't make work for the guards. It won't do you any good to holler and yell anyway, no one can hear you."

Alex and Jack looked around their cell. Their bed of straw stank of urine and had been used so long it was crushed into bits about two inches long. As they moved farther into their cell, near the back wall, their nostrils were assaulted by the putrid odor emanating from the refuse of previous captives. Yes, the Old Tolbooth deserved its reputation.

17

Ian wrapped his plaid about himself, grabbed Henson and sat down, legs crossed, arms snug against his sides. "Henson, we're going to move quickly now. Ye'll get used to this way of traveling, and ye'll like it—eventually."

Bowing briefly, as Wabi had taught him, he closed his eyes, lifted his face to the sky and began a faint chant, one that would only be heard by others of his ilk. His concentration wandered momentarily and he thought about his plan. He was using Caitlin's map as his reference point, but it was so very old. Would the markings still be the same today? Would they lead him to Master Wabi? Would he be able to sense Wabi's presence as usual? And if not, then what?

Knowing to entertain these thoughts would prevent him from traveling, he became centered and once again began his chant, and the earth began a rhythmic throbbing Ian could feel in his soul. A blinding light flashed and lit the sky all around as a whirlwind encircled the young wizard and lifted him from the ground. It slowly began its frenzied, spinning, tornadic pace—he was on his way.

The few moments of unease and vertigo that always accompanied time weaving were worth the experiences that came next. The singing always came first, soft voices that blended so perfectly you never knew when one stopped and another began. A magnificent kaleidoscope of colors followed with an array of hues the human eye could never discern. Each time Ian traveled in this manner, he experienced a brief interval when he wished to stay in this place, this paradise of sounds, colors, and feelings. But the whirlwind had other ideas, and with a final unexpected thrust, he was deposited at the top of a lush green meadow with sheep grazing in the distance. To say it was a rather unceremonious landing would be exactly right.

He rubbed his backside and at first wondered if he had landed on his moor in the Highlands. For a second he thought he spied someone in the distance, but then they disappeared as if into thin air. Perhaps he hadn't seen anyone. The aftermath of time weaving often left one a bit disoriented for a few moments.

Henson had apparently survived the trip, but his fur stood on end in every direction. Ian laughed, then placed his feline friend down on the grass.

Taking his map out once again, he began to look closely at the various markings. According to the map, there should be several stone structures, apparently erected by peoples of ancient times, near where he had landed. To the east he saw a stand of oak trees, and to the west he could see the roiling sea, its whitecaps splashing upwards reaching for the seabirds as they dove and circled above.

"Henson, there's a cairn somewhere nearby. We need to find it. Beneath it is a series of deep caverns within the earth. It would be a perfect place for Druids to practice their rituals. Mam always said they were to be revered and certainly ye shouldn't offend them. Even Julius Caesar believed them to have great power and respected them. Wish I'd read more about them, now."

It was only moments later that his ears detected a musical sound coming from an area just in front of him. Walking to the top of the moor, he discovered he was actually standing atop a cairn, but it had been overgrown by grass over the years.

"Then the map is right. This is the Druids' cairn, right here under my feet."

Henson ran off, as usual, but Ian wasn't concerned.

A cairn would have marked the site of burial for one or more persons. That being the case, Ian was careful to keep an attitude of reverence as Mam and Wabi had indicated. The climb down the side of the cairn was quite steep and Ian lost his footing more than once in his descent.

"Dang it. A bloody knee and scraped elbows, just what I need." He finally got to the base of the cairn and looked about. If there were caverns here he saw no entrance, but did see a small stream that ran along the cairn, so he stopped to drink.

He may not have seen anything, but suddenly he certainly felt something—a vibration was pulling him, beckoning to him, filling the air around him. Was it Master Wabi? No. Master Wabi's call was unique and Ian knew it from all others. Someone was calling, but who? There was no decision to make about whether to answer the vibrating call—he could not resist it.

He came closer to the exterior wall of the cairn, but still saw no entry. Eventually, making his way along the wall, he came to a tall stand of grass and thought to sit there for a moment, perhaps long enough to discover the nature of the vibration. As he sat down, he almost fell backward. Just behind the tall grass there was a steep flight of grass-covered steps that seemed to go downward forever.

As Ian stood and began to make his way downward, Henson returned and went bounding along in front of him.

"Wait, Henson. We don't know where these steps may lead." But Henson turned a deaf ear to Ian's warning. The farther down Ian went, the stronger the vibration became, and at the bottom of the steps he came upon an arched doorway with a thick wooden door. When he raised his hand to knock, the doorway opened slightly. Before him stood a young man, perhaps only a few years older than himself. He was dressed in a long, sand-colored tunic and his hair was just a fringe around his skull. Ian stared at the young man. Never had he seen anyone like this.

"Welcome, Master Ian. Please follow me."

"What? I'm no master, sir. And who are you? Why should I follow you?" Master Wabi had taught Ian to always know where you are going and never to follow blindly.

"I am called Jobaer. Come, young master. Our leader will explain all you need to understand. Come now. Follow me. All will be well."

Ian slowly followed, taking in his surroundings as he did so. There were several tunnels leading off the main one, and hundreds of candles lighted the way. Occasionally he felt a draft of wind as they passed an adjoining tunnel. The music he had heard earlier was here as well. Perhaps it was a flute, certainly a woodwind instrument of some kind, and the sound was enticing.

Finally the young man stopped and pulled back a colorful,

finely woven curtain hanging at an entrance to one of the tunnels. Jobaer then bowed and quietly walked away. From within, a voice called to Ian.

"Come. Come now."

Ian hesitated, then followed Henson, who darted through immediately.

The words were spoken by a tall, thin man whose very presence filled the room. Ian felt the vibrations coming from this one, much like what he felt in Master Wabi's presence.

"I am called Danaan. Join me. Master Wabi indicated we may have a visit from you, Master Ian. He will be most pleased you have completed your assigned task."

"I am no master, sir. I am only an apprentice of Master Wabi."

"Yes, of course. But if Master Wabi has chosen you to follow in his path, then the title of master will most certainly be yours soon."

"Where is he, Master Wabi?"

"He has come to us as he has come before, and we are humbled to assist him in his time of need. A great one such as Master Wabi has need to hibernate at various intervals in his lives. We are simply his friends, his brethren of a similar ilk, and it is our pleasure to offer our assistance to him."

"I must see him. It's important, ye ken? My family's in trouble and Wabi can help them if only I can find him."

"No, young master. He cannot help you at this time. His power must be regenerated and he must go deep within himself and begin to renew his energies. Have no fear young Ian, the Creator will be with his chosen one."

"But there's no time. I must—"

"If you wish, you may abide with our order while your master is here. We spend much time studying nature, the ancient ones, their beliefs, and their rituals. Master Wabi suggested you might gain knowledge and experience through time spent with us. It is, of course, your decision."

"I should stay here? Master Wabi says so?"

"Yes. He has begun his hibernation already and will return if and when the Creator so desires. Until such time, we would be honored with your presence." He leaned down and scooped Henson up, cradling him gently in his arms.

"I see you've brought a companion with you."

The large cat purred and Danaan smiled and scratched him behind his dark ears.

"Ah, so. Of course. A special one as well."

He placed the cat on the floor, bowed to Ian and called for Jobaer, who was there instantly.

Jobaer smiled. "Come, young wizard. I'll take you to your quarters and clean your wounded knees."

Before he departed, Danaan turned his attention to Ian once again. "You should join us for our evening meal and meditation time. I think you'll find the food delicious and the prayers comforting."

Ian had no other plan. He had thought to convince Wabi to come help him, but this was not to be. Reluctantly, he accompanied Jobaer to a small chamber that had been carved into the walls of the cavern. It was complete with a small cot, several candles, and to Ian's delight, a stack of books stood in the corner.

"You have books? Most folk don't have any, much less as many as I have seen since coming into this cavern."

"Yes. Danaan reads to us each day, and we are all able to read ourselves. But when he reads from the ancient scrolls, the message comes with a greater emotional understanding than we are able to muster as yet. He is a great leader and you should listen when he speaks. He is not of the same ilk as Master Wabi, but he has great knowledge and understands more than we novices."

That evening, the food was just as Danaan had said it would be—delicious. Ian hadn't eaten very well since leaving the lodge in the Highlands, and he ate his fill, pinching off tidbits and hand-feeding them to Henson.

The evening prayer service was also most interesting. Ian knew there were cultures that had unusual rituals and had read about many of them. But to actually see a ritual being performed firsthand was an exciting adventure for him.

Danaan had taken his place on a small raised dais made of wood that was covered with a fabric similar to the curtain in the cave, with numerous animals created from colorful threads. Certainly this exquisite stitchery was the work of a woman, but Ian had seen only men so far. Danaan had changed from his beige tunic into a long, white one that dragged the ground as he walked along, and two young novices walked quietly in his wake.

In preparation for the lighting of the Beltane fires, the ritual this evening was dedicated to cleansing oneself and purifying the body to be more acceptable to the various gods. This preparation was done in order to transcend earthly things for the life of the spirit.

As always, the Druids practiced their worship in the open air. In this instance, they gathered under the grove of oak trees near the mound.

When the ceremony ended, Danaan and the two young novices began their walk along the path among the others. When Ian looked up from his own prayers, his head jerked up even higher. He found himself staring. He had never seen anyone as breathtakingly beautiful as the young woman who walked at the end of the procession. She too wore a long, white tunic very similar to the one like Danaan wore. Flower petals clung to her long, white-blond hair that flowed down her back as she moved gracefully down the path. He reached out as if to touch her as she passed by.

Jobaer quickly grabbed his arm and pulled it back. "No, Master Ian. She is not for you."

"But who is she? I must meet her. She's beautiful."

"Her name is Arduinna. She is a young priestess of our order. She is pledged to celibacy and has dedicated herself to being one with nature and not with any man. She is not for you."

Ian was speechless and stared at Arduinna until she disappeared in the distance.

The next day, when the great fires were lighted across the land, prayers were offered for all peoples, the animals and all beings found in nature. Each village had its own specific rituals, but all were centered around a spirit of renewal and rebirth, well-being throughout.

There was much celebration, dancing, and sharing of foods. As the sun began to slide down the sky and daylight faded into night, the villagers were exhausted from their activities and the day came to its end and the rituals ceased.

As was common at the end of the celebration, the villagers rushed their cattle over the dying flames of the sacred fires. As the last cow rushed through the smoky haze, suddenly a roar came from the crowd. The final flame jumper was not a cow, but rather a huge mountain lion with dark ears and a long dark tail.

"Oh! Where did he come from? I've not seen a mountain lion

for many years. They roamed our caves here for eons, but none have been seen for ages. Danaan, is this a spiritual omen of some kind? Should we be afraid?"

"No. There is nothing here to be afraid of. It is simply one of our fellow creatures making his own celebration of the Beltane. He is not to be feared. He is chosen."

Ian knew the moment Master Wabi returned to them. His very soul felt a stirring and relief flooded through him. A sharp tingling down his spine had him up and running across the mound toward his friend and master. The old one took long strides and met him quickly.

"Wabi! Are ye all right then? Do ye still have ye powers? Are ye hurt?"

Wabi smiled and embraced his young apprentice. "I am well, Ian. The Creator has been generous with his gifts and I am myself once again. Now, young one, it appears you met my challenge and found me. That was quite a feat, and now it's time we moved on. You have much more knowledge to be gained. Come. Let's be off now."

"But Wabi, ye've got to help me. The Brits are scouring the country looking for Jacobite supporters. How do I know they aren't looking for my brothers, and me too? There's a lot of confusion everywhere I go."

"Ian, hear me now. Your brothers are very capable men. They would prefer you be with me. There is nothing you can do to help them at this moment. We'll return to Skye and try to get information about the situation with the British. Come. Gather Henson. Time's wasting."

The dervishing whirlwind that dipped from the sky sent leaves scattering and caused branches to fly about. With a nod of Wabi's head, smoke from the dying fire encircled the two and they disappeared in a fiery trail of red flames licking about them as they departed.

18

Caitlin looked to Robbie. "We'll stick to the forest as much as possible. This map shows a clear path and my compass will keep us on target."

Robbie nodded. "I may not be such a good rider, but I can read a map and know how to use a compass. The library in Edinburgh has a room that's filled with nothing but old maps. I've spent more time than you would believe in that room. If I can manage to stay on this horse, we'll get there alright."

"Of course we'll get there. We have no choice. Alex and Jack have certainly been taken or they would have returned by now. You and I will have to figure out a way to find them and bring them back with us."

"We can go to my home there, I suppose. Mattie, our housekeeper, will still be there. She's been with us as long as I can remember. She'll help us. She's quiet as a mouse but knows everything that's going on in Edinburgh. She'll know the latest on the talk about town."

"But, Robbie. We've got to find out where they are. Is there more than one prison in Edinburgh? Or did they send them off already?" She shook her head in exasperation.

"First of all we must get there, then we'll tackle those problems. Let's be off now." She slapped Soldier on the rump and prayed Robbie would keep up with her

~ ~ ~

It only took a couple of hours of riding for Robbie to realize that if he relaxed his legs his backside didn't bounce around so much, and the fact he had very long legs seemed to be to his advantage. Plus, Caitlin was right. Goliath was surefooted and seemed to know exactly where they were headed.

He wasn't certain how long it would take them, and neither was Caitlin. If they'd been able to talk to Da he'd have given them some details that could have been helpful. But Caitlin knew Da would have tried to stop her, and she was determined to do this.

"Let's walk the horses for a little. My rear end is tired and I'm sure yours must be too. We'll stop at nightfall and rest a bit longer."

"I don't think we should stop, I think we should keep moving."

"Well, I think we should just walk on for a little now. We're being followed."

"What? Followed? How can you tell? I don't hear anything."

"I don't actually hear anything, but I sense something or someone. I'm sure we've been followed for some time now. As soon as it's dark, we'll find a place to get off and see who's trailing us."

Robbie didn't like the sound of that, but had no better idea himself. "What do we do if it is someone?"

"I have a pistol. Alex always insists I take one anytime I go by horseback." She spoke with authority, which was her way of trying to sound sure of herself in order to convince Robbie she could carry out this impossible plan. "And I can tell you, he's gruff with me if I don't do what he asks."

At this moment she would give anything to have him putting her in her place for not following his rules about traveling. Even better than that would be his strong arms holding her close and telling her all would be alright and to "trust me, *mo chridhe."*

Night was beginning to close in on them and Caitlin decided now was the time to find out who was close on their heels.

"Let's stop here. There's a stream where the horses can drink and we can stretch our legs. We'll have a quick bite to eat and then move on."

Robbie dismounted and led Goliath over to the stream. The animal was truly a man's horse, being at least eighteen hands high. Only someone with legs as long as Jack's or Robbie's could straddle his great girth, and Robbie was learning that riding was not quite as difficult as he had thought it might be. But it did feel good to be on his own two feet for a while.

Caitlin walked behind him and led Soldier to the water also. She got to her knees and Robbie came over to kneel next to her. She put a hand on his arm, indicating he should be still and quiet.

"What? Do you hear someone?" he whispered.

"No. But there's someone close, very close. I feel them."

Then, before either of them could see it coming, a large dark shadow reared its frightening head out of the darkness and flew through the air toward them.

WHUMP!

Caitlin was flat on her back, struggling to get her breath. It happened so quickly that Robbie fell over trying to get to her.

"Caitlin! Caitlin!"

The healer sighed and finally was able to speak, her nerves on fire.

"Willie? What are you doing out here? I told you to stay with Millie!"

But Willie had other ideas apparently. Presently, he licked his master's face as he stood over her with his fur standing on end and his tail wagging vigorously. Caitlin hugged him and held him close a moment.

"Alright then. Looks like we're stuck with you. No doubt you may be helpful to us. Should have known you wouldn't want me to go without you."

Robbie was almost relieved the wolf had come. He'd watched him follow the bairns at the lodge. The large beast was ever mindful of where everyone was and often knew when things were happening before all others. Yes, Robbie was very glad Caitlin's protector was here.

After a brief rest they were back in the saddle and on the path to Edinburgh, but they still had no real plan of action for what to do when they arrived.

Caitlin had never asked Robbie anything about his mother. She felt he would bring her up if and when he wanted to discuss her. That he did so now was a bit of a surprise to her. They continued to move along, and Robbie began to speak with more ease than usual.

"My mother left a letter for me before she passed away. I brought it with me when I came to the lodge, but I had not read it until last evening.

Mother's father is Lord Robert Wellington, a British citizen of course. He lives in London, but has properties in Scotland as well. In fact, according to her letter the house I have always lived in belonged to him, but he deeded it to her when she insisted on leaving London and moving to Edinburgh. She says she had her solicitor deed the house over to me, so I guess it belongs to me now.

One other fact I should probably tell you is that Lord Wellington is not particularly fond of me. Even as a small child I could feel his anger when I would come into the room. I wasn't old enough to understand, but I was aware of his dislike for me.

Apparently he knew who my father was, and that caused a great rift in his relationship with Mother. I don't think he knew the name, but he knew she was keeping company with a Scot, which in his mind was beneath her. But in her letter she says if I am ever in true need, I should go to him. Even though he despised she had a child by a Scot, he made sure she never wanted for anything and visited, even if infrequently. But he always frightened me, so I doubt I'll ever make contact with him."

"Families can cause great pain, but then also bring the greatest joys. I never had anyone but Uncle Wabi, but he was enough. Now, being part of this MacKinnon clan, I see what I have missed by not having sisters or brothers. I know you must understand that, even if only a little bit, since you were an only child yourself."

"When I first arrived at the lodge I was so scared. I didn't know what to do or say. Still don't sometimes. There are so many people at the lodge, or were. At my home it was usually very quiet and I kept to myself, either in my room or at the library. But I'm getting use to lots of folk and I can see that Alex's, er, Da's family is most important to him. But I'm not sure I'll ever fit his idea of what he wanted in a son."

"Alex is a very complicated man. But you'll find he is fair at all times and will never turn his back on anyone he cares for. He is truly the finest man I have ever met. I knew from the first that I wanted to be with him. Now, he is my life and I don't plan to let the Brits take him away from me."

With that statement she kicked Soldier's side and hurried on down the trail, with Robbie keeping pace every step of the way.

19

Making his way to Edinburgh in the dark of night was not such a chore for Hector. He'd always done Da's legal negotiating with their solicitor and was very familiar with Edinburgh. Of course, since the Battle of Culloden no one had ventured in that direction. Even now he would rather have stayed at Cameron Castle with Reggie. His mind kept returning to the embrace they had shared when he had left.

"You must hurry back. I want you by my side, Hector MacKinnon."

She smiled up at him and he felt her warm body next to his.

"That's exactly where I want to be, Miss Reggie Carmichael. So ye can count of me returning shortly."

But, of course, he wasn't sure what he would find in Edinburgh. It wasn't like he could just walk up to a stranger and ask where the Jacobite supporters were being kept. That being the case, he decided to remove his kilt and dress like a highwayman, a vagabond of sorts, and visit a couple of pubs and see if he could learn anything. News travels fast in the dark corners of pubs, and a few coins dropped in the right place always helped too.

Tying his horse at the back of the pub, he walked around front and took time to carefully see where the doors opened out to, what the surroundings were, and what was the best route to make a quick getaway should he need to do so. He enjoyed his role at the Sanctuary keeping track of the financial details, but he hadn't forgotten Da's lessons of survival. He could take care of himself. But would he be captured as well?

Hector hoped his highwayman persona would keep him disguised somewhat and he'd move on as soon as he knew anything that would help locate Alex and Jack. He remembered those two extricating him from an uncomfortable predicament once when an Englishman, whose wife made advances toward Hector, had come after him with murderous intent. A long time back now, but he recalled being greatly relieved when his brothers came to his rescue. That was a tight spot, certainly, but it couldn't hold a candle to this situation.

He kept his weathered hat pulled down around his ears and made his way to the farthest corner in the pub. There were a dozen or so men huddled together around the end of the bar, all talking at the same time, throwing dice, and laughing at something one had said.

"Yep. They bringing 'em in every day now, ye ken? Just yesterday I watched as they paraded a couple of Highlanders by on horses. Said they was taking 'em to the Old Tolbooth. The Brits seemed to enjoy marching 'em past us, as if that's a spectacle we would enjoy. Damn scoundrels. Why can't they just go back to they own country and leave ours to us?"

Downing another pint of ale, they were all back to their game of dice and Hector walked out the back door and was on his way once again. Two Highlanders could mean anyone, not necessarily Alex and Jack. But even so, the fact the captured men were seen means the Brits were becoming more successful in their task. He had to get to Edinburgh quickly, and the Old Tollbooth was at least a place to start his search.

As he passed through the villages, he saw numerous fires along the way. He had forgotten it was time for the great Beltane fire rituals. He stopped at one small village with the intention of finding an inn where he could get a decent meal, and again listen to the local talk.

A huge fire had been built in the village square and Hector heard music, loud talking, laughing, and women snickering in the background. He slowly made his way to the square, and as he ambled along a young woman grabbed him by the arm as he passed by. She was quite attractive. Her long, dark curls hanging down her back and her frock of dark green sprigged with lace at the neck and wrists made for a most pleasing appearance. Yes, she was dressed in her finest for the occasion.

"Come! Come dance with me, handsome fellow. Here, drink my ale and dance around the great fire with me. This night can be one you remember."

Pretending to enjoy her overtures, Hector grabbed her hand and began to swing her around in a slow dance. She stopped and insisted he take a swig of her ale before they continued. Hector drank deeply and laughed as she pulled his face down to hers and planted a very wet kiss on him.

"Beltane is for lovers, don't you know?" She kissed him thoroughly once again then lifted the mug to his lips.

"Here, one more taste for you then we'll find a quiet place in the forest where nature will give her blessings to all who celebrate the great fire."

Hector drank once again, hoping he might get her to tell him of happenings in the village.

"Lass, have ye seen many travelers today? Anyone that ye didn't know?"

"Oh, listen to that Highland brogue! Aye. We have travelers every day in our village. It's only a short distance to Edinburgh from here, so we get them as they pass through."

"Have ye seen any of the captured Jacobite supporters?"

"Oh, aye. There be lots of supporters about this area, but they stay hidden as much as they can. The British are searching every street and hollow looking for them."

Hector was pleased the woman was beginning to offer a few tidbits of information. Just as he was about to inquire a bit further, his head began to swim and he found himself sitting down to keep from falling over.

"I'll sit here for just a minute, lass, if ye don't mind."

"Aye. That's some fine ale old Jem makes if I do say so. It can put you on your tail if you're not use to it! Ha!"

She tried pulling Hector to his feet, but he was a large man and she couldn't budge him.

"Aw, now, come on. Dance about the fire with me, big fellow. Celebrate with me. We'll share the night. That's what the Beltane time is all about, renewal!"

But Hector slumped to the ground and she was not sure what

to do with him. Looking about, she called over a couple of young lads to help her.

"Here, Aidan, Seamus. Let's get this one tucked up over on the haystacks. He's done for. No good to me tonight. He'll come round in the morning, I reckon."

Hector was quite a large man and the two lads struggled to get him out of the way of the dancers. They stretched him out atop a large hay bale and went on about their own frolicking. The young woman left, still laughing, hoping to find another partner for the evening.

20

Hearing the sobs of the woman in the cell down the hall was the worse part of being in the prison. Alex and Jack had both seen the inside of a few jails during their time, but never anything as disgusting as the conditions in the Old Tolbooth.

"Wouldn't ye think the guards would at least give the lass a blanket? Did ye notice that when we walked by? She had nothing but that fancy red dress and her shawl—silk it looked like to me. She's gotta be cold."

"Aye, I did notice. I also saw she was wearing ankle irons, too. At least we've been spared that ordeal, so far. Let's try to think this situation through and come up with a few ideas that might help us get out of here."

"Aye. But, Alex, I think we're on our own now. Da's too old and Hamish and Kenny are too young. Robbie's no help either. Maybe if Hector gets wind of our predicament he might come looking for us."

"Hector's got his hands full at the Sanctuary. At least he's not out in the general public like we've been. He may actually be safer where he is, in a house full of women and children. It's not likely the Brits will be looking for Jacobites there. Let's hope he stays there. I believe yer right—we're on our own. So, what do we know?"

"Well, I know it stinks to high heaven in here and if I see that snake again I'll tear these bars down with my bare hands."

21

The great Beltane celebration was over and the villagers were occupied about their places of business, trying to get things back in some sort of order. There had been much gaiety, laughter and dancing, and a lot of ale had been drunk as well. So, finding a highwayman with his head held over between his legs was not surprising.

"You got a big head this morning then I guess, eh?" The old man had seen the aftermath of celebrations before and knew what it felt like himself. He was too old for such shenanigans now, but could empathize with the man sitting on the bale of hay.

"Aye. Looks like I must have had quite a time. Can't actually remember much about it, though."

"Then I suggest you find your horse and get on back home, wherever that is. From the brogue, I assume it's in the Highlands somewhere."

That statement had Hector's mind reeling. He'd taken pains to try and speak like the Lowlanders last evening. But this morning his head hurt too much and he knew without question that he was feverish. This was more than just a hangover from a night of celebration. He was intelligent enough to realize he was in no shape to help anyone, and had no choice but to try to get back to the Sanctuary and recover before he could help his brothers.

Just standing up was a real chore, and for a moment he was overcome with dizziness and all was dark. If that gentleman had noticed his brogue, then he'd better move on quickly. Not all Highlanders were Jacobites, but some were, and there were even some down here. And there were some folk who were quick to turn the Jacobites in for a small reward.

It took him a few minutes to locate his horse. Thank goodness he'd had the sense to turn him in at the local livery. At least his horse would not be hung over and struggling with fever.

~ ~ ~

Reggie busied herself about the Sanctuary, which wasn't difficult. There was always a problem with one of the children or the women, or the kitchen staff. But at least Ethel pretty much handled that area. However, the kitchen was not quite the same without Aileen. The woman might have been quiet and prone to crying, but she was a marvelous cook and they all missed her dishes.

Old Clint came by for his morning coffee and a quick chat with Ethel. They'd shared a cottage for some time now and the arrangement worked for both of them. Even at their advanced age, a warm person to lie next to on a cold winter's night was comforting.

Their morning ritual of coffee and a chat had started many years ago when they were both married to others. Time had a way of altering lives and it was just a truth they accepted. Both lost their mates and had to learn to pick up the pieces of their lives and move on, and they had. Now, at this stage of their lives, there was a quiet happiness and contentment they may not have expected, and both were thankful.

Reggie came to the kitchen just as Clint walked in.

"I didn't see Mr. MacKinnon, uh Hector, this morning, Reggie. He always takes a turn around the castle. Is he alright then?"

"Aye. He's gone down to Edinburgh. Something to do with seeing his da's solicitor about some property deeds. He'll be back in a day he said."

"Then I'll walk about the place, just to make sure nothing's amiss, ye ken?" This old one hailed from the Highlands long ago and his speech pattern never did change.

When the next morning came, Clint once again made rounds as Hector still hadn't returned. Later, just as the sun was slipping behind the distant hills, Clint saw a rider coming. It was dusk so he couldn't see the face very well, but he recognized the horse right away.

It's Mr. MacKinnon. But why's he leaning over on his horse?

He hurried down the lane to meet him.

"What's wrong, Mr. MacKinnon? Are ye hurt?"

Hector had insisted Clint call him Hector, but the old one still had difficulty with that particular request.

Hector slowly climbed off his horse. "Nae, Clint. Just sick I think. Some sort of fever I guess. Better just help me to the bunk out in the tack room. Don't think I'd better go inside where the women and bairns are. I don't know what's wrong, but Da was just getting over Scarlet Fever when I was at the lodge. Could be I picked it up; but whatever it is, no need to be spreading it around the castle."

"Yessir. Ye just come on back here. I'll get Ethel. She'll know what to do. Here, now. Rest a bit and I'll be back shortly."

Hector went inside the tack room, collapsed on the bunk, and was asleep before he could even get his boots off.

~ ~ ~

"What? Hector's back? Where is he?" Reggie searched Clint's old weathered face trying to read what he wasn't saying aloud.

"He's out in the stable, resting on the bunk in the tack room."

"Why's he out there? What's going on Clint?"

Reggie prided herself on remaining calm even in situations that were often trying. She'd been able to maintain her composure and keep a semblance of order at the Sanctuary even when pandemonium broke out, which it did occasionally. Whenever a new family, a mother and her children, showed up at the door it always caused something of a furor as they scrambled to find beds, clothing and to deal with the distraught women. But this problem today had even the ever-calm Miss Carmichael rattled.

"He's not feeling himself just at the moment, Reggie. He's got a bit of a fever, ye ken?"

"Fever? What kind of fever? Are you sure?" Even as she spoke, she started toward the kitchen door headed to the stable, picking up her long skirts in order to move more rapidly.

"No, lass, ye don't need to go out there. He says his da was just getting over the Scarlet Fever when he was at the lodge. Not sure that's what he has, but ye gonna be in here working with the women and bairns. Ye don't need to spread it."

Ethel spoke up. "I'll go see about him, Reggie. If it is the scarlatina, then I've already had my turn. It struck my family when I was a wee girl. Took my baby brother from us. But it won't bother me now."

"But I must see him. He means everything to me, Clint!" She grabbed at the old man's hands as if to gather strength from him in some way.

"Aye, lass. We all know that. Ethel will know what to do, she's seen a lot in her time. Ye just keep everything going inside here. Mr. MacKinnon, Hector, he's young and tough. He'll be alright."

Reggie tried her best to go on about her business, and when she heard a sharp, hard rap on the front door she headed in that direction. As much as she wanted to help the widows and offer them relief, she truly hoped it wasn't a new family needing a place to stay. She could hardly keep her mind on her duties, as the mental picture of Hector lying on a cot perhaps dying of fever would not go away.

When she opened the door, she unconsciously stepped back. This caller was not a woman in need. She now wished it had been. Rather, it was a couple of British soldiers, fully outfitted in their uniforms, and armed. Reggie dug deep and found her calm, reasonable self and spoke in a soft, quiet voice.

"Good morning, sirs. May I help you?"

One of the soldiers just stared at her, but the other one, a very young one with dark hair, actually had enough manners to remove his tricorne as he bowed slightly to her.

"Ma'am. We've been authorized by the Crown to search any and all residences, barns, stables, castles, and any other buildings we suspect may harbor Jacobite supporters. This castle is one of the properties we are to search today."

"Why on earth would you wish to search Cameron Castle, sir? We are a place of refuge, a sanctuary for widows and their children. We do not harbor Jacobites."

The older soldier spoke up. "That will be for us to decide, madam. Are there any male workers here?"

"Yes, of course. We women can't possibly do everything alone. We have several men who help with the chores, care for the animals, and our gardeners help with the vegetable harvesting."

"How many do you have?"

"Oh, well. That number varies. If the vegetables are in season then we may have half a dozen or more gardeners. But if the growing season is over we may only have a couple. But, of course, we have sheep that have to be sheared, and someone has to feed and water the animals. Clint's in charge of keeping the workers on task, so I suppose he may have a better idea than I of exactly how many workers we may have right now."

The young soldier was having difficulty staying on task. He was taken with Reggie's beauty and wished he could find a way to talk with her longer.

The older soldier spoke up. "Then I'd like to see him, the one you call Clint."

"Of course. I'll see if I can find him. He's usually about somewhere. Excuse me."

Reggie closed the door, gathered her skirts, hurried through the kitchen, and fairly flew down the steps headed for the stable. Clint met her halfway across the bailey and one look at her face told him something was off.

"What? What's wrong?"

Gasping for breath, she finally found her voice. "Soldiers at the front of the castle. They're searching for Jacobite supporters, insisting they be allowed to search all buildings. Actually, they're demanding it."

"Aye. Aye. Then let them search. I'll take them around and show them whatever they wish to see. They'll not find Hector, Reggie. I'll see to that."

She nodded, took a deep breath, squared her shoulders and put her calm face on again. She slowly walked back to the front door and invited them in.

"Please come in, gentlemen. Clint will join us momentarily. May I offer you a cup of tea? Or perhaps you would care for one of Ethel's scones? She excels in her baking skills."

The young, dark haired soldier would like nothing more than to share tea and scones with this striking woman. "Thank you. We'd like that very much."

His companion glared at him.

"No. We don't care for tea. We have a duty to perform. Where is your man?"

"Clint's on in years, you understand. But he's quite capable and we depend on him greatly. He knows every inch of this castle and the outbuildings. I'm sure he'll be of assistance to you. Please, just take a seat."

Clint rushed back to the stable and found Ethel pouring some concoction down Hector's throat. His flushed face and trembling hands told Clint a lot. But at least he was conscious now and nodded to Clint.

Ethel stood and motioned Clint to come closer.

"Don't think it's the scarlatina. He's fevered alright, but there's no rash and I know that when I see it. I think he's just got a light case or some other kinda fever. But he's gonna be on his backside for a few days, and he's a mite weak. I'll keep giving him this tonic and I'll stir up some of my partridge soup. That'll give him some strength."

"Aye. But we've got a new problem at the moment. A couple of British soldiers are at the front door, and Reggie says they're demanding to search all buildings looking for Jacobites. I'll try to steer them away from here, so ye just keep quiet and tend to Hector. I'll come back later and see how he's doing."

Hector tried to speak up, but the effort was too great and he fell back on the cot, exhaustion overtaking him.

Clint whispered to her, "Ethel, did ye notice Hector's clothing? Wonder where he got that outfit? Looks like he stole it from a beggar, I say. Might be more to his trip than we know about."

"Huh. Maybe," Ethel said as she began bathing Hector's face with her cloth.

Clint finally walked to the castle and entered the great room where Reggie had kept the soldiers. The older one was obviously put out with her and Clint's measures to detain them.

"I say, let's get on with this search. We've other places to inspect today also. Show us each building, old man."

Clint took his time, taking his steps slower than usual. He even took them upstairs where the women and children were going about their daily routines. The soldiers noted the ragged condition of the clothing the women were wearing, and couldn't miss the vacant stares coming from most of them. They were accustomed to seeing men in such conditions, but were uncomfortable seeing women in a similar state.

"That's enough in here. Take us to the barn, the stables."

"Aye. This way. The barn is just out yonder a ways. James and Gordy are cleaning up in there this morning. One of the ewes has a wee lamb and they're trying to get it to nurse, but she's not cooperating. We may lose her I'm afraid."

"Take us through the building." The soldiers walked around the stalls and kicked at various corners where layers of sheared wool had been piled.

'That's enough in here. Take us to the stable."

"Certainly. Follow me."

Clint started at the front of the stable, ushering them up the ladder to the attic where the young stable hands sometimes slept.

The soldiers carefully walked from one end of the attic to the other, pulling hay bales away from the walls. Nothing.

Clint nodded to them. "That's everything. Ye've seen it all. Can we help ye any other way?"

"What's that room down at the end of the building? You didn't show us that."

"Oh, well, that's just the tack room. We keep our saddles, reins, and currying tools in there."

"I said take us in every room."

Clint had no choice but to obey. Some things were just out of his control. Slowly opening the door, he saw Ethel leaning over Hector, crying softly. Clint was just as surprised as the soldiers.

"What's going on here? Who's this man?"

Ethel looked up, taking her handkerchief and dabbing at her eyes as she did so.

"It's me son, Thomas. He's had the scarlatina ye see? I put him out here to keep from spreading it. It just goes like wildfire, ye ken? But he's at peace now. He can rest and I'll have the vicar say some special prayers over him." She allowed a sob to accent her last words.

The soldier turned quickly to Clint. "You idiot! Why didn't you tell us there was fever about? Are all Scots as stupid as you?"

Reggie watched from the front window and saw the soldiers mount up, kick the sides of their mounts and take off at a fast pace. She finally took a breath and knew she'd never been so afraid. If they had found Hector she'd have never seen him again. As she had said to Clint and Ethel, he was most important to her.

Rushing outside, she met Clint as he was returning to the stable.

"Did they find him?"

Clint smiled. "Oh, aye, lass, they did. Ethel put on a

performance that would have pleased the king himself! But Hector's going to be down a few days according to Ethel. She's tending him and feeding him her special partridge soup. He'll be back to himself, Reggie, and one thing's for sure, those soldiers won't come back here again!"

Clint didn't mention Hector's strange clothing to Reggie. He thought it better to discuss the matter with Hector first, but wondered if the clothing might have something to do with his trip to Edinburgh.

22

In spite of her concerns about Alex and Jack, Caitlin found herself trying to recall everything she knew about Edinburgh. Most of her knowledge came from books in the library at the lodge, and from the pamphlets and news articles Uncle Andrew would often bring back from his visits to the city.

More than anything, Caitlin was interested in the medical community in Edinburgh. Andrew had told her of a number of physicians who resided there who were making tremendous progress in diagnosing illnesses and coming up with treatments for some of the most dreaded illnesses, such as typhoid, diphtheria, and of late, even treatments for cancer. If only she could go there and learn from these physicians, she would be even more helpful to the Highlanders and her family. Presently, however, she needed to dwell on finding Alex and Jack and getting them to safety.

Robbie reined Goliath in and looked to Caitlin. "We're just on the outskirts of the city now. Look up to the skyline. That's Edinburgh Castle. In early times royalty lived there. I heard Mother and Mr. Bowers discussing it a while back. They were saying that before the Culloden incident, Bonnie Prince Charlie and some of his supporters tried to recapture the castle, but they failed. There's a dungeon there, too. I've been in it."

"A dungeon? Do you think that could be where Alex and Jack are being held?"

"No. My bet is they're in the Old Tolbooth. That's where

most prisoners are taken these days."

Caitlin sighed and studied Robbie's face, so like Alex's.

You're alive, Alex. I know I would sense it if you weren't, and we'll find you.

"I've heard horrendous tales of the Old Tolbooth. Are there any other prisons besides that one?"

"Yes, there's Canongate Tolbooth also. And a couple of other small jails where prisoners, usually the less dangerous ones, are kept. I've actually been in the Old Tolbooth and Canongate. Mother would have skinned me alive had she known. But I'd read about them in the library and was curious. They've been in existence since medieval times. King Robert II granted Edinburgh a charter giving land for the Tolbooth and the records tell of the inhumane treatment the prisoners received in their confinement there."

"I don't think I need to hear those stories, Robbie. Let's just concentrate on where Alex and Jack are most likely to be."

"Then I say we should try the Old Tolbooth. It's located on the northwest corner of St. Giles's Cathedral on the High Street. It's been used as a prison and place of execution for a long time now. When Mary, Queen of Scots, was reigning it was in such poor condition she demolished it and had it rebuilt."

"I see you've spent time reading about that as well. Well, I don't think we can just walk through the front door. So let's think about how to get in without being seen."

"Oh, there are several ways to get in besides the front door. There'll be guards at each entrance for sure, but there's one other place to enter where I know there won't be any guards."

"An entry without guards?"

"Yeah. There's a very large stone in the cobblestone street near the west door of St. Giles Kirk. In early times, that exact spot was where the public executions took place, and now it's an entry to the sewer and tunnels underneath the city. You have to look closely to find it, but Paul Brampton and I discovered it one day when we were messing about."

"How does knowing about a sewer opening help us?"

"As I said, the opening in the cobblestones is near the west door of St. Giles. The original Tolbooth was there according to the records in the library. But on that spot, the large central stone can be lifted up and you can get to the sewer that way. The sewers were built long ago, something from the Romans I believe. If we can lift the center stone, then we can go down into the tunnels that run below the city and lead to the bowels of the prison. I went down that way with Paul a few times.

We would sneak down there and leave packets of food and sometimes some sweets that Mattie made. Somehow she knew what we were doing, but she never told Mother. I think Mattie knows some of the guards. Not all of them are bad, they just need a job, and working at the prison is better than starving."

"It's a place to start then. If we can just get in, then Willie can find Alex and Jack. He's a better tracker than either of us. Robbie, it occurs to me that you were not exactly the quiet, bookish lad your mother thought you were. These escapades you talk about are exactly the kind of things Alex and his brothers would have pulled off."

"Oh, most of the time I stayed in my room or the library. But occasionally I would walk down the street and wonder what it was like to be free like Paul was. He could just go anywhere, any time. His mother didn't seem to know or care what he was doing."

"Well, whatever the reasons for your friend having such freedom, your mother took good care of you and she did a fine job of teaching you how to care for others. I have no doubt she was a special lady."

Robbie nodded but didn't trust himself to speak. Just being here this close to the city had his head spinning. Where would they go? What was the first step to freeing his da and Jack? What would his mother think if she saw him today? Robbie was young, but he wasn't stupid. This woman married to his da was a brave one. He just hoped he could be brave himself when it became necessary, and that time would come, of that he had no doubt.

"I think we should go to my home and talk to Mattie. She's been with Mother and me since I was born. She's someone we can trust and she'll know everything that's going on in the city. She goes out every morning and does her shopping and talks to all the shop owners."

As they got to the entrance to the city proper, they reined their horses to a walk and slowly made their way up the steep hillside that led to the High Street. Caitlin took in all the sights, which she found appalling. Hordes of people seemed to just mingle about talking, laughing, and standing around fires that were built on every corner, even though the weather was warmer here than in the Highlands. They all looked to be wearing rags and many were actually barefoot. Children darted from one side of the cobblestone street to the other, oblivious to their ragtag appearance. Suddenly, Caitlin's keen nose was awakened rudely with unbelievably vile odors. She pulled her reins in quickly, causing Soldier to come to a complete stop.

"Oh, good glory! What is that smell?"

"What smell?"

"You surely must smell that odor. Like human waste, unwashed bodies, and maybe even dead animals."

"Oh, well, that's just the smell of Edinburgh, Caitlin. I guess I've grown up with it and don't pay much attention to it. But it definitely smells different than the Highlands."

Looking around, Caitlin saw what looked like houses on top of houses. They were so close the inhabitants could see inside their neighbors' homes. But oddly enough, there might be one shabby shanty and next to it a fine, well-built home with a small garden attached. She again made note of the number of people crowding the streets. There was hardly room for one to walk without stumbling over another.

"Is it always so crowded here?"

"I guess so. I never thought about it. But you get used to it I suppose. Come on. My home is just another few blocks up the High Street. The homes there are much more comfortable and there aren't so many people. But you need to know that our neighbor is a British major, Major Lloyd Ashford. He's actually a kind man, but we might want to avoid him if we can. We'll go the back way, behind the major's house and on to ours. Then we'll go through the kitchen and find Mattie."

"This is not how I pictured Edinburgh. I know it's a city of great medical achievements. I thought it would be cleaner, I suppose. But with so many people crowded into one place it can't be clean, and I bet disease would run rampant in these surroundings. We need to find Alex and Jack quickly. This is no place for any of us. Now I understand why Alex was so keen on getting back to the Highlands when he studied here."

As Robbie had said, the closer they got to his end of High Street the homes were indeed more appealing. In fact, some of them were very fine.

"That's my home there, the one with the tall, black doors with the lion's head knocker. Let's get off here and sneak to the back."

Robbie's home was a stately two-story building with columns supporting the porch on the second floor. The two front doors were exceedingly tall and painted a lustrous black. As he pointed out, the doorknocker of a lion's head stared out at anyone who got close enough to use it. They both dismounted and slowly made their way along the street.

"The next house down is where Major Ashford lives. He often has soldiers in his home and we don't need them to see us. His is the last house on the street, so we shouldn't have to worry about anyone else seeing us. Come on, let's find Mattie. She'll be mad as a wicked witch with me. I left while she was sleeping and didn't tell her I was going."

"Yes, I can see that she might be a bit perturbed with you."

Tying the horses to the large birch tree behind the house, Robbie led the way to the kitchen door. There were several candles burning in the windows, so he was hopeful Mattie was still up. She had no family and he assumed she would just live there until she died. But, as he had told Caitlin, he didn't expect she would greet him warmly.

Quietly twisting the doorknob, he found what he knew he would find, a locked door.

"Just as I expected. Locked. Mattie is particular about keeping all doors locked at all times. We never had a robbery or anything of that sort, but Mattie took it upon herself to be the keeper of the house."

"Then why don't you just knock and perhaps she'll answer the door?"

"Uh, of course. Yes, that's what I'll do." Robbie squared his shoulders and stood tall then knocked lightly on the door.

They waited for what seemed like ages to Robbie. What was taking Mattie so long to get to the door? Was she ill? She was getting on in years, but Robbie's impression of her was that she was still very spry and her mind was as keen as it had always been. She'd been more than just a housekeeper for his mother. She was a friend and confidant as well. Now that he knew more about the circumstances surrounding his birth, he suspected she knew many secrets he didn't know.

Finally, he heard a tap-tap-tap.

"That's Mattie. She always uses a cane. I'm not sure she really needs it to walk, but I saw her use it to whack a couple of dogs that were chasing us one day. She's a tiny woman, but I'd rather not have her truly angry at me."

Holding a candle in one hand and her cane in the other, Mattie came to the door and called out. "Who's there? What do you want?"

"It's me, Mattie, Robbie. Let us in."

"Who? I don't know anyone called Nobbie."

"Robbie! Robbie! It's me, Mattie!"

"What? Oh, Robbie! Is that you, my boy?"

"Yes, Mattie, it's me. Hurry now, let us in."

Fumbling with the candle and her cane, she eventually opened the door and stood staring at them for a moment.

"Oh, Robbie. I thought you were gone forever! Come here, dear boy!" He walked forward and she pulled him to her bosom. He stood more than a head taller, but allowed her to hold him. He knew a moment of great relief, as he had thought she might use her cane on him.

"Are you alright then?" Pushing him away from her, she looked him up and down and, satisfied he was in good condition, she held him close once again.

"And just what explanation do you have for disappearing in the middle of the night? And where have you been? And who is this lad with you?"

Robbie grinned at Caitlin and proceeded to make the proper introductions.

"Mattie, this lad is Caitlin MacKinnon, my stepmother as it happens."

"What? You're a lady?"

"How do you do. Yes, I'm Caitlin MacKinnon and I am indeed Robbie's stepmother. I don't usually dress in this manner, but we find ourselves in a desperate situation and that sometimes means you have to take desperate measures."

As Caitlin made her way inside, Willie followed right behind her, insisting on standing between her and Mattie.

When Mattie spied Willie, she jumped back and raised her

cane high in the air. "Oh dear! A wolf!"

She brought her cane down and Robbie caught it just in time before she struck Willie.

"No, Mattie! It's only Willie. He's Caitlin's protector and he'll not hurt you. Be calm now. He's harmless, at least until he needs to be fierce."

Mattie took a deep breath and looked from Robbie to Caitlin then back to Willie. His hackles were standing on end and he was watching her with blazing eyes that held hers in place.

"That's the largest wolf I've ever seen. And I've certainly never been this close to one." She gathered herself together. "Well then, come in to the kitchen. I'm quite sure I can find something to fill your stomachs."

She moved very quickly—without her cane Caitlin noticed—and they followed her through to the kitchen. Just as Robbie had said, she was very tiny and thin, and had an abundance of totally white hair piled up in a bun on the back of her head. Her spectacles dipped low on her nose and she peered over them most of the time. When she did push them up, Robbie always thought she looked like an owl, as her blue eyes were enormous then.

"Young man, you have some explaining to do first. Where have you been?"

"Mattie, Mother told me about my father before she died. She told me if I ever needed any help I should find him and he would not turn me away. Well, when she was gone I didn't know what to do, or how to get on with my life. So I read all her notes about my father and found my way to the Highlands. That's where I've been all this time."

"What? You actually found him?"

"Yes. It really wasn't so hard, as the MacKinnons are well known in the Highlands. I took the coach to the nearest village and walked some miles from there and found their lodge. My father, my da, lives there with his entire family, which is quite large. He has a wife, Caitlin, who you just met. And he has several brothers, and there are some orphans, and an uncle and his lady friend."

"And how did you know which one of them was your father?"

Caitlin spoke up. "It wasn't difficult to tell who had fathered this young lad. He is so like Alex it's uncanny. He's a MacKinnon no doubt."

"What did this MacKinnon have to say when you showed up?"

"Uh, he was very surprised I think, but treated me well. It's a long story Mattie, and I don't have time to tell you all the details just now. We're in trouble and need your help."

"What have you gotten yourself into now, young man? I've saved your hide more than once and never let your mother know. Don't tell me you and that Brampton boy have pulled another stunt! Getting you out of that prison was not so easy. If I hadn't known a couple of the guards you'd still be there today. I know the two of you thought taking food to the prisoners was a good deed, but in the end it wasn't such a bright idea."

"I haven't seen Paul in some time, but I need to find him. He might help us."

"He's bad news, Robbie. He's just a street urchin who doesn't know right from wrong. He's not had much in the way of parents if you recall. Who knows where he even is anymore."

"Mattie, just listen. Alex, my da, and his brother, Jack, have been captured and we think they may be in the Old Tolbooth. I don't know how much you've kept up with the happenings here, but the British soldiers are rounding up the Jacobites and either executing them or sending them to the islands where they'll be sold as slaves. We've got to get my da and Jack out before they're shipped off."

"Oh, saints above! Your father's a Jacobite? That could make things difficult. I hear a lot on the High Street when I make my daily rounds. I've not told anyone you've been missing—well, except for Ned, the old gent I get candles from. He's almost totally blind now, and his candles aren't as fine as they once were, but he needs every pence he can get."

"And how about you, Mattie? Are you able to get along in this big house without Mother being here?"

"Oh, Robbie. I miss Fiona tremendously. But she's at peace now and I'm getting along. You know your mother. She made provisions for both of us long before she passed on.

"Lord Wellington was most angry with her when she told him she was with child, but he sent her away long enough that no one knew any of the details. When she returned she concocted her story of your father being a soldier and dying in a battle.

"I believe she truly loved that Scotsman, but she never told him about you. That was her decision and I accepted it as well. She could never have left the city, and he couldn't have stayed away from the Highlands. She was intelligent enough to recognize that fact.

"She and Lord Wellington made their peace long ago, but he was not one to show his emotions. Still, he made sure she was well provided for and that was his way of forgiving her, I suppose."

"I barely remember him. He always seemed angry any time he came to visit."

"I saw him briefly at your mother's funeral. He remembered me of course and asked about 'the boy.' But as you had left and I had no idea where you were, I couldn't tell him anything. Then he walked away before the vicar even finished his final prayer. Lord Wellington was always a bit difficult to converse with, but he's very old now, Robbie. He's not as fearsome as he might once have seemed."

"Yes, well, I doubt we'd have much to say to one another anyway."

~ ~ ~

Caitlin had sat about as long as she could manage. "Robbie, we've got to get moving. Time is not something we have a lot of. Now, about that stone in the cobblestones you told me about. Can you find it in the dark?"

"Oh, certainly. Finding it will be easy enough, but lifting it will be difficult. It was all Paul and I could do to get it open ourselves. We finally pried it up enough to put a stone under the edge, then we dropped down and got to the tunnel."

"What? You don't think we'll be able to lift it? We have to find a way. Come on. Let's just find the place and then we'll figure out how to lift the stone."

"Mattie, if we can find Jack and Da, we'll sneak them back here so they can get a couple of hours of rest and maybe some food. As I recall, they only get a bit of gruel and water twice a day. They're bound to be weak and tired. So if you can get some food ready for them, and maybe have a tub of water ready? That place stinks to high heaven and they will, too."

"You two must stay hidden. There's been a lot of activity over at the major's place yesterday and today. Don't know what it's all about, but something's up. But go now. Everything will be ready when you two get back. And Robbie, be careful son. Your mother will turn over in her grave if anything happens to you."

Caitlin pulled at Robbie's arm. "Robbie, the major lives right next door. Don't you think it's dangerous to bring two escapees here?"

"No, Caitlin. Think about it. If the guards even learn they're gone, they'd never think to look at a home close to a British major's place. Plus, the major has a small paddock behind his house where he keeps some very fine horses. That may come in handy too. Right now, though, we've got to find Paul. He can help us I know."

As they started out the back door, Mattie called to them. "Here, take this small lantern. You'll need it if you get inside the prison."

Robbie took the small lighted lantern and they left out the back door, looking about before they started out. Noise from next door got their attention.

"Mattie's right. There's a lot of activity at the major's place. Look."

Caitlin saw several Redcoats prancing about, drinking ale and laughing.

"Looks like he's having a celebration of some kind. The soldiers all seem to be enjoying their evening."

Robbie nodded but made no comment.

"Do you know your way in the dark?" Caitlin was even more worried about Alex and Jack now that she had seen Edinburgh and the throng of people.

"Of course. Paul and I know every inch of this city. We actually made a map of the underground tunnels once. Some of them are probably not even known to the officials. One of them winds its way under the chapel of the kirk on the south end of the castle, and another one runs underneath Cowgate Street. We could always use one of those if we can't get out and go above ground."

"How are we going to find this lad called Paul?"

"Oh, that won't be hard. I know where he's probably staying. His mother walks the streets most nights, if you understand what I'm saying. He'll be hanging about the back room of the pub. The pub owner sorta looks after him, keeps him pretty well fed, and I used to bring him stuff from home, too. Mattie knew about that too, but she'd never admit it. Paul's pretty self-sufficient, much more so than I am."

The streets were lighted by oil lamps and the lamplighters were busy now extinguishing them. The official time for them to be used was five to nine, and it was well past that. But there were several still burning, which helped Caitlin even if Robbie didn't need them.

"The pub's just around the corner here. Paul sleeps on a cot next to the window. He'll hear me tapping on it." He rounded the corner and walked gingerly across the cobblestone street, then got down on his knees.

Rapping quickly, he waited a moment. It was only a second before a face appeared and lifted the window.

"Robbie! Where've you been? I've looked all over the city for you. You just disappeared. Thought maybe that lord fellow had come and taken you back to London with him."

"No, I've not been to London. I'll tell you about it later. Right now I need your help. My father, my real father, is a Jacobite. He's been captured and I think he may be in the Old Tolbooth. I need to get him out of there."

"What? Your father? I thought he was dead."

"Yeah, well, so did I. But that's not important right now. I need some help lifting the cobblestone, you know, the heavy one in the middle of the others close to St. Giles."

"You mean the one where we got trapped and Mattie had to plead with the guards to let us go?"

"Right. That's it."

"Robbie, we could get trapped again. I don't know if that's such a good plan."

"We've got to try Paul. My da's in there. I just know he is."

Paul nodded, then without further discussion grabbed the long, wooden stick he never went out without. He'd learned early on he may have to defend himself, especially when he stole food from the merchants.

"Then let's go. Haven't had any fun since you left. I even tried going to the library and reading like you do, but that's pretty boring stuff if you ask me."

Robbie smiled at him as he climbed through the window and was on the street with them. As Paul stood he saw Caitlin, then he saw Willie and immediately stepped back.

"Whoa! What is that?" He stood very still, pointing down at Willie who was keeping close to Caitlin but aware of everything around him.

"Oh, never mind him. That's Willie. He's a friend. Nothing to worry about with him."

"Huh. If you say so. He looks pretty vicious to me."

"Well, but he's on our side. And this is Caitlin, my stepmother."

"Ma'am." He nodded to her.

Caitlin looked at the young lad, much smaller than Robbie, and far too thin. He had a head full of auburn hair—in need of a good washing—pulled back and tied with a leather thong. Not at all someone she would have expected Robbie to have been acquainted with. But at this moment she'd take any help she could get.

"It's getting late. Most people will have gone home by now, except for the few who never go home and sleep on the street. But they won't bother us. Probably won't even know we're around," Paul commented.

"We need to hurry, Paul. We've got to get down below the streets before daylight gets us."

The three night crawlers and Willie began working their way to St. Giles Cathedral. Most of the streetlights in that area were out now, so they weren't quite so visible.

"Ma'am, did you know this was where the first Tolbooth was built a long time back?" Paul asked.

Robbie smiled at his friend. "Guess you learned that from some of your trips to the library?"

"No. But I do remember you telling me about it. I don't read a lot, but I've got a memory that never fails me."

"Trips to the library can be good, Paul. There's a whole section on the landmarks about the city. You might want to look at those sometimes."

"I know where most of 'em are. Just don't know the history of 'em like you do."

The central stone was actually fairly large and Caitlin was amazed the two young lads had found this entryway. But just one look told her it would be extremely heavy.

"Robbie, we'll never be able to lift that!"

"Oh, yeah we will," Paul said.

Running to the edge of the cobblestone street, he returned with an iron bar about one meter long.

"This should do it. Just like before, Robbie, I'll pry the edge up and you and the mistress drop down. You'll have to hurry, as I can't hold it very long. Come on now, get moving."

"Paul, if we're not back here in a half hour, then come to the tunnel at the kirk, at the end of Cowgate. This exit and that one are the only ones not sealed off. This one is closer, but if we can't get back here then we'll use the Cowgate exit and then make our way home from there."

Robbie then turned to Caitlin. "It's about a two-three meter drop from the top to the floor. Can you do that?"

"Guess we'll see."

"OK, ready now?"

Paul put all his weight on one end of the iron bar and the central stone lifted the slightest bit, just enough for Robbie to slide his body through. He dropped, and called out to Caitlin.

"Alright. Come on now. Hand the lantern down and I'll try to catch you."

Caitlin didn't hesitate. She sat down at the edge, handed the lantern to him and lowered herself into the opening. She quickly let go and found herself lying flat on her back on the cold, wet ground below, struggling to catch her breath.

"Sorry, Caitlin. I couldn't grab hold. You came down so quickly."

Then, in a move that had Robbie scurrying backward, Willie fell through the opening. But unlike Caitlin, he landed on his feet, as he always seemed to do. And it was none too soon, as the stone above them crashed down heavily and they were trapped below the street.

"Now what? Where do we go from here?"

Caitlin needn't have asked that question. Willie lifted his snout and moved his large ears from one side to the other, hearing from all angles. He let out one deep growl then took off down the tunnel on the right.

"Wait, Willie, don't leave us!"

Caitlin had no doubt Willie's sense of smell would find Alex and Jack long before she and Robbie could begin to. Presently, all she could smell was the disgusting stench of raw sewage close by, accompanied by the odor of a rotting animal. Whether that was an animal or whether it was a human being wasn't clear. But the smell of death was everywhere.

"Do you think he can find them?" Robbie had never known an animal that was this intelligent.

"If anyone can, then Willie can. Our problem will be to try and keep up with him."

"Watch where you walk. The sewer is a few meters to the left and some sections are open. Paul and I found a flight of stairs at the end of this tunnel. They lead up to another level where they keep the prisoners that will spend a lifetime here. Those are the ones we tried to get food to. If that's where Willie's headed, then we can find him. But there are several floors above this one, too."

Robbie raised the lantern above his head, hoping to light their way. For a brief moment the lantern blazed brightly, then a gust of wind coming from one of the adjoining tunnels had it flickering. In another second, it sputtered and finally died out completely.

This was a moment when Caitlin wished she had learned to light torches and candles with a nod of her head as Uncle Wabi and Ian could do. Something she needed to work out with Uncle Wabi when she saw him. She still didn't understand him not answering her call, and she greatly feared something had happened to him. But that was a problem for another day. She had enough to handle at the moment.

"There, at the end of the tunnel, see that soft light? There's a torch there that lights the stairway leading up to the next floor. That's where the guard station is. We have to get in there and get the keys somehow." Robbie had no idea how they would accomplish this task.

"I see. I'll use this pistol if I must, but I'm a healer, Robbie. Killing is not something I wish to do. But I will if I must in order to save Alex and Jack."

She held the pistol with both hands. Alex had given it to her explaining that it was smaller than some. But right now it felt very heavy, and she wasn't sure she could pull the trigger.

Robbie looked at her and shook his head. "I'm quite sure you can use it better than I can. Maybe one day I'll be better at shooting, but not yet." Robbie was woefully aware of his inadequacies in this endeavor they had undertaken.

What now? Did I think I'd just burst in here and take the keys from the guards? Alex, my Da, would know exactly what to do, but I certainly don't.

"I don't see Willie anymore. He's going too fast for us to keep up. Can you call him, Caitlin? Will he hear you?"

"Oh, he can hear me alright. But he may not listen. He's got a mind of his own in situations like this. Trust me, he can take care of himself."

No sooner had she said those words than a scream coming from the guardroom echoed throughout the hallway. In fact, it was so loud it was probably heard on several floors.

"What was that?" Robbie asked, not daring to move another muscle.

"That, dear Robbie, would be Willie announcing his arrival at the guardroom. We'd better hurry and hope we get there before he eliminates anyone who gets in his way."

Rushing down the tunnel, they watched as a very young guard darted from the room and scooted up the stairs just as they reached the doorway.

As they entered, they saw another guard backed into a corner as far as he could possibly be, and his face registered the fear he felt within. He was unarmed, so had no way of defending himself.

In order to leave the room he would have to go past the wolf, and he didn't think that was a good move. Another guard was lying on the floor and Willie's tremendous jaws were clamped solidly on his throat. Blood gurgled from his wound as he tried to push the wolf off and he was quickly losing all strength. Finally he refrained from his struggles and his eyes closed.

Caitlin handed Robbie the pistol and got down on her knees.

"Willie, good boy. Come here now." Caitlin wrapped her arms around her great protector.

How could I possibly have thought I could do this without you?

Caitlin turned then to the guard cowering in the corner. "Robbie, let me hold the gun and you get the keys and tie this one up. There, up on the wall, a set of leg irons should do the trick." Next she tore a sleeve off the uniform of the guard on the floor and handed it to Robbie.

"Now stuff this in his mouth." Then, unable to stop herself, she returned to the guard on the floor and lay her fingers against his neck, feeling for a pulse.

"Aye, there's a pulse. He's not dead, but he's not going anywhere any time soon." She stood, looking at Robbie as if he would know the next steps to take.

"Uh, I think we should go up one flight of stairs to the main floor. That's the most likely place they would hold them."

"Alright. Come Willie. Find Alex. Go now!"

With that instruction, Willie flew through the door and bounded up the stairs to the left, with Caitlin and Robbie hurrying to keep up with him.

23

The prison confinement was getting to both Alex and Jack and their nerves were on edge.

"Alright, the guard just made his final round for the evening. If we're ever going to try this, now's the time."

"I don't know, Alex. Even if ye can get through the hole, ye'll have a hard time pulling me up."

"Aye, that could be a problem. Then maybe ye ought to be the one to go up first. Maybe ye can stand on my shoulders and once yer up there ye can pull me up. It's worth a try. We don't have any other plan."

"Aye. Just know that ye may have a shoulder ache the rest of yer life, brother. Don't say I didn't warn ye."

"Then, just like we did when we were lads, I'll bend over a bit and ye can put yer foot on my thigh, then up on my shoulder. Make it quick, brother. I don't relish holding a sixteen stone weight very long."

"Alright, here goes."

Jack quickly stepped from Alex's thigh and onto his shoulders. But as soon as he reached the opening, he knew it was hopeless. There was no way his broad shoulders would go through the tight space.

"I'm coming down now. Easy does it." Jack stepped back down on Alex's thigh and onto the floor. "It's no use. You might could get through that hole, but I can't."

"Then let's try that. If I can make it through I'll make my way to the guardroom. If I can get there, mayhap I can overtake the guard and get his keys. Then I'll come get ye out."

"I don't know. What if the guard comes by again? He'll notice yer missing, don't ye think?"

"But his routine is that he never comes back after he delivers the gruel and water. He's just done that, so I don't think we'll see him again until morning. That leaves all night for us to work our way out of this place."

"Then come on. Get up on my shoulders. I'll wait quietly, but I'd appreciate ye moving quickly if ye will."

Alex put an arm around his big brother. "Ah, Jack. We're not done in yet. And we don't want to make Caitlin and Millie young widows either. They'd figure out some way to punish us even in our next life." He smiled at his brother and both knew this plan might go haywire.

Alex had no trouble getting to the opening. Jack was just a tad bit taller and his shoulders were plenty wide enough to stand on. In just a matter of minutes Alex was hefting himself up through the hole, but it was really tight even for him.

Good glory. This opening must have been put here for some reason, but I may not be able to get through it. Why would they put it here anyway?

He pushed harder against the right side of the opening, and he felt the skin on his shoulder tear as he continued to push. Finally, with his shoulder bleeding and his sleeve almost torn off, he managed to squeeze through. He stood and immediately hit his head on the ceiling.

Good Lord! I'll have to crawl on all fours to get out of this place.

Now down on his knees, he felt numerous pipes running across the floor in all directions.

Some kind of water pipes? Certainly not heating as this place is frigid and it's not even winter. What do they use this space for?

Still on his knees, he called out to Jack. "I'm in. Sit tight and I'll come for ye as soon as I can." Listening for a moment, he heard critters skittering about and felt something warm brush across his fingers.

Probably a good thing Jack didn't get up here. Pretty sure that was a snake that just crawled over my hand.

It was so dark in the room that Alex had to feel along the wall to find the door and was relieved to find it was not locked from the outside. Stepping out into the dark hallway, he saw one small torch at the other end. That would have to be the stairway to the guard station. He put his back against the wall and began to make his way slowly in that direction. Holding his dirk in his left hand, he was prepared to do whatever was necessary to get the keys and return for Jack.

24

Standing at the top of the moor, Daniel looked about. The sun was setting and a warm red glow covered the entire farm. How many times had he stood here over his lifetime, watching the seasons change, and observing the rituals that made them official.

Of course...the Beltane fires.

Alice had particularly enjoyed this ritual that marked a time of renewal. She had always insisted on a large fire on that occasion and she'd recite several passages from some of her favorite readings. Beltane was a time for celebrating many things she'd said. Some folk gave thanks for their crops, their homes, and their animals.

"But, Daniel, we should always give thanks for our family. That's more important than anything. Without that nothing has any meaning."

He strolled slowly through the circle of stones, and for a brief moment he stood at Alice's grave and said his usual prayer. After his prayer, he began to talk to her as he always did.

"*Mo chridhe*, I know ye can hear me and I can feel ye when I come here. Ye always told me if I would learn to listen then I'd hear what ye were saying to me. Well, I'm asking ye to listen to me now, and I expect ye are better at that than I ever was. We've been blessed with a fine family as ye always reminded me. And yer right about that. Our lads are fine men, ones to be proud of. And their women, Caitlin and Millie, would make ye smile. Then there's the bairns. But I've

Grrrr! Grrrr!

The hoarse, throaty sound had Alex's skin prickling. If the guards had let the dogs out on him he was done for. He'd seen what a pack of angry dogs could do to a man, and he hadn't forgotten the sight. He had his dirk ready and looked from one side of the hall to the other. Nothing.

Then even more unsettling sounds filled the air—another angry growl followed by another scream. And this time the growl and the scream ended as quickly as they began.

Glory, how many dogs did they let loose?

A very small torch placed high on the wall lighted the hallway, but as he entered the stone stairwell it was totally dark. He approached the bottom stair and quickly found himself being slammed up against the wall, his breath completely knocked out of him. He doubled over, then, finally catching his breath, tried to stand. A whimper caught his attention just before a large wet tongue found his face.

"Jesus Christ! Stop you mangy dog!"

He struck out with his dirk, but missed his target. Then, as his eyes adjusted to the darkness, he was astounded.

"Willie! What are ye doing here? Ye scared the daylights out of me!" He took the wolf by the jowls and looked at him.

"If yer here, then ye've either tracked us on yer own or Caitlin's close by. Good God, I hope she's not here."

His heart was already racing from having been flattened by Willie, but now he could feel his pulse pounding in his head as well.

"Where is she Willie? Find Caitlin."

Willie immediately bounded back up the stairs. Suddenly the blast of a whistle tore through the air and the incessant blare had Alex covering his ears trying to escape the sound. It never stopped and no doubt was heard throughout the prison.

Then the guards know there's been a breakout, which means every entrance will be closely guarded and I still have to get Jack out. How am I going to do that? I must get those keys!

He began to make his way up the stairs and as he did so he caught a whiff of lavender. That could only mean one thing.

"Caitlin! Are ye here, *mo chridhe?"*

He almost wished she wouldn't be. At least she had been safe at the lodge. Now he had her to worry about also.

About half way up, he found himself flattened against the wall again, but this time his arms encountered softness and lavender—Caitlin.

"Oh, lass! What are ye doing here? Ye should be at the lodge where I left ye."

"Alex, you're alive. I knew you were. Thanks be to the Creator." She held on to him for dear life and thought she would never let him go again.

"Aye, we're both alive. But Jack's still in a cell at the end of the hall on this floor. I've got to get the keys somehow and get him out of there. The guards must have discovered I'm on the loose, so this could be very difficult."

He quickly raised his head when he saw someone rushing through the door, heading down the stairs in their direction.

His dirk was drawn and before the man could say a word, Alex had him down on his knees with his arms held behind him.

"Hold there, fellow. What's yer hurry?"

In the darkness he couldn't see facial features very well, but he knew the voice.

"Uh, Da, it's me, Robbie."

"What? Robbie? How in heaven's name did ye get here? I almost killed ye, lad!"

"It's a very involved story, Da. But Caitlin and I took the keys from the guard and were looking for you and Jack."

"What? You have the keys? How? Never mind. Let's hurry then and get to Jack before this whole place is overrun by Redcoats."

Down the hall the three of them fled, with Willie leading the way. He knew where Jack was and reached him several seconds before the others did.

"Willie!" Jack kneeled down and reached through the bars to ruffle Willie's fur.

"Glad to see ye fella. But, how'd ye get here?"

He stood as the others arrived, out of breath from their dash. As Alex was fiddling with the keys, two guards appeared a couple of cells down from them.

"Hold there! Stop I tell you!" The men began to run toward the group.

Alex turned to Caitlin, quickly reaching for her hand. The look on her face was one he'd seen before, like the calm before a storm.

Dear heaven, be with us all.

Intuition told him to be still and let this moment be hers. The healer was in charge now. He watched as she dropped the pistol and turned to face the guards.

Caitlin was acutely aware, every nerve in her body was on fire, but her mind was still and calm; it was as if the events all about her were taking place in slow motion.

Focus, Caitlin, focus your mind. Your powers are at your fingertips. The Creator gifted you with them to be used when necessary. Don't question, just direct your energies to your hands and release the power at the right moment.

This was a moment of decision for the healer. Finally she was in control of these powers, and had no qualms about using them now.

Instantly, a searing, sizzling bolt of jagged lightning flashed from her fingertips and raced across the room. In a matter of seconds, the two guards were on the floor, writhing as their clothing began to burn their bodies.

"Aieeeee! Help me! Stop it! No! No!"

One of the guards lay still, never moving a muscle. He watched his hands as his fingers melted together and then were just nubs of charred skin and bone. The other one watched in disbelief as his boots turned to liquid and he felt the fire as it raced up his leg. Eventually they both were quiet—deathly quiet.

Caitlin had once again found her power when she most needed it, and this time it didn't frighten her. This time she controlled it.

Robbie's face was as stunned as the guards' had been. He'd never witnessed Caitlin's powers, even though he had heard Jack talking about how she had saved him at Cameron Castle. Surely there was some explanation for this. He'd need to ask Ian more about this event. He recalled Ian had told him if he was ever in real trouble to call on Caitlin. Now he understood why.

Alex nodded, he too realizing she could now control her powers. He tried several keys, finally found one that worked and Jack was out of the cell.

"Come on, let's get out of here."

As they started back to the stairwell, he stopped long enough to throw the keys to the prisoner in the next cell.

"Here, let yerself out and help the others. And don't forget the lady in the last cell! We've got to get out of here. Good luck to ye."

Alex started toward the stairway again when Robbie called out to him.

"No, Da. This way. There's an escape tunnel out this side door."

Everyone followed Robbie as he took them out the door, down a short path, then back inside the prison. This time he had them going down a steep flight of stairs that seemed endless.

"Are ye sure ye know where yer going, lad?" Jack asked. He'd never run so fast in his life.

"Yes, I've been here before. I know where we're going."

For another twenty minutes they ran from one tunnel to another before they finally came to a door at the end of one of them.

"This will bring us up onto Cowgate Street. Paul will be there waiting for us. Then we'll backtrack to my home on the High Street."

~ ~ ~

Kicking his horse in the sides harshly, the young guard rode like a madman to Major Ashford's residence at the end of the High Street.

He was actually a soldier, but had been assigned to the prison when the British took it over. The local guards had all been replaced by young recruits such as him, and they all knew to follow the major's orders to the letter or suffer the consequences. He didn't relish the tongue lashing he knew would be coming from the major, but the sooner he told him the news the better.

By the time he'd found a superior officer at the Tolbooth to give him instructions, the whistle had sounded. They all knew that meant an escape was underway.

"Go, Johnson. Looks like it's the two Highland fellows, the big red-haired one and his brother. Scully saw them headed down to the tunnel with a couple of others, maybe young lads. Oh, and Scully swears they were being led down the hall by a wolf!"

"I saw that wolf myself. I watched him tear Donald's throat out. He's a huge devil, and vicious!"

By the time he arrived, the celebration at the major's place was well underway. Apparently Major Ashford had been selected for another promotion and was to be sent to his new post in London shortly, so a celebration was in order. The guard was personally glad the man would be leaving. He was a thorn in everyone's side and tried to run the prison like a military establishment.

After tying his horse around back where the other horses were tethered, he walked to the front door and knocked.

He saluted the officer answering the door.

"Lt. Johnson to see Major Ashford."

"Wait here. I'll see if he's available." It seemed forever before the major presented himself at the door.

"Yes, Johnson? What brings you here?"

"Uh ..."

"Come on, man. I don't have all day."

"Yessir. There's been an escape at the Tolbooth, sir."

"What? That's impossible—no one can get out of there. There are soldiers guarding every entrance and exit."

"Yessir. I know. But it appears two prisoners have escaped."

"Two?"

"Yessir. The Highlanders that were brought in last week, the two who caused such a ruckus when they arrived. The big one smashed Gordy's front teeth in the fracas and he's got a broken collarbone as well. He's still mighty angry about that, sir."

"We have many Highlanders in the Old Tolbooth, Lt. Johnson."

"Yessir. These two were the ones you identified from that lodge far up in the Highlands. MacKinnon's the name, sir."

"The MacKinnons? Damn their heathen souls! Then get a move on, man! Start a search of the entire city. They can't have gotten far yet. Which door did they leave from?"

"Uh, I don't believe they used a door, sir. They were seen headed down into the tunnels beneath the prison. From there I don't know where they'll go, sir." He stopped short of reporting the incident with the large wolf. The major probably wouldn't believe him anyway.

Ashford threw his head back and let out a laugh that had the soldier wondering if he were mentally deranged.

"Ah, ha, ha, hee hee!"

"Sir?"

"Idiots! There are only two exits from the tunnels. Those were left open in case of flooding from the firth. All the others were sealed off centuries ago. They're trapped for sure now. All we have to do is wait patiently for the tunnel rats to crawl out of their hiding place. They will either exit at the large stone near St. Giles or at the old kirk at the end of Cowsgate. We'll put men at each exit."

Laughing aloud once again, he went back inside and resumed his drinking and celebrating with his men. A short while later he made an announcement.

"Attention, men. I'm going to have to leave you now, but you may continue with our celebration. Two Jacobites have escaped from the Tolbooth and I must be there when they're apprehended."

Looking around the room, he called out to one of the officers.

"You there, Harrington, come with me. The two of us should be able to handle the escapees. They're Scots, so they're not very bright to begin with." Laughing again, he grabbed his tricorne and walked out the door.

"I can't wait to see MacKinnon's face when he realizes he's been caught again, and by his 'farm hand' no less. I wouldn't miss this for the world!"

~ ~ ~

After forty minutes had passed and Robbie had not returned to the cobblestone exit, Paul followed Robbie's orders and made his way through the city over to Cowgate Street.

The kirk at the end of the street was small and had been built sometime in the 1400s. The original builder had the foresight to include a priest's hole in the floor, which led to the tunnel where Robbie was bringing his entourage. The tunnel, therefore, could be reached from inside the kirk or from an opening outside near a large oak tree a few meters behind the kirk. The opening was covered by a sewer cap and grass, and most folks never even knew it existed. Of course Robbie and Paul had found both openings.

As he sat down on the curb with his back to the kirk, Paul chewed on his fingernails, a habit he had developed long ago, sometime in early childhood. He no longer feared for his life as he had in those days, but the habit was still with him. In those days he never knew if his drunken father might batter him about just for being there. But those days were over. Today he pretty much took care of himself, with the help of Mick, the pub owner who gave him a cot to sleep on. Sometimes he even saw his mother, though she spent most of her time with one drunken mate or another.

Some time ago he and Robbie had run into each other along the water's edge down near the firth. Robbie was trying to float a very crudely made wooden boat, with not much luck. The small boat refused to stay upright and Robbie found that frustrating.

Paul watched as Robbie worked at making the sail tighter, thinking perhaps that would help. Paul could make anything out of wood. In fact, he had made several small wooden boats for himself. One of them even had a sail that he'd made from one of his mother's tattered petticoats.

Once Paul had shown Robbie how to balance the boat, the two of them spent a lot of time together. Robbie would go to the library and come up with a new design for them to try, and Paul would steal a few pieces of wood from one of the merchants. Robbie never questioned his friend about where the wood came from, but had an inkling he'd stolen it.

After that they went about the city, each showing the other things they had missed. They created a map of the entire underground tunnels of Edinburgh and now they both knew it from memory. So, just now, he didn't worry about Robbie. He'd get everyone here safely. Paul would just wait patiently then see what else he could do to help his friend.

He'd heard the blare of the whistle when it had started blasting out. He wasn't surprised as he knew there were several guards on duty, and lately he'd seen more and more prisoners being marched through the city. Apparently two of them had been Robbie's da and his uncle.

He decided to lie back on the grass and rest a bit 'til Robbie and his crew got to the kirk. When he leaned back, however, something cold and hard stuck him in the back.

"Get up you little sewer rat! What did you think? We know all about you and your friends. They'll be running through the tunnels about now and coming out here then I suppose?"

"I don't know what you're talking about."

"You don't huh? Then we'll just hang around a few minutes and see if they show up."

The young soldier was excited to be in on this capture, as he'd heard some of his fellow soldiers had received rewards from Major Ashford. He was determined to round up every Jacobite in his territory and nothing would stop him.

The major was particularly interested in these two Jacobites. He'd spent a couple of weeks working for these Highlanders at their lodge during the lambing season. He'd heard they may have been supporters, but he wanted to be sure before he brought them in. Plus, by working at the lodge for a short while he learned the names of quite a few other Jacobites in the area as well. Bringing in a goodly number of prisoners would go a long way toward his making rank and perhaps being sent to London as a special envoy, which was the position he most desired.

While working at the lodge he had seen how the MacKinnons lived—their fine lodge and their close-knit family. Compared to his own lonely military existence, it was quite appealing.

But he'd take them down a few notches and send the two leaders, Alex and Jack, off to be slaves. Then he'd go back and convince that lady with the long, dark hair that she would live with him now. She was a lady, he could tell that. He couldn't understand how she ever could have seen anything in that huge heathen she called her husband.

Ashford had made overtures to her while he was there, but she'd rebuffed him soundly, which had come as somewhat of a surprise to him. He was considered quite handsome and a real catch for some lucky woman. But somehow he hadn't managed to find a woman who would spend much time with him after their initial meeting.

The other woman, the one with the fiery hair and a big wolf who followed her around, there was something about her that bothered him. When she looked at him it was as if she could read his mind. No, he'd not take her. Best to leave her behind to care for that brood of children he saw running about the lodge.

But all that would change with the two Highlanders gone to the islands. He'd have that dark-haired woman if he had to resort to capturing her as he had these two. Then, too, that lodge would serve nicely as a regimental station for them in the future. Yes, he'd enjoy finishing off these ruffians.

Major Ashford and a contingent of soldiers arrived and Lt. Harrington had spotted the young lad laying back in the grass. He quickly made a show of sticking him with his bayonet.

"Light those torches, Harrington. All of them. I want Alex

Lloyd Ashford, taking you two Jacobites back where you belong—the Tolbooth."

"Not in this lifetime, you Redcoat bastard!"

Jack was ready to pounce on him then and there, but Alex put out an arm to hold him back.

"My lieutenant has a pistol and a bayonet at the young boy's back. Do you want to see him die? Plus, I'm brandishing my own pistol and am quite a marksman, if I say so myself. I don't think you want to test me on that point, surely.

"I believe the lieutenant and I can take care of two unarmed, escaped, Highland fools, don't you? Now, just march yourselves inside the kirk and be seated on the front pew. We'll have a short service of sorts, and then you'll put on the leg irons I've provided for each of you. That should keep you in place until my men get back.

"Harrington, let that street rat go. I've no quarrel with him. It's these Highlanders I'm interested in."

Ashford watched as Paul scooted off and kept running into the darkness behind the kirk.

"He's so scared he won't stop running until he finds whatever hovel he hides in. Just another little street beggar."

He turned his attention back to his captives.

"Inside with you, now. MacKinnon, you first, then your brother."

Alex and Jack moved forward slowly, with Caitlin holding onto Alex's shirttail. The major stopped Robbie as he walked near.

"Robbie, you disappoint me greatly, young man. Do you think your mother would approve of your companions? Of course, apparently she had very close relations with one of them some years ago. I find that most disturbing. I had thought she was a perfect lady. Indeed, I had hoped she might even find time for me eventually. But she's gone now, so I must look elsewhere."

He then walked closer to Jack.

"Speaking of ladies, the two that grace your lodge are truly lovely, but I believe my favorite is the one with that flowing mane of dark hair. I believe she's your wife, big man? She'll be the perfect escort for me when I take up my post in London."

That comment had Jack jerking the major's collar, lifting him off the floor and squeezing him by the throat.

"If ye touch Millie I'll tear ye limbs from yer body! You pile of sheep shite!"

He had the major firmly by the throat, and before Alex could stop him, he slammed his very large fist into the major's stomach causing him to double over in agony.

Young Lt. Harrington was at a loss as to what he should do, but he managed to point his pistol at Jack.

"Get back, you two! Get back! Sit down on that pew, now!"

Alex spoke under his breath to his brother.

"Hold on, Jack. We'll find the right time. Keep your temper under wraps. He'll make another mistake. Right now that pistol's pointed at yer head and that young soldier might just be green enough to pull the trigger."

As they took a seat on the front pew, Caitlin murmured quietly to Alex.

"Alex, where's Willie? Did we lose him in the tunnel?"

"I rather doubt Willie could be lost anywhere. If I know him, he's following your scent and will eventually find you. Don't worry yerself about him, lass. Just keep quiet and we'll make a move soon. Watch for a signal from Jack or me. Ye'll know when it comes."

Outside, behind the kirk, Paul lay on the ground and began to slowly inch his body along through the damp grass. He'd never think of leaving Robbie and the others without at least trying to save them.

But what was he to do? He racked his brain, but nothing was coming to mind. He was almost to the edge of the tall grass when he heard a deep growling sound coming from the open sewer.

"Willie! Is that you? Over here! Robbie says to trust you, but I have to say you scare the knickers off me. Come here, now. Maybe the two of us can come up with some way to help them."

Willie jumped out of the opening, rubbed his nose against Paul's hand, then darted off toward the kirk. He knew exactly where Caitlin was and he'd get to her or die trying.

"Wait! Don't rush in! They'll shoot you for sure!"

But Willie's ears were closed to anything but the sounds inside the kirk, and he was moving at a pace Paul couldn't begin to keep up with.

After a few very uncomfortable minutes, Ashford had managed to stand upright and was sensible enough to take a few deep breaths before trying to walk. Then he slowly made his way to the front of the nave and stood facing Alex.

"MacKinnon, I often told you that you didn't have good command of those in your employment. Looks like your brother needs a few lessons in following orders, too. If he'd listened to you there would be no need for this little exercise we must perform now."

He took another step, which brought him in front of Jack. "You really do need to bridle that temper of yours. It doesn't serve you well, as you will see shortly."

He walked away, then paced the floor for a moment, mumbling to himself, apparently lost in thought.

As if speaking to some unseen person, he nodded his head. "Yes, this is a good plan. It will make a lasting impression on these two men. They are certainly both brave and would have made good fighters for my regiment. Yes."

He walked back to the pew and ambled over to stand in front of Caitlin.

"This attire, these trousers you're wearing, make for quite an alluring look I must say, Mrs. MacKinnon. You do wear the outfit well." He ran his hand slowly down her arm as if to make his point. "Now stand and look at me."

When Caitlin remained seated and looked the other direction, totally ignoring his order, he jerked at her tam and her curls came tumbling down her back. Then he yanked her up by her tunic, causing her to gasp. Slowly he lifted his hand to his lips, removed the ever-present cheroot with its glowing end and pressed it to her neck, just long enough to leave a burn mark to show he meant business.

"Aieeeee!"

Caitlin reacted as anyone would—she screamed out in pain.

Alex came flying off the pew, placing himself between Ashford and Caitlin.

"You British bastard! Stop it! Take yer rage out on me, not her—a woman! Yer nothing but a bloody British coward, Boder!"

Now it was Jack's turn to hold Alex back.

Ashford pointed his pistol at Alex, then reached for Caitlin's chin and pulled her forward. With one hand he ripped her tunic, exposing her thin camisole. This time he held the glowing cheroot close to her face.

"I'll do whatever I—"

Ashford's words were lost when a blinding flash of lightning streaked from Caitlin's fingertips, lit up the entire kirk and found its primary target—Ashford. Ashford's terror-filled face revealed that he knew there was no hope of escape. Immediately the stench of burned flesh lay heavily in the kirk.

Lt. Harrington had been repulsed by the major's actions. He never liked his commander, but surely he thought him to be an officer and a gentleman.

As the major ripped the lady's tunic he looked away, which meant he took his eyes off the captives for a moment. Just one. It was long enough for Jack to knock Harrington's pistol out of his hand and have him on the floor, struggling to no avail. Jack clocked him on the chin and he was out like an oil lamp without any oil.

Alex was at Caitlin's side, grabbing at Ashford's pistol. But there was no need. Everything that needed to be done had already been done.

Ashford grabbed at his legs, which were literally on fire and burning beyond belief. He felt the bottoms of his feet searing as if he were walking through campfire coals.

"My feet! Help me! Please!"

He fell to his knees, then was assaulted again. But this time the assault wasn't from lightning, and it was so quick he never saw it coming. All he saw was a blur of dark fur and huge, gnarling, gnashing canines reaching for his throat.

Willie had perfected this move—one giant leap from the floor, then his large canines embedded themselves in the throat and his large body brought the victim down to the floor where he would finish his kill.

"No! I can't breathe! Get the beast off me! Please help me!" His pleas went unanswered as he struggled with his feet of fire and his rapidly depleting supply of oxygen.

Robbie felt planted to the pew. He'd observed Caitlin's power twice in one day now and it was something to behold.

"Come on, Robbie. Let's get out of here before his men get back. Hurry!"

Robbie stood and followed as Alex, Jack and Caitlin made a beeline for the open door. He took one last look at Major Ashford and Lieutenant Harrington, and stopped abruptly.

"The lieutenant, he's not dead! He's not dead!"

"Never mind him, Robbie. Let's get out of here, now!"

But Robbie saw Lieutenant Harrington reaching for his pistol, which lay just a short distance from his hand.

"No, I won't let you hurt anyone else!"

Then, seemingly without thought, he reached down inside his boot and drew out his dirk, the smaller one Da had given him. He held the dirk in his left hand, and in one smoothly executed move let it fly through the air. He watched as the dirk sailed quickly, without wavering, and heard the sickening thud as it went through the lieutenant's hand, pinning it soundly to the floor.

Alex stood at the rear of the kirk, his mouth open in amazement.

"Robbie! I'd say ye hit yer target, lad. Come on now!"

He grabbed the boy by the shoulders and practically dragged him out of the kirk, trying to put some space between them and anyone who might be after them.

~ ~ ~

Paul led the group as they made their way back to Robbie's home. He was so excited he could hardly keep still. This Robbie was not the same friend he had known for years.

"Robbie, where'd you learn to throw a dirk like that?"

"Uh, my da and grandda have been working with me. But I've got a ways to go yet. Takes some practice to be as good as Da and his brothers."

Alex grinned at his son.

"Looks to me like ye've got it down pretty well, lad. And I saw ye threw it left-handed. Now when did ye start that?"

"Grandda made that suggestion. Guess it might have been a good one."

Alex nodded.

"Yeah, well, Da's a fair hand at most anything he tries. But I imagine ye've found that out already."

The back door opened before they even knocked.

"Robbie? Are you hurt boy? Let me look at you. Come in here."

"I'm alright, Mattie. We're all fine. Right now we need to feed my da and Jack. They're starved after being in the Old Tolbooth for a week."

He made short work of introducing everyone to Mattie as she brought out a Shepard's pie and some freshly baked bread. Tea was served in mugs and everyone hurriedly scoffed down enough food to help them endure the long night ahead of them. She even laid out some bits of beef tips for Willie.

"Mattie, Major Ashford's men may come here looking for us. You say you haven't seen me since I left a few months ago. The major's unable to tell them anything now, so they'll believe whatever you tell them. I don't think you need to worry about him bothering you. He's moved on to his next duty station."

"Oh? Then good for him. Never was very fond of him myself. He was just too nosy. Your mother tolerated him as best she could, but he was never her cup of tea I tell you."

"We've got to have horses, Robbie. Any idea where we can find some?" Alex looked at his son, this young lad who had just helped save their lives.

Paul was standing next to Mattie, who had insisted he stay and eat too.

"I can probably come up with a couple if you give me a few minutes."

"Oh no you won't, young thief!"

Mattie gave him a quick slap on the back of his head.

"No need, Mr. MacKinnon. I took the liberty of visiting the major's corral while the soldiers were celebrating. Most of them are full as a goat and won't realize until tomorrow they may be walking instead of riding."

"Mattie? You stole horses? Mother would never believe you'd steal!"

"And she'd never believe you'd run through tunnels full of rats either, my boy. I've filled a tub as you asked, Robbie, but I think it might be better for you all to get out of here. But, you're right, these two do smell to high heaven!"

They all laughed and she led them out behind the house where she had tied two horses next to where Robbie and Caitlin had left Soldier and Goliath.

"Guess I'll let you have Goliath, Jack. He's quite a horse, and he kept me from falling off more times than one."

"Yeah, he's quite a fellow, he is." Jack stroked Goliath's face and for a moment thought only of getting back to Millie and little Midge.

Alex took the larger of the two horses Mattie had stolen. "I'll take this sorrel. Looks like he's fit enough for a trip to the Highlands.

Robbie, that leaves the chestnut with the white blaze for you."

"I think I'll manage to stay on this one. He doesn't look too frisky."

"Oh, I think you can manage to stay on any horse now, Robbie," Caitlin chimed in.

"Your days of saying you can't ride or throw a dirk are over, my lad."

Alex took Mattie's hand briefly. "Mattie, yer a lifesaver. We're in yer debt. Mayhap we'll have a chance to repay it one day."

"You just take care of my boy. He's a fine one, sir. Don't keep him away too long, though. I need to see him once in a while."

"Aye. That can be arranged."

Robbie hugged his old nursemaid, and only now did he realize he had never even considered staying in Edinburgh. He was headed back to the Highlands again, and this time he wasn't traveling alone hoping to find his kin. This time he was with his kin and he was as much a part of this family as any of them.

As they quietly rode off—a small, aromatic group with a wolf leading them—they could hear Mattie, her voice carrying on the soft breeze that had come up.

"Now, you'll just rest here tonight, young laddie. There's a tub of hot water in Robbie's old room. A good scrubbing wouldn't hurt you none either. And then ..."

26

Dawn was creeping across the top of the moor as the four weary travelers arrived at the edge of MacKinnon land. The sky appeared endless, draped in a pale pink glow. The air itself glistened with a dewy morning mist that felt good on Alex's cheeks, like a soft caress. He took a deep breath, inhaling the scents that surrounded him. He reined his horse in, dismounted, pulled up a sprig of heather and rolled it between his fingers, taking a quick whiff of it.

"What's wrong? Did you hear something?" Jack asked, reining Goliath to a halt.

"Nae, didn't hear anything. But have a need to stand on my own land again. Just for a moment."

He inhaled deeply again.

"The scent of the Highlands, the scent of home."

He was acutely aware these scents he had known all his life, those of pine, birch, rowan, and the delicate scent of the heather, were more than just scents.

"These scents, these Highland smells, they speak of freedom, a place in time, and a way of life. No matter how hard the Brits may try to take this land and our way of life from us, it's embedded in this place, and in our Highland blood. In all Scots. There is no taking it away."

~ ~ ~

A short while later, not quite yet sunrise, they arrived at the lodge, which was aglow with lighted candles at every window. The sight was so warming to them that they forgot their aching backs and legs. They were home now. Nothing else mattered.

Before they could climb down from their very tired horses, Millie came tearing out the back door, Midge on her hip.

"Oh, you're home! Jack! Jack!"

She threw herself into his huge arms and he had to refrain from hugging her as hard as he wished. Little Midge held up her hands to him as always and he gathered her close, too.

Finally, Millie looked to Caitlin and smiled, then answered the question on Caitlin's face.

"She's sleeping in her crib now, but then she's been awake most of the night so I suppose that's to be expected."

Caitlin nodded, unable to speak, as she knew tears were just waiting to spill over. She was almost afraid to go in and see her bairn. Leaving her had been the most difficult thing she'd ever had to do.

Millie stood back from Jack, taking in his bruised face and black, swollen eye. She began a litany of questions that seemed very important to her at the moment.

"Are you alright? Are you hurt? Any broken bones?"

"Nae, Millie. I'm not hurt, lass. It takes more than a few foppish British soldiers to do me in."

He appeared to be well, but Millie felt him tremble as he held her once again.

They all looked up as another figure made an appearance on the back stoop. Alex stood very still and quiet as Da slowly made his way down the steps and started toward them, carrying his latest grandchild close to his chest. He had always been at ease with the bairns, and this one was no different.

Alex looked down at Caitlin, who was smiling at the sight of her newborn being cradled by Da.

"Is he fully recovered, lass?"

"Yes. He's getting older now, Alex. He's a tough old Highlander, but even those must learn to take life a bit slower at some point. He's alright, though. He'll not leave us for a long while yet."

Not willing to wait for Da to get closer, Alex took several long strides and was at his side. He relieved him of his bundle and held her in the crook of his arm. After one long MacKinnon embrace, he looked Da in the eyes.

"So, ye survived the fever then. Caitlin says ye'll be back to yer old self shortly."

"Well, I wasn't sure I wanted to survive it for a while there, ye ken? When Andrew took his leave, I thought for a bit that perhaps I'd just go with him. We were mates for a lifetime. But I know yer mam would tell me that we all have a reason for being here, and when we're no longer needed then we'll go to our next home. Still, though, it's not the same without him."

"Aye. He'll be sorely missed and that's as it should be. The real problem is that now we don't have anyone to keep records of our family. None of us are what ye'd call good with keeping detailed accounts of anything."

"Oh, I believe we might have someone who can step in for Andrew. He's quite a hand at writing stories, and from what I see today, he's becoming one of us. That, too, is as it should be."

Alex took a quick glance over at Robbie, who was surrounded by the three orphans.

Dugald was pulling him toward the stable.

"Robbie! Ye gotta come see the kittens. Their mam died so we've been feeding them with a dropper, but one of them looks poorly," Dugald reported.

Bridgette found Alex's leg and wound herself around it. She was rewarded with a hug and off she went again.

Willie stood close to Caitlin, still in his protective mode apparently. It always took him a couple of days to move any distance from her following an episode that had her in danger.

Caitlin had given Alex time with his daughter and his da, but now she stepped forward, reaching out to take her child.

"Looks like you've been in good hands, my precious. These are my two favorite men. But for the next few minutes, you belong to me!"

She pulled her close and inhaled that special scent of her infant, a scent that is forever etched in a mother's memory.

"Millie, where's Charlie?"

Caitlin was so in hopes that he would eventually try to speak again. But, only time could heal some wounds.

"Oh, he'll be along any minute now. He's doing his 'kitten duty,' which he really likes. Having his mam has helped more than to Aned Favre's cottage. "I believe I'll just check on Aned first thing. She wasn't quite herself when I left. In fact, she was most evasive, which is unlike her."

"And I'll look in on Merlin. He's probably grown fat as an old ewe grazing on that grass in your field."

Wabi knocked lightly at the door and waited quietly, expecting Aned's smiling face to greet him. But several minutes later she still had not appeared.

Trying the doorknob, he was surprised to find it unlocked. She lived alone and was in the habit of keeping her doors locked, especially if Wabi was gone on one of his adventures.

As he walked into the room, he looked about. Everything was in place as usual. Her teapot was on the kitchen table, a recipe for cappuccino soufflé lying next to it. She was forever coming up with a new dish of some sort and he always volunteered to try them out for her.

Walking down the hall to her bedroom, he wondered if she had perhaps taken ill and was resting. Her door was ajar so he walked in. He was right, to some degree. There was someone resting on the bed, but it wasn't Aned. Old Groucho was stretched out with his head between his paws, sleeping so soundly he didn't even know Wabi was there.

"You old reprobate! Sleeping in a lady's bed when she's not even here."

He picked the old feline up, stroked his head, and walked to the kitchen again. He then went to Aned's breadbox, where she always kept something scrumptious—freshly baked bread, or perhaps some scones.

He was disappointed. There were no pastries, but there was an envelope addressed to "Wabi."

He had to smile. She knew exactly where to leave a message for him. He read the short note, then put it in his pocket.

Groucho pushed his face into Wabi's hand, hoping to get his head rubbed, and of course he was successful.

"I see. Well then, Groucho. Aned has gone to France for a while. To see family, she says. I thought she had no family left there. Of course she's free to go where she pleases, but I do wish she had discussed whatever has been on her mind lately."

He left then, making sure he locked the door behind himself.

He found Ian out in the pasture talking with Merlin, Henson at his feet. Wabi was relieved the lad had found him and they could now get on with his training.

The old wizard would never have children of his own, but he'd had the pleasure of teaching Ci-Cero so many years ago, and now this young one, Ian. Ci-Cero had certainly been granted gifts beyond what others had been given, and he had great hopes for this Highland lad. He may have been chosen for greatness too.

But, presently the country was in a state of unrest and that had Wabi worried. He'd seen much in his many years and knew this too would pass, but in the meantime there would undoubtedly be great sorrow for so many. He was lost in his thoughts when Ian spoke up.

"Master Wabi? Are ye alright then?"

"Yes, yes, of course. Just thinking I suppose."

"Yeah. Me too. Wabi, do ye think we could go to the Highlands soon? I'm verra worried about my brothers, my family. I know we need to get back to my training, but if we could just go up for a day or so and find out if they're alright. Things there will most likely be as boring as always, nothing ever happens up there, but just wait 'til I tell them about my experience with the Druids!"

"Maybe you should keep some of that information to yourself, Ian. Not everyone understands them, and some folk are actually afraid of them. Most of their fear comes from the same place all fear comes from, ignorance. But still, you must learn to filter what you reveal about some events. It could be you'll soon be called on to make decisions that may not please everyone, but as long as you have assured yourself you are following the path the Creator has set for you, then you should continue."

"Do ye truly think I've been called for some special reason?"

"We've all been called for some special purpose, Ian. Not everyone has your gifts or my powers, but all are called. But not all answer the call."

"But ..."

"To answer your first question, lad, yes, we'll go to the Highlands and see how everyone fares. I've been unavailable to Caitlin for a short while, so no telling what kind of trouble she's managed to get herself into."

"Do you think she could get into trouble, Wabi?"

28

Clint nodded to Hector. "Off with you now. Me and Ethel and Winston can take care of this place for a few days. Dorothea's got the little ones sorted and she's got several women who can step in if she needs more help. Go now. Go see about yer brothers and yer da."

"But if the soldiers return, they could cause trouble." Hector had concerns about leaving these older hands to run the Sanctuary, although he knew each one was as capable as he and Reggie.

"They were scared to death of that fever when they were here last time. I don't think they'll get anywhere near this place!" Ethel laughed as she rubbed butter and herbs on the turkey she was preparing for the oven.

"I lived through the '15 uprising, Hector. Eventually they all just get tired of fighting and things settle down again. For a while anyway. Go on with you, now," Clint said.

"Reggie? What do ye think, lass? We'd be gone for a few days, but I really would like ye to go with me. My da will hide me if I don't bring ye to meet them before I marry ye."

"Hector MacKinnon! I haven't agreed to marry you yet, I said I'd think about it, that's all."

But she smiled as she said it and knew she'd go anywhere with this Highlander. He was so very different from her first husband, and that was probably a good thing. This time around she was older and much wiser.

Hector had known from the first moment that this woman was meant for him.

"Then we'll be off early tomorrow. We'll return as soon as we've made sure everyone is alright. Clint, my fear is that Alex and Jack were sent off already. But before I go running down to Edinburgh again, I want to know if anything has happened at the lodge. Caitlin and Millie may have heard something that might help me find them."

"Aye. That's not a bad idea. If I recollect correctly, those brothers of yours managed to get their women and themselves to safety when that lord and lunatic soldier was after them. They're not men I'd like to cross meself, 'specially that big one."

Hector laughed. "Ye've got a point there, Clint. I don't particularly like to cross them either, and we have our moments when we're all at the lodge."

"Another thing, too. My bones are aching like the very devil himself, Hector. That means there's weather brewing, somewhere. It might be a good idea for you to take the small, one-horse covered carriage for the trip."

"A covered carriage? I didn't know we had one. Where'd it come from?"

"The Mistress Cameron. She had it brought up from London some years ago. After one trip to the village in it she had us put it in the back of the barn and keep it covered with bales of hay. She thought it was just too "fancy" to be used here. So that's where it's been for some years now."

"That would be a lot more comfortable than the cart I used to take Aileen to the lodge. At least we'd be somewhat protected from the weather you predict may be coming. Why didn't ye tell me about it?"

"It completely slipped my mind, Hector. And, too, we had to make sure ye were as honest as our Millie seemed to think. Ye could have just taken off in that posthaste and we'd never see ye again."

Hector shook his head and laughed. "Well then, I'm glad to see I've finally gained your approval, Clint. Reggie will enjoy the trip if we travel in that. Thank ye. I'll take ye up on that offer."

29

Chaos was the only word to describe the scene at the lodge this evening. With the arrival of Alex, Caitlin, Jack and Robbie a couple of days ago, any semblance of order was lost.

Earlier in the day, Aileen had taken Charlie by the face and looked directly at him.

"Charlie, I know you can hear me, son. Get yourself back to the classroom now."

Aileen pushed the little lad out the kitchen door and he laughed as he ran along. He had been so excited to see Willie and would much rather spend time with the wolf than be in the classroom. The two had forged an unusual bond and Charlie was thrilled the wolf was back.

Since the Scarlet Fever had abated, Millie and Caitlin were struggling to get the children back in school doing their studies again. Today, Dugald and Bridgette dragged the four kittens into the classroom, which brought shrieks from the other children making it almost impossible to conduct any kind of instruction.

Aileen had taken over the kitchen and ran it even better than Millie had. This clan needed her and she was already becoming indispensable. The end of the day found her in the kitchen, Millie closing the school for the day, and Caitlin gathering up her herbs from the stable where she kept them in an unused stall.

Alex and Jack were coming in after a long day of herding

sheep from one pasture to another. They had barely gotten inside before the thunderstorm that had threatened all afternoon finally arrived.

"Well, one good thing has come from our time in the Tolbooth," Alex said, brushing the rain off his shoulders.

"Yeah? What's that?" Jack asked.

"I used to think the sheep smelled bad, but after the Tolbooth I won't complain about them anymore."

They both laughed and headed to the bath.

A little while later they were coming down for their evening ritual, a wee dram and conversation around the dining table, when the back door opened and Caitlin rushed inside.

"Holy Rusephus! A thunderstorm this time of year?" She'd had to make a run for it from the stable.

The next one to make his way to the kitchen was Da, whose health had improved markedly since his lads had come home. He spent a few minutes rocking Flinn to sleep and placed her in her crib, still located in the corner of the kitchen. Willie, her self-appointed protector, was back in his preferred place keeping watch from beneath her crib.

Millie handed out mugs of cider and watched as Aileen filled the table with scrumptious looking dishes, one after the other.

"Aileen, you are amazing. It would take me a week to prepare that many dishes."

Jack laughed. "But don't stop, lass. We've been starved for more than a week and need to build our strength up."

A banging on the kitchen door had everyone looking in that direction. Jack opened the door and stood there staring. After a long minute, the visitor said his piece.

"It's raining out here, brother. Ye think ye could let us come in?" Hector smiled at his big brother.

"Hector? Yer alright, then? Yer alright?"

Alex and Da came closer and embraced him.

"Aye, I can see yer alright, lad," Da said. "But I do believe yer mam would tell us we've forgotten our manners." He bowed to Reggie, who'd been standing there watching as the scene unfolded before her.

"Good evening, ma'am. I'm Daniel MacKinnon and these three oafs are my sons. Please come in."

The laughter that filled the room was music to everyone's ears.

Reggie removed her long, hooded cloak and looked about. "So then, this is the family you speak of so often. As you said, there are a lot of them!"

Reggie had a brother, but he had died as a youngster so she'd grown up in a relatively quiet home.

"And this isn't all of them," Hector told her.

"Oh goodness! Who's missing?"

"Ian, the youngest. He's off with Uncle Wabi," Caitlin informed her.

"But take my word for it, he looks like all the others and is just as loud."

"Here, let's close the door. The rain's really coming down now and with this wind it'll be blown inside," Millie said.

"Oh right. Certainly." Hector stood back, and just as he was about to close the door a booted foot stuck itself through—a boot with a prosthesis.

"Ian! Our long lost brother! Didn't expect to see ye. How'd ye get here?"

Then, seeing Uncle Wabi standing behind him, he quietly nodded.

"I see. Uncle Wabi. So glad to see you, sir. Please come in."

Caitlin's tears began the minute she saw Wabi.

"Uncle Wabi, I thought something awful had happened to you. I've called and called but you didn't answer."

Wabi gathered his niece in his arms. "Yes, dear girl. There was a problem for a short while, but all is well now. I can hear you now should you call again."

Wabi was relieved to find Caitlin and the MacKinnons had endured their escapade at the Old Tolbooth. He knew what the place was like and he shuddered to think of Caitlin running through it.

He walked over to the crib where Caitlin's bairn, Flinn, rested, then knelt down and lay a finger against her cheek. He was not surprised to feel a vibration coming from the child, but he was very surprised at the intensity of it.

Oh, my sweet one, such strong vibrations mean challenges for sure. What lies ahead for you? Only the Creator knows for sure. But you and I will be together, of that much I'm certain.

Caitlin walked over and smiled at her uncle.

"She's very special Uncle Wabi, very special."

"That she is, dear girl, as are you. Of course, all your ancestors were special. I strongly suggest you find time to read Ci-Cero's entire journal, The Wolf, the Wizard, and the Woad. Learning about your ancestors may be of great importance, Caitlin. We often are better able to face the future when we understand the past. And I have an inkling that young Flinn, the latest in this line of healers, will bring her own special talents and have her own challenges. Again, you must read the journal."

Hector was also relieved.

"So, looks like yer all in one piece. I had heard the Brits were all over the place and I feared ye'd all be in prison or learning how to behave like slaves by now."

There were nods all round, but no laughter. They were all glad Alex and Jack were safe, but the problem still existed—how to escape being caught by the British. There'd been much discussion since their return to the lodge, but no solutions had been found.

Ian wasn't sure he understood everything that was going on, so thought he'd change the subject.

"Wait until I tell ye about my trip down the Highlands to Wabi's cottage. I was followed by a mountain lion, then I rescued some folks from a highwayman, and learned how to talk to an owl."

"Of course ye did, lad. And it pleases me to see ye've learned to tell tales just like yer brothers did at your age!" Da put an arm around his youngest.

Ah, just take a look down here, mo chridhe. Our lads are safe and looks like Hector is bringing us another lovely lady. The Creator is merciful.

Ian sighed. "No, it's true! All of it! Where's Robbie? He'll believe me."

A voice from above rang out.

"Ian? Is that you? Come up here, quickly!"

Ian raced up to the attic, anxious to see his nephew again. As he stepped into the room, however, he began to roll with laughter. Robbie was in the middle of an undertaking that was totally beyond his comprehension.

"Here, let me help ye with that. Stand still."

When the two lads entered the kitchen a few minutes later, no one laughed. In fact, no one said a word for the longest moment.

Finally, Alex stood and walked over, taking Robbie by the shoulders and turning him around slowly.

"Aye. Lad. Aye. It becomes ye. Ye wear the kilt well."

He blinked back a tear and put his arm around Robbie. "Miss Carmichael, this is Robbie. He's my son."

"...just one more thing"...

Holy Rusephus — you made it! I'm very grateful you took the time to read my work and your feedback is essential to improving my writing. Therefore, if I could ask for "just one more thing"...go to **amazon.com/dp/1943369119** *to favor me with your review.*

If you would like to know more about Caitlin, Wabi, the MacKinnon brothers, the animals, and how all this started, go to **amazon.com/dp/B016CF7I4C** *to get your copy of Highland Healer, Book 1 in this series.*

In Book 2 in the series, Highland Circle of Stones, the healer weds her Highlander and the family struggles to accept her and her magickal powers. You may find your copy at **amazon.com/dp/B01FKI3QS4**.

For information regarding future projects, blogs, and useful links about Scotland and its history, use the contact button at **florencelovekarsner.com** *to join the mailing list.*

Thanks so much for reading my novels and "lang may yer lum reek."

ABOUT THE AUTHOR

Florence Love Karsner is a fifth generation Floridian who grew up in a rural Panhandle village near Tallahassee. In the late 60's, she married a Navy Ensign and followed him to the South Pacific. In her travels she experienced different lands, peoples, and cultures all of which would forever influence her view of the world and provide creative ideas for painting, pottery, and writing.

Today, she is retired from nursing and clinical research careers, and spends her time writing, painting, and creating pottery. She lives with her husband on the Intracoastal Waterway in Ponte Vedra Beach, Florida. Her Highland Healer Series is set in the 18th century Scottish Highlands following the Bloody Battle of Culloden.

Made in the USA
Middletown, DE
16 March 2018